Praise for *Beautiful Little Fools*

'Cantor's shifting kaleidoscope of female perspectives makes F. Scott Fitzgerald's classic tale of Jazz Age longing and lust feel utterly modern. A breathtaking accomplishment."

—Fiona Davis, *New York Times* bestselling author of *The Lions of Fifth Avenue*

'Cantor gorgeously captures the complex lives of the women in *The Great Gatsby*, creating a delicate and intricate story that dovetails perfectly with F. Scott Fitzgerald's."

—Jill Santopolo, *New York Times* bestselling author of *The Light We Lost*

'Glittering with intrigue, full of fast-paced tension, and saturated in Jazz Age decadence, this powerful exploration of the women of *The Great Gatsby* will forever change the way you see the American classic."

—Kristin Harmel, *New York Times* bestselling author of *The Forest of Vanishing Stars*

'Lush, beautiful, and dazzling, Cantor transports readers back to an era of hot summer nights, jazz music, and lounging poolside at one of Jay Gatsby's infamous parties."

—Shea Ernshaw, *New York Times* bestselling author of *A History of Wild Places*

"Cantor beautifully re-crafts an American classic in *Beautiful Little Fools*, placing the women of *The Great Gatsby* center stage. Both fresh and familiar, this page-turner is one to savor!"

—Kate Quinn, *New York Times* bestselling author of *The Rose Code*

Also by Jillian Cantor

Beautiful Little Fools
Half Life
The Code for Love and Heartbreak
In Another Time
The Hours Count
Margot
Searching for Sky
The Transformation of Things
The Life of Glass
The September Sisters

The
FICTION WRITER

JILLIAN CANTOR

PARK
ROW
BOOKS

**PARK
ROW
BOOKS™**

Recycling programs
for this product may
not exist in your area.

ISBN-13: 978-0-7783-1083-9

The Fiction Writer

This edition published by arrangement with Harlequin Books S.A.

Park Row Books
22 Adelaide St. West, 41st Floor
Toronto, Ontario M5H 4E3, Canada
ParkRowBooks.com
BookClubbish.com

Printed in U.S.A.

For Jess and Laura,
this fiction writer's dream team

Out of the ash
I rise with my red hair
And I eat men like air.

—Sylvia Plath, "Lady Lazarus"

PROLOGUE

Last night I dreamt I went to Malibu again.

I stood barefoot on the sand, the cool water nipping at my ankles. And there, high above me, perched on the edge of that magnificent cliff, his stunning house sat as it once had, alive, whole. It had ten bedrooms and was on three private cliffside acres, with a lap pool, a tennis court, and a garden blooming flush with pink-and-white bougainvillea. But from the beach down below all I could see was its long wall of privacy-tinted glass windows, slanting out toward the sea.

He could see me here, out on the beach. I was certain he could, even in my dream.

He was still behind those windows, watching my every step. Though I couldn't see him. The glass was one-way. But I imagined him there behind the glass so vividly, it had to be real.

Until it wasn't. Until the heat from the flames would shatter all the windows, break them apart, send smoke spewing from the piano room, down the cliff, evaporating in wisps into the lonely Pacific.

But in my dream, the flames hadn't existed yet. Or, maybe they never would. He and his house were there, watching me. Wanting me. Haunting me.

"Come back!" His voice was a desperate echo, my undoing. The smoke was so thick, even out on the beach I couldn't see, and I couldn't breathe.

So that's why I did it, in my dream. I turned away from the house, and I walked into the bone-chilling water. It was so cold, it numbed me, but I walked into the sea, up to my shoulders, my neck, my chin. Until I could no longer smell the smoke or hear his voice.

And then my entire head was underwater, and the tide was strong. It sucked me in, held me there.

But I wasn't trying to drown. I really wasn't. I was merely trying to escape the fire.

ONE

One year earlier

To say I was shocked to see my agent's name, Charley Bingham, pop up on my phone that morning in early March would be an understatement. But truly another word to describe how I was feeling escaped me. *Aghast? Stunned? Astounded?* None of them. All of them? I was a writer; words were supposed to come easily to me. But lately not much had. Why should this be the exception?

"Hey, Charley," I answered, forcing a brightness to my tone I certainly wasn't feeling. The last time Charley and I had spoken on the phone, six months earlier, was when she'd called to tell me that the last of the editors she'd submitted my third novel to had passed. *What are you thinking for your next book, Olivia?* she'd asked me then.

My next book. As if my ideas and words sprouted fully formed from our rooftop garden each summer, the same as my tomatoes. As if I didn't need to actually sell a novel to eat and pay my rent. And what about my poor third novel, a *slightly* semi-autobiographical coming-of-age story, which was now destined for no more than a dusty drawer? It had drained every bit of creative life out of me to write it; I'd poured my whole self into it for nine months, ignoring everything, and worse, everyone, in my life, until it was too late. And then having it out on submission for months had been its own special kind of hell. Charley had forwarded me lovely note after lovely note from passing editors who *just weren't the right fit*. They used words like *beautiful writing* or *gorgeous prose*, followed by *can't break her out*, *too quiet*, or perhaps the most honest one, who'd said that *following the lackluster sales of* Becky, *is there really a place for this new book in the market*? Harsh, but maybe that was fair. My second novel, *Becky*, had sold about a thousand copies to date.

"Olivia," Charley said now. "How's the new book coming?"

"Great," I lied. "Almost finished the first draft." If you considered fifty (well, forty-six to be exact) rambling pages close to a first draft, then that wasn't a complete lie. But creativity was an emotional well, and mine had run dry, even as the generous advance I'd received for my first and second novels had too, almost run dry from my checking account.

"Great," Charley echoed. "Can't wait to read it."

She paused for a moment, and the line was silent. Was that really why she was calling, to check on my progress? Charley had too many other clients, important ones, to have the time to hold my hand.

"Anyway." She cleared her throat. "I have an interesting offer in for you."

"An offer?" I repeated, not quite understanding. Book three was no longer out on submission. The disaster that was *Becky* certainly wasn't causing any subsidiary rights folks to knock on my door. And though my first novel had gotten a little bit of nice press and was even an *Indie Next* pick, no one was still thinking about it (except for me) five years later.

"A write-for-hire gig," she said. "A very well-paying one."

"How well-paying?" I asked, quickly.

"Fifty thousand up front, and then twenty percent once it sells to a publisher," she said. "Twenty percent of all of it— advance, subrights, royalties," she clarified.

But all I really heard was *fifty thousand up front*. "Okay, I'll do it," I said, not asking any of the questions I should've asked, any of the questions all writers *know* to ask: *who, what, why, where, when?* These past six months, a fuzzy sort of desperation had come over me, where everything I used to know about writing felt ephemeral. Fifty thousand dollars? Great. Sign me up.

Charley laughed a little. "How about I send over the NDA, and after you sign it, we can discuss the details."

I agreed. But how hard could it be? And fifty thousand dollars would go a long way toward rent and groceries and giving me time to figure out what the hell I was going to do next.

TWO

I refreshed my inbox, eager for the NDA to land, still in disbelief that Charley had called with something that might actually be *good* news.

The last time I'd spoken to Charley before today was the same day Jack had moved out of our apartment. Charley had called that morning to tell me my third book was dead. Charley was too tactful to actually use the word *dead*, though. Instead she'd said, *how about we put a pin in this project for now?* The pin felt more like a knife, as I'd tried to digest what Charley was saying while simultaneously staring at the boxes Jack had haphazardly stacked up by our front door. They were shoddily labeled—the top one was simply Sharpied with the word **STUFF**. (At that point, why had he even bothered to label?) And it occurred to me in that exact moment when Charley was talking about *a pin*, that Jack was so desperate to get out of here, to get away from me, that he hadn't even taken the time to properly pack his *STUFF*.

What felt worse? The death of our relationship or the death of my book? *The book.* Definitely the book. It was my entire life, my career. The words had felt like my blood for a year, running through me, keeping my heart beating. But, later that night, lying in our bed all alone, knowing that all the boxes were gone from the front door, I'd suddenly wished I'd never written the book at all. If I hadn't, I might've noticed what Jack had already seen for months, if not years, that *we were growing apart*. I might've held us together, before we were too far gone to fix things. Jack was the one who left, but as he'd said, quietly, just a few nights earlier as I'd downed half a bottle of pinot grigio in our tiny kitchen, I was the one who'd stopped trying. It wasn't true, though. I'd simply gotten caught up in my story, in my fictional world, in my desperation to overcome those depressing *Becky* sales numbers and resurrect my fledgling career. Writing was my blood, but it was also my addiction. I hadn't necessarily stopped trying with Jack. I'd just *forgotten* to try, for a while. For too long. And by the time Jack actually left me, I couldn't even necessarily remember if I truly loved him, or if I more just loved the idea of him.

My inbox suddenly dinged with an email—Charley!—and I pushed Jack out of my mind again. It felt impossible that an offer could come out of nowhere, just like this, and for the first time in months, an excitement pulsed through my veins. Writing was still my lifeline.

Charley's email called the NDA *industry standard*, and *okay to sign*, so I skimmed it, signed it, and emailed it right back to her. My phone rang almost as soon as I hit Send.

"Okay, are you sitting down?" Charley asked.

"Yep," I lied. I was, in fact, standing up, watching my fish, Oscar, flutter through his massive tank. After Jack moved out, I'd needed something to fill the space where his sixty-inch TV once sat, and I'd landed on an aquarium after the internet told me watching fish swim could improve my mental health. I'd started with six fish, but five of them had already perished.

"Henry Asherwood," Charley said.

"What about him?" I watched Oscar flip through a tiny pink coral like an acrobat.

"That's who wants to hire you."

I laughed because Charley definitely was joking. Henry Asherwood, reclusive mega-billionaire, twice-named *People*'s Sexiest Man Alive, and heir to the Asherwood store chain—wanted to hire me?

"Olivia, I'm serious," Charley said, and I remembered that Charley was always serious, always working, not at all prone to kidding around. But how could this possibly be right?

"I don't...understand," I stammered and then sat down for real, bracing myself against the arm of the couch.

"His manager called me this morning. Henry Asherwood wants *you* for this project." If I wasn't so surprised myself, I might've been offended by how surprised Charley sounded.

"Why me?" I finally asked a question, though I inwardly chided myself for its self-deprecation as soon as it popped out of my mouth. *Why not you?* my friend Noah used to say back in college, when I'd doubt myself or worry that my writing would never be good enough to be publishable. "I mean, how does Henry Asherwood even know who I am, much less want to hire me?"

"His manager didn't say," Charley answered. "But maybe he read *All the Little Lights*?" My first novel had sold nearly one hundred thousand copies, so I supposed it was possible. But it also came out five years ago. "He thinks your writing is perfect for this project," Charley added.

"And what is the project?"

Charley was silent for a few seconds, and then she said, "Well, that's the catch. He didn't exactly tell me what the project was. He wants to meet you in person first. Asked if you'd fly out to LA. He'll pay five thousand now for your time and transportation. And if it works out, after you meet, we'll set up a contract for terms. He'll pay the fifty thousand and you can do the project."

So the fifty thousand was far from a sure thing. I sighed.

"Are you up for this, Olivia?" Charley's voice softened a little, and it occurred to me maybe she knew I'd been lying about my first draft being almost done earlier.

I stared at poor lonely Oscar, and then glanced around my half-empty apartment. Fifty thousand dollars or not, maybe *this* was what I needed. To get away, out of this apartment, out of Boston, which, even in March, was still in the depressing throes of a dark winter. LA sounded far away, warm, and sunny. Someone was handing me a free trip. And meeting Henry Asherwood! How could I possibly say no?

THREE

Much later I would think, *I should've just said no*. There were red flags, even from that earliest conversation with Charley, that, had I not been in such a desperate, awful state, I would've recognized.

But stepping on the plane at Logan a few days later, that was the furthest thought from my mind. I was thinking about (1) the Pacific Ocean. I'd used the money Charley had deposited in my account to book my plane ticket as well as an ocean-view room at the Malibu Heights Inn. (2) The fact that *the* Henry Asherwood III now had *my* email and we had actually written back and forth last night. Granted, he'd only asked where I was staying and what time he should send a car tonight to pick me up. I'd responded with that simple information. But still! And (3) Noah.

Noah Weissman had been both my best friend at Brown and my critique partner in our writing seminars. We'd both planned to get our MFAs after college, but then I'd ended up moving to Boston with Jack after we graduated instead, and Noah went to get his MFA at UCLA. He stayed out in LA after, and now taught as an adjunct while (still) trying to get his first novel published. While I'd written *All the Little Lights* in the two years after college, had signed with Charley, and then got a publisher for it, almost right away. My two-book deal hadn't exactly caused tension between me and Noah, but in the years since college, we'd gone from hourly texts, to daily, to weekly, to checking in twice a year on birthdays. Now I couldn't even remember the last time we'd texted, much less talked. I hadn't told him about Jack leaving or my third novel not selling, and as I settled into my seat on the plane, my finger hovered over his contact in my phone. I wondered if I should even bother to text him and let him know I was coming to LA.

But no, that was silly. This was Noah. If he were coming to Boston and didn't text me, I'd be hurt. I shot off a quick text: Hey, will be in LA for the next week. Would love to see you if you're free? I stared at my phone for a few minutes, expecting him to immediately text me back, but he didn't, and then I had to put it in airplane mode.

I settled into my seat and pulled out the thick copy of the biography I'd purchased last night: *From the Ashes: The Rags to Riches Story of America's Wealthiest Family.* I knew a little about the Asherwood family, as much as anyone who was a devout reader of *People* magazine did. I knew that Henry Asherwood III's grandfather had been a decorated navy hero during World War I, and that he had started the Asherwood store chain with one store outside of LA in the early 1930s. (Today, the Asherwood chain had more stores than Costco and Target combined.) I knew that his son, Henry II, nearly bankrupted the company before his untimely drug-fueled death in the '90s, and that in recent years, Henry III had brought it back to life. But tragedy seemed to follow the family generationally, from Henry III's grandmother, who'd died young in an accident, to his father's drug overdose, to most recently, one year ago, the death of his wife, leaving him a widower at the age of forty. He'd allegedly holed up at his Malibu estate ever since, and even the tabloids had barely gotten a photo of him.

And now I was on my way across the country to *meet* with him. To potentially write something for him. It felt so improbable that had it not been for the deposit in my bank account from Charley and the email in my inbox from Henry himself, I might've thought that I'd dreamt the entire thing.

Six hours and one Lyft later, I was in my room at the Malibu Heights Inn, sitting out on the balcony, reveling in the warmth of the sunshine on my face. Waves crashed against the rocks in front of me, and I was close enough to the water to feel a fine mist of sea spray dance across my bare arms. I inhaled deeply, and it smelled like summer. So amazingly different from the stuffy air and hissing radiator inside my apartment back in Boston. I closed my eyes, and I sighed. This trip, this write-for-hire job, were exactly what I needed to get myself back on track. Soon, the words would flow easily from my fingertips again, and after I finished this project, maybe I'd even write something of my own good enough for Charley to sell at auction.

I opened my eyes just in time to see a dolphin jump out in the surf, and then suddenly I remembered: Oscar! He couldn't go a whole week without eating, and I'd been rushing this morning to get to the airport. Had I even fed him before I left? Keeping him alive felt like the one good thing I'd done these past few months, and killing him now, because I'd gone on this trip, felt like it would be a bad omen for the Asherwood project and the easier future I'd just imagined.

Jack still had a key to the apartment. We hadn't talked since he'd moved out, but if I texted him now and asked him to feed Oscar, I wouldn't mind also having to tell him I was in LA for the week. Subtext: *I've moved on. I have an amazing life!* The truth, of course, was another story.

Can you do me a huge favor? I quickly texted Jack before I could change my mind. Can you stop by the apartment a few times this week and feed Oscar? I had to go to LA for the week.

His reply came back immediately. And I was relieved that he wasn't avoiding my texts, as much for my pride as for poor Oscar's well-being. Who's Oscar? Did you get a cat?

I'd been born and raised a cat lover, and grew up in a house with four cats, but Jack was allergic. So why hadn't I gotten a cat after he moved out? Maybe deep down I'd clung to the notion that someday, Jack might move back in. Or maybe I just didn't have it in me right now to care for a real pet.

No, allergen-free pet! Oscar's a fish, I typed.

You got a fish, seriously?

What? He's good company!

You replaced me with a fish? Was he trying to be funny, or was he trying to be an ass? It was hard to tell which one over text.

I ignored the question. Please, please can you feed him? I've already managed to kill his five friends. Food is next to the aquarium. Just sprinkle a few flakes a few times this week. I'll be back next Saturday.

What are you doing in LA? Visiting Noah?

Jack and Noah had a long history of disliking each other, all the way back to senior year at Brown, when Noah told me Jack wasn't right for me and Jack told me Noah was secretly in love with me. I'd rolled my eyes at both of them, positive they were both completely wrong. But still, it would give me a sadistic sort of pleasure to lie and tell Jack now that yes, I was here for Noah. In truth, Noah had yet to text me back, but the NDA I'd signed also prevented me from telling Jack exactly what I was actually doing in LA. My fingers hovered over my phone for a minute before I replied. Novel research, I finally typed. I swallowed hard; it was only half a lie.

Jack didn't comment on that or question me. Why would he? Instead, he finally texted back: Okay, I'll feed Oscar for you. Three dots popped up for a second, then disappeared. Then reappeared. How have you been?

I stared at his words for a moment, thinking of all the truthful ways I could respond. Pretty miserable. I missed him. Oscar really was honestly a shitty replacement for a guy who used to regularly wash and fold my laundry.

But it was easier to lie than to get into any of that over text. So instead I quickly typed: I'm great!!! Busy. Gotta run. Thanks for saving Oscar!

FOUR

Henry Asherwood's estate was only a fifteen-minute ride from my hotel, but the road leading up to it was so winding and deserted, it almost felt like my entry into an entirely different world.

I mean, this *was* an entirely different world from the one I inhabited back in Boston. Not just the sunshine, the Pacific Ocean, the damp salty air, and the cliffside views for days. A well-dressed driver in a black Tesla, *Nate*, had come to pick me up at my hotel promptly at six, and after offering me a small bottle of Pellegrino, he tried to engage me in small talk the whole drive. *Have you ever been to Malibu before, Ms. Fitzgerald? Do you want any restaurant recommendations? Do you want to know the best place to surf?*

No, no, and no, though I nodded politely, sipped my Pellegrino, and held on to the door as we turned off the busy Pacific Coast Highway and then took the steep turns sharper than my stomach liked. We spun through the final bend, and there in front of me was the unbelievable and sprawling Asherwood mansion, a large one-story expanse of floor-to-ceiling tinted glass that hugged the edge of a cliff and seemed to stretch for as long as a city block in Boston. The word *estate* popped into my head, but that didn't seem to do this justice. *Wow. Someone actually lives here?*

"It's something, isn't it?" Nate chuckled, and only then did I realize that I'd actually said my thoughts out loud.

I put my hand to mouth, swallowing back embarrassment, but he didn't say anything else as he walked around and opened the car door for me. "Come on, I'll walk you to the door," Nate said kindly. "He's eager to meet you."

Standing in his marble-and-glass foyer, Henry Asherwood III looked exactly the same in person as he had on the cover of *People's Sexiest Man Alive* issue: tall, tanned, athletic, with striking curly black hair, and blue-green eyes brighter than the Pacific. Only, in person there was something else about him that didn't quite come across in a magazine photograph, even a high-gloss one. He exuded a certain warmth, a strange sort of magnetism that drew me inside his house and made me feel eager to win his good opinion.

"Mr. Asherwood," I said. (*No*, embarrassingly, I *gushed*). "It's so great to meet you. Thanks for bringing me out here. I'm really excited to hear about your project."

He laughed a little, and the magnetism sparked, turning electric. My skin felt hot as he reached behind me to shut the door, and I looked away from him, past him, into the house. In front of us was an immaculate living room with high wood-beamed ceilings, white leather couches, a gleaming white grand piano, and then a wall of glass that showcased the sparkling blue Pacific. I wondered if there was any place in this house where you couldn't see or hear the ocean.

"Please, call me Ash," he was saying now, as he gestured for me to follow him into the living room. "All my friends do. Mr. Asherwood was my grandfather."

It struck me that he said his grandfather, not his father, but I had read in the biography on the plane that his grandfather had practically raised him, his own father too wrapped up in partying. I nodded. "Okay, sure. *Ash*. And call me Olivia, please."

He stopped walking, turned to face me again, and smiled easily, like he hadn't considered anything else. "Ms. Fitzgerald is your mother? Or your mother-in-law?" He laughed again, but raised his eyebrows slightly like he genuinely wanted to know.

"Neither one. Fitzgerald is actually a pen name." Charley's invention, and as a twenty-four-year-old writer eager to go out on submission, when Charley told me my real last name, *Finkemeier*, was both too clunky and too hard to spell, who was I to argue? Sometimes lately, though, I wished I had. *Olivia Fitzgerald* felt unreal like everything else with my writing career, a fantasy, like any glimmer of hope I once held that I might be successful.

"I sense there's a story there," Ash said, and I felt almost unsettled, like he knew exactly what I'd just been thinking.

But I shook my head, brushed him off with a smile. "Not a very interesting one."

"Well, if you wrote it, I'm sure it would be. I just love your writing, Olivia. I'm a huge fan."

I was full-on blushing now, transparently beet-colored from the neck up. "I'm honestly so honored that you read *All the Little Lights*, and that you're interested in working with me." I realized even as I spoke that he probably wasn't going to continue to want to work with me if I couldn't stop blushing and stammering like a teenager in front of him.

But it didn't seem to faze him. Maybe he was used to it. Other people falling to pieces right in front of him. I now fully understood what it meant to be starstruck.

He smiled. "To be completely honest, Olivia, I haven't had a chance to read the *Lights* book yet."

"Then…how do you know my writing?" I let out a nervous laugh as I thought through the few personal essays I'd been able to publish alongside the release of *All the Little Lights*, talking about the impact of my mother's death on the novel. Did Ash read *Lit Hub*? Seemed unlikely.

"I loved your other novel." He said it so easily, so lightly, that for a moment, I couldn't really process what he was saying: *"Becky."*

FIVE

In the months leading up to *Becky*'s release, two years ago, Charley had high hopes. *All the Little Lights* had gotten good reviews and by all accounts sold very well. And *Becky* had, as Charley put it, an amazing hook: a modern-day retelling of Daphne du Maurier's *Rebecca*, told from the point of view of the first Mrs. de Winter's—Becky's—ghost.

But then several, what Charley would later refer to euphemistically as *very unfortunate events*, occurred. First my editor quit, and my book fell into the hands of her kind but very overwhelmed assistant. Then, in the crucial months when the sales and marketing teams should've been pitching my book for store placement, my imprint folded and I was shuffled off into a much larger sister imprint, where no one working there knew my name, much less had read my book. The death knell was the *Kirkus* review that came a week later, calling *Becky* "a shoddy, ridiculous knockoff."

Kirkus is always tough, Charley noted unhelpfully at the time. (They'd given *All the Little Lights* a starred review.) But a few days later, *Publisher's Weekly* echoed the same sentiment: "Fitzgerald's sophomore novel is a mess of contradictions." And then it seemed that *Becky*'s fate was sealed. It was doomed to be badly reviewed in the trades, and the book released into obscurity, stocked hardly anywhere. Based on those two terrible reviews, deep down I wondered if maybe it was a blessing that no one even knew it existed. Maybe it was better for a book to be universally ignored than universally hated.

But there was more to it than that. At the time, I didn't yet understand how this failure could bloom and grow, how it would follow behind me, define me, suffocate me. *Becky* had failed so spectacularly on so many levels that now, a few years later, I wondered if I'd ever be able to write my way out, no matter what I did next. And that was most paralyzing of all.

"Wine?" Ash asked me, interrupting my thoughts. I'd followed him out to a large veranda and had taken the seat he'd offered at a wide plank table, formally set with china for our introductory dinner. Below us, waves crashed against rocks, and up ahead, the orange-pink sun was sinking into the ocean. But I barely noticed the scenery. I couldn't stop thinking about what he'd said inside, that he'd loved *Becky*.

Now he held a bottle of red, poised just above the crystal wineglass set out on the table in front of me, and he raised his eyebrows, waiting for my answer.

I didn't really want wine. I was already struggling to think clearly, but I didn't want to seem impolite either, and as I'd learned from my years working with Charley, nearly all publishing relationships were forged over glasses of wine. "Just a little," I finally said, to which he smiled, poured a rather large glass, and then took the seat across from me.

He raised his own full glass toward me. "To new friends and new projects," he said.

"Cheers to that." We clinked and I took a small sip. "So, I have to be totally honest." My words tumbled out in a rush.

"I'm pretty sure you're one of the only people who has actually read *Becky*. It barely sold any copies. How did you even find it?"

He didn't answer for a moment. He took another sip of wine, then turned off to stare at the sunset. When he turned back toward me, he was smiling wide. "It's an amazing novel, Olivia. Really, you're very talented."

"Thank you." I was blushing again, and I swallowed back my snarky reply that *Kirkus* would beg to differ.

"As soon as I read it, I just knew you would be the exact right writer for this project. I called up my manager and said I had to have you. He called your agent and now, here you are. Just like that." He snapped his fingers as if I'd just appeared magically, out of thin air, and I wondered if most things in his life had and did appear for him. *Just like that.*

"I'm flattered," I said, and I was. "But I still don't understand..."

"Why don't we eat dinner, and then we can talk more about the project. I'll explain everything. But first, I hope you like gazpacho. I made it myself." His voice exuded self-pride, but in a charming way. "I've been taking these cooking classes, and I've gotten pretty good, if I do say so myself."

I despised gazpacho. Cold soup? Nope. Soup was by its very nature meant to be a hot food. But I nodded and told him I loved gazpacho.

So maybe it wasn't just him being dishonest that night, but me too. Maybe from the very beginning, everything about our entire relationship was built on a lie.

"Okay," Ash finally said, sipping his second glass of wine. The sun set, and twinkle lights suddenly illuminated, strung all along the edge of the balcony, clearly on a timer. "Are you ready to talk about the project?"

I nodded. I'd choked back a whole bowl of gazpacho and was more than ready.

"When my grandfather died ten years ago, I had his papers packed up, shipped here. They sat in boxes in the attic, gathering dust for a long time, but then, last year, after…after the accident…" His voice trailed off, and I nodded to show I understood. Or, at least that I understood the *People* magazine version of what had happened—his wife, Angelica, had died after a tragic one-car accident. "Well, suddenly I was here all alone with a lot of time on my hands, and I finally went through all the boxes. There were these journals. My grandmother's journals, from the 1930s. And they tell this incredible story that would make an amazing book. And a film. I definitely see it on the big screen…"

Who was I to tell him how hard it was to sell movie rights, much less get a movie made? But maybe for a guy like Ash, it actually wouldn't be very hard at all. And it occurred to me that this bizarre job interview, or whatever this was, could be about much more than fifty thousand dollars. Maybe having my name attached to Henry Asherwood's sure-to-be-a-success project would turn my sales track around and resurrect my failing career. This could be my golden ticket.

"Okay," I said. "I'm really intrigued. What *is* the story?"

"Ah, well, that's where you come in, Olivia. You're the Daphne du Maurier expert."

"Hardly." I laughed. Sure, I knew *Rebecca* inside and out, but writing a retelling of that novel did not make me any sort of expert on du Maurier herself.

"But you know *Rebecca* better than anyone, don't you?"

"I know it pretty well," I admitted.

"Right, and that's why you're the perfect writer for this story."

"Why?" I was still confused, and in spite of myself, I'd finished the whole glass of wine. My head felt foggy. I had this pervading sense that something was wrong, something was very wrong, but it felt ridiculous too, because here was Ash, about to offer me the world, and so didn't that make everything just right?

"Because, Olivia," Ash finally said. "Daphne du Maurier stole my grandmother's story."

SIX

There was only one short chapter on Emilia Asherwood in the biography I'd read on the plane—just eight pages singularly devoted to Ash's grandmother. She'd died fairly young, at the age of thirty-seven, when Ash's father was only two years old, but the book mentioned her death in just a few words *(tragic accident)*. All I could glean from those eight pages was the tiniest picture into her life. She was born in France, met Henry Asherwood by chance on a trip abroad to the US, married him within weeks and moved to California with him. Seven years later, she was dead.

Daphne du Maurier stole my grandmother's story.

Back in my hotel room later that night, I turned Ash's words over again in my head. What did they even mean? I'd asked him to explain more before I'd left. And he promised he'd go through the story in more detail if I'd agree to another dinner at his house, tomorrow—he was trying an all-day paella.

What I'd said to Ash was the truth. I was hardly a du Maurier expert. I did know a little, but it had been a few years now since I'd written *Becky*, so once I got back to my hotel, I sat on the bed with my laptop and googled to refresh my memory.

Daphne du Maurier was born in 1907, so she would've been about the same age as Emilia, who was born in 1905. Daphne lived the majority of her life in England, though. She grew up the middle of three sisters, in a family of artists—both her parents were actors. But their ancestry was French, and she did spend some time in France as a teenager. I wondered now if she had ever crossed paths with Emilia there?

But also, maybe more significantly, Ash was not the first person to accuse du Maurier of stealing a story. She'd defended herself against a plagiarism claim in New York in the late 1940s, brought by the heir of the late Edwina MacDonald, a lesser-known American author. Her son sued, saying Daphne du Maurier had plagiarized his mother's novel, *Blind Windows*, in *Rebecca*. But the claim was ultimately dismissed. Then, there was a Brazilian author, Carolina Nabuco, whose *A Sucessora* was strikingly similar to *Rebecca* and was rumored to have had been submitted (and passed over) for English translation by Daphne's publisher years before *Rebecca* was published.

Charley and I had actually discussed all this when I'd first broached doing a retelling of *Rebecca*. I'd felt a little strange about entering a space myself that was already rife with questions of ownership.

"There are no new stories," Charley had insisted to me, waving my concerns away over a glass of sauvignon blanc after I'd worried out loud that retelling a classic novel, a novel I'd loved and admired since I first read it at the age of fifteen, almost felt a little bit like stealing. "And anyway," she'd added, "aren't *Rebecca*—and those other two novels—really just a retelling of *Jane Eyre* to begin with?"

There are no new stories. Her words had settled the anxiety I'd been feeling, enough for me to go ahead and write *Becky*. But now as I rehashed it all again in my mind, as I thought about what Ash had said earlier tonight about his grandmother, something twisted inside of me, leaving me feeling unsettled.

I awoke before dawn the next morning, my body still on Boston time, and saw I had a text from Noah. He'd finally texted back at midnight, long after I'd fallen into a weird nightmarish sleep. I blinked, half remembering my dream now, a vague creeping recollection of a dark and twisty cliff-side road.

Heyyyy Livvy! I smiled—Noah was the only one who ever called me *Livvy*. Seeing it typed out like that on my phone, I suddenly remembered how much I'd missed him. Coffee in the morning? I teach a class at 9. Text me where you're staying—I'll come pick you up after?

I sighed happily at the thought of coffee with Noah this morning, but it was too early to text him back now. Purple light slowly seeped through a crack in the curtains, and I decided I'd go down to the beach for a walk first.

Everyone else in Malibu was still asleep but me, and the open-air hotel lobby—and beach—were quiet, empty. It was a different kind of quiet than back in my apartment in Boston, though. A nicer, calming quiet. The beach was damp, foggy, a gray haze hugging the horizon, but I walked barefoot along the surf, stepping over rocks. And for the first time in a long time, my mind ruminated on a story, on possibility.

I walked and I walked, and made my way down the beach, lost in thoughts of Emilia Asherwood, Daphne du Maurier, the nameless narrator in *Rebecca*. I got so caught up in my own thoughts that I didn't quite realize how far I'd walked until suddenly, I glimpsed a familiar wall of glass off the cliff up ahead: *Ash's house.*

I walked toward it, curious how Ash's world appeared from down here, at the ocean's edge. His house looked even larger, looming, more towering glass than it had seemed up close. My eye caught the veranda where we'd eaten dinner last night, and a woman in a white dress stood there now, leaning against the edge of the railing. I was too far away to make out her face, but she had long wavy auburn hair that swirled from the wind coming off the water. I imagined her white dress was sheer, though I was too far to know that for sure. Did Ash have a girlfriend who rose before dawn, like me? He hadn't mentioned her last night, but why would he have?

I quickly turned back to look at the ocean, not wanting to be caught staring, even from far away. But as I turned around to walk back toward my hotel, I glanced at the veranda one last time. Now, though, it was empty.

Excerpt from *The Wife*

I will tell you exactly who my husband is: a fraud.

You might think you already know him. You've seen him, and you've loved him from afar. You might think that he is beautiful and perfect. Wealthy and divine. You might think that as his wife, I have everything.

But nothing about him is what it seems. You have never really known him at all. And the truth is, neither have I.

So where do I begin?

First there is a story, and then there is a thief.

But before that, there's just me: the wife.

Sometimes I can still remember how I used to be a woman on my own in the world. How I was young and pretty and smart, and life glittered with so much promise and possibility. And now, all I am is the wife. Which means exactly nothing. And everything.

So I am going to write my story. His story. Our story.

I am going to tell you everything that happened up until the moment he killed me.

SEVEN

"Fancy hotel," Noah said a few hours a later, raising his eyebrows, as I got into his old college-era black Honda in the circular drive of the Malibu Heights Inn. "Now I'm dying to know what brought you to LA."

I laughed, accepted the hug he offered as I got into his strangely familiar car. Just sitting in the passenger seat suddenly took me back ten years, and for a moment I remembered what it was like to feel happy, to be filled with this strange thing called hope.

"No matter why you're here, it's just great to see you." Noah grabbed my hand and squeezed it for a second, before putting both hands back on the wheel and pulling onto the Pacific Coast Highway.

I leaned back against the seat, relaxing into the way it was always like this with Noah and me. *Easy.* Even when time passed, even with distance between us, whenever we saw each other again, it was like we instantly both remembered our connection, and suddenly all the years since college evaporated just like that.

"It's great to see you too," I said. "How long has it been?"

Noah didn't answer, but I was pretty sure that like me, he remembered exactly how long. I could still recall the exact frown on his face as he'd walked away from my book launch party for *All the Little Lights*, five years earlier.

Jack had picked a fight with him. I'd glanced up from signing books to see the two of them arguing in the corner of the bookstore, and then I'd watched Noah storm out of the party. *Let him go*, Jack had walked over and whispered in my ear. *He's just jealous*. Though whether he meant jealous about my book or about something else, it wasn't totally clear. And I was annoyed that whatever issue he'd had with Jack, Noah had left without saying goodbye to me.

That was it, the last time I saw him before now. And that was exactly how long it had been, *five years*. The truth was, I was hoping Noah wouldn't bring up the book party, and I felt relieved when he ignored my question.

I glanced at him—we were stopped at a light, and he seemed laser-focused on the directions on his phone. We were driving to a coffee shop nearby. Just down the road from where I was staying, and he'd heard good things, he'd said when we'd texted earlier. We'd driven in what felt like a large circle after pulling out of my hotel, and I was fairly sure we were lost now, but also, I didn't care. I was just happy to be here, in this car, with Noah again.

"Aha! There it is." He pumped his fist in victory, and I started laughing. "Are you seriously laughing at me right now, Livvy?" He smiled a little and shook his head as he made a U-turn and pulled into a small (and perhaps unsurprisingly for Malibu, cliffside) parking lot. Everything was just on the edge of the world here, even coffee.

"I'm not laughing at you. I'm laughing *with* you." It was a distinction we'd made many times back in college. *Prepositions*, as Noah was fond of saying, *always do the heavy lifting*. I laughed a little again thinking about how college Noah felt exactly like this Noah, and how it brought me back to college Olivia too. That girl who loved words, who loved to write more than anything. I laughed again, this time more with a sense of nostalgic glee. Noah shot me a faux pout. "With you," I emphasized as he parked and we got out of the car.

We ordered two Americanos at the little window out front, then took them around back to a picnic table, where suddenly the whole Pacific Ocean spread out wide, all-consuming, below and ahead of us. The fog had begun to lift, just the haziest line of gray hugged the horizon, and the sky above us had turned a bright and sparkling cerulean.

"God, it's really beautiful here," I said. "I totally get why you live here now."

"Well, I don't live *here*." He gestured out in front of him. "Malibu is for the extra-fancy and ultra-wealthy." He whistled a little under his breath. "Of which I am decidedly neither." I blushed a little at the implication that maybe he thought I was. "So what are you doing out here anyway, Livvy? Film meetings?"

A laugh caught in the back of my throat but came out sounding more like a strangled cry. The idea that I'd be out here for film meetings felt downright preposterous right now. Noah had no idea how badly my career was faltering. And why would he? I hadn't told him anything real in years. Maybe that feeling I'd had in the car, that familiarity, that comfort, that ease in falling back to who and what we once were, was actually nothing more than an illusion. A false feeling of closeness.

I opened my mouth to tell Noah about Ash, but then I remembered the NDA. I thought for a moment about how to parse things in the most general way so I wouldn't be violating anything. "I'm actually out here for a write-for-hire job, but I can't exactly tell you the specifics since I signed an NDA," I finally said.

"An NDA?" He raised his eyebrows and sipped his Americano. "Very fancy, Livvy. Very Malibu."

"Not fancy. *Industry standard,*" I said, repeating what Charley had written in the email when she'd sent the NDA over.

Noah blushed a little, like maybe he thought I was talking down to him from inside an industry he'd longed to be a part of but wasn't quite yet. I wasn't really either, not anymore. I wanted to tell him that, but for some reason I didn't. Instead I said, "This is my first write-for-hire gig, so it's all kind of strange to me too. I mean, it might be my first, if it all works out. That's why I'm out here, to kind of test the waters, learn about the project."

"But won't that take you away from your own work?" Noah sounded genuinely concerned, and I didn't have the heart to tell him that my own work was not in demand at the moment.

I shrugged. "I have a little time now. And it's good money," I added.

"Ah." He nodded. "Did I tell you I got a new agent?"

I shook my head. Of course he hadn't told me—we'd barely talked these last few years. Noah had signed with an agent after he got his MFA, but that agent had failed to sell his first two novels, and then had broken up with him. Last I'd heard, Noah had been querying again with a new book.

He told me his new agent's name now. I didn't recognize it (which meant nothing), but for some reason, I nodded and pretended like I did.

"Yeah," he said, finishing off his Americano. "We're working on edits right now, and then she seems to really believe she can sell it. But you know...we'll see."

"Noah, that's great. I'm excited for you." I pushed the words out with so much cheer they sounded forced. But I was truly excited for him. Mostly. I felt a little something else too—jealousy, maybe?—but not because he might finally sell a novel. I wanted that for him, I really did. It was more that everything was still fresh and shiny for Noah. Possibility still sparked. There were no bad sales numbers to bring him down, no *unfortunate events* to make him feel tired and jaded like me.

"And what about you?" he asked. "When does your new one come out?"

"Oh, well…" My voice faltered a little, and I couldn't exactly lie to him. "I'm kind of in between projects. It's why this write-for-hire job would be ideal."

"In between?" He frowned but didn't push it. "But Boston, Jack? Both are still amazing, right?"

"Jack and I aren't together anymore." Finally, I said something completely honest to him, and it felt like such a relief to say it out loud. I exhaled, like I'd been holding my breath ever since he'd picked me up. No, maybe ever since Jack had moved out.

"Oh, Livvy." He reached across the table for my hand and squeezed, like he felt sorry about the whole thing. Surely he wasn't. He'd never liked Jack. The feeling was very mutual.

"Well, you know, maybe it was a long time coming," I said, and that felt pretty honest too.

Noah nodded. "I get it. I actually think I'm having a midlife crisis," he added, almost nonchalantly.

"Noah, you're thirty-two! You're too young to have a midlife crisis."

"If I die at sixty-four, it tracks."

"I forgot how morbid you are," I said, finishing off my Americano.

"How could you forget?" Noah smirked. "Considering it's one of my finer qualities."

I laughed, and then a silence settled between us. We'd run out of coffee to drink and things that were definitely safe to say. We stared at each other for another moment, and Noah opened his mouth like he wanted to say something else, but then closed it again, as if deciding against it.

He finally cleared his throat. "Well, on that note, I guess I should get you back so you can get to work, huh?"

I stared into my empty coffee cup, wishing I'd sipped it more slowly so I had an excuse to stay longer, talk more. But I wasn't sure what else I would say anyway. Maybe Noah's star was finally rising and mine had been dimming, and even though we were both right here in Malibu, we were further apart than we'd ever been.

EIGHT

All-day paella beat gazpacho by a mile, and back on Ash's balcony, I complimented his cooking skills, and meant it this time. My jet lag had won out over the caffeine, and I'd taken a long nap this afternoon. Now, well-rested, I felt infinitely more relaxed and prepared for our second meeting tonight. I also made sure not to drink the wine he'd poured for me, aside from a polite sip. My head felt clearer, my senses sharper. I'd come with a notebook and a list of questions about his grandmother, about her journals, and about her connection to Daphne du Maurier.

But every time I tried to ask a question about Emilia, about the story he wanted to hire me to write, he changed the subject.

Me: "Tell me exactly why you think your Daphne du Maurier stole something from your grandmother?"

Ash: "Can you taste the saffron? The recipe called for a pinch, but I added two."

What the fuck does saffron taste like?

Me: "Yep, tastes amazing. So, your grandmother...did she actually know Daphne du Maurier?"

Ash: "But I think more saffron next time, don't you?"

We went around for nearly half an hour, Ash obsessing over the saffron, then the bread—he should've offered a sourdough loaf instead of wheat. Also, the wine. He'd set out a Spanish red, but he liked the Italian varietal better.

I remembered what Noah said, about having a midlife crisis, and Ash was decidedly in the throes of one. Noah would get a kick out of this. If I could ever actually share any of it. And it would be funnier if it didn't also feel like this write-for-hire job—and any money or career boost that would come with it—was moving further and further from my reach by the second.

"Everything about the dinner was perfect," I interrupted him, my voice louder and more forceful than I meant it to be, "but if you want me to write this book for you, I really need to know more about the story."

Ash drained his wineglass and smiled sheepishly. "Olivia, forgive me. It's been a while since I've had a woman's company in this house. I've turned into a bit of an eccentric this last year, I'm afraid."

I thought about the woman in the sheer white dress, out on his balcony earlier this morning, and I wanted to call him out on it, ask him why he was both lying now and avoiding discussing the very reason he'd asked me here. But I once again remembered the fifty thousand dollars, and I bit my lip. "No forgiveness necessary," I said. "And dinner is delicious, really. But...your grandmother?"

"My grandmother," he repeated.

"If you want me to write her story, I need to know everything."

"Everything," he repeated softly, and I wasn't sure whether it was a question or a promise.

"I'd love to see her journals, read her story for myself."

"Do you speak French?" he asked, so abruptly that it felt like he was changing the subject again, and I closed my notebook and sighed a little. "Her journals are all in French. That's why I'm asking. I'm in the process of translating them. I can email you over what I have so far, but it's incomplete." *Of course he speaks French.* "Obviously I'll send you the full translation over the next few weeks, and then you'll have it to write from."

"Okay," I said. "So, let's start there, for now. What is the story you want me to write exactly?"

"Her story. Her untold, incredible story." He paused for a moment, and finally he gave me something. "My grandfather met her in the early 1930s, and they fell in love quickly and got married just like that." I nodded. I knew that much already from the biography. "After she moved to California with him, she lived in the shadow of his dead first wife. And she penned a story about her experience," he said. "Her story, it *is Rebecca.* Even Grandfather's first wife's name was Rebecca."

"Wait, hold on." I was trying to process what he was saying, and though I heard all his words, I was struggling to put it together. "So, you're telling me your grandmother wrote a story, in French, in these journals of hers about her life with your grandfather. But it reads and plays out just like *Rebecca*?"

"Yes!" His voice was effusive. This definitely excited him more than saffron. I wasn't sure why he took so long to spell it out.

"So, she actually lived the story of *Rebecca*—and then wrote out her day-to-day experience in her journals? Or she wrote an actual novel in her journals?"

"It's her story," he said, sounding so certain.

"But is it possible," I asked gently, "that it could have been some kind of very early fan fiction?"

"No." Ash shook his head. "Grandmother Emilia's journals are from 1934. But *Rebecca* wasn't published until 1938. It was Emilia's story first," he said firmly.

And Carolina Nabuco's, and Edwina McDonald's, and Charlotte Brontë's. I heard Charley's voice: *There are no new stories, Olivia.* But I kept my mouth shut and let Ash keep talking.

"If anyone was writing *fan fiction*, it was Daphne du Maurier. Grandmother Emilia's story deserves to be told. I owe her that much. She died so young." His voice broke, and he abruptly looked away from me, out toward the ocean. "It wasn't fair," he added.

He was suddenly far away, even though he was still sitting across the table from me. His grandmother died when his father was a baby—Ash never knew her, never even met her. But I wondered if this wasn't really about his grandmother. If this deep dive into his grandmother's journals, this write-for-hire project, was more about him needing to work through his own private grief over his wife.

And for the first time, I felt a flicker of something real for him. Understanding.

NINE

Like Ash's wife, my mom also died in a tragic car accident.

Except my mom had been high on prescription pills at the time and had killed a teenager in a head-on collision after her car crossed the median. It happened my senior year of college, and none of it made any sense. No matter what my dad or what my older sister, Suzy, said afterwards, in my mind, I just couldn't process what had happened. Ever since, I had avoided spending more than a weekend at home, and in my head, I often still thought of my mom back there, in my childhood house in Connecticut, baking vegan cookies, doing yoga, and volunteering to read to sick and injured kids at the hospital. (Ironically, she was on her way there when she'd had her accident.)

I wrote *All the Little Lights* about her, about a woman who burns her whole life down for Vicodin. But no, really it was about me, for me. Trying to understand it, trying to make the absurdity of what happened in real life make any sense whatsoever in fiction. Maybe I wrote *Becky* about her too— because by the time I started it, Dad had already remarried

Shawna, and maybe my narrator, Becky's ghost, was really more about my mom's ghost than a *Rebecca* retelling. That's what writing fiction was, wasn't it? Processing your own life, answering all those questions in any way you wanted to, since fictional worlds operated with their own language and their own rules and their own timelines. They offered their own answers.

But sitting across from Ash, watching his face turn when he spoke about his grandmother's story, I understood, for the first time, why this project was important to him. He wanted meaning where there was none. A story that made sense, when his own didn't. And suddenly too, I understood why I was exactly the right person to write it.

Back in my hotel room later that night, I refreshed my inbox, waiting for the email Ash had promised me—the partial translation of his grandmother's journal. He'd promised to send it before bed, and by 10:00 p.m., I yawned, realized I was still on Boston time, and wondered exactly how late he planned to email.

While I was waiting, I couldn't help myself, and I googled his dead wife, Angelica Asherwood. I remembered when the accident happened last year. It had been all over the news, social media, and every celeb gossip site I followed as a means of procrastination. But they'd been a very private couple, and I realized now I knew barely anything of substance about Angelica, who she was, what she had done for a living, even what she looked like. I remembered only the headline I'd seen again and again: *Angelica Asherwood Dead at 31 After Tragic Car Accident.*

I found a few old pictures in Google images now. They were all snapped from far away—her and Ash holding coffees on the beach—both in baseball caps and sunglasses—the photos clearly taken in secret by some paparazzi trailing them. It was hard to see her face, hard to tell if she was pretty, though I imagined she was. But I suddenly wanted to see her, wanted to know her in some strange way, wanted to imagine exactly what it was Ash was missing when he woke up alone each morning. Like Noah, morbid was one of my finest qualities. It was why I'd really leaned on him, senior year of college, after my mom died. Noah got my darkness.

I kept searching, until I found myself down the Reddit rabbit hole. There was a whole subreddit on the Asherwoods (of course there was), and I spent a good twenty minutes scrolling through. There was everything from people complaining about their store coupons to people speculating if Ash was dating again and whom. *(Was he?)* Then a post from a few weeks ago caught my eye: *ANGELICA ASHERWOOD IS ALIVE!!!*

u/Malibulandscapeguy—13d
   Okay, I *just* saw Angelica Asherwood on Carbon Beach. I'm telling you, it was definitely her!!! I used to do landscaping on their property and I talked to her a few times before she "died," so I know exactly what she looks like. I said hi to her on the beach, and she immediately ran away all scared like she knew I caught her. Husband is intense. Dude always gave me the creeps. Did she fake her death????

A knock on the door made me jump, and I dropped my laptop on the bed before I could read the replies. It was 10:30 p.m., and no one really knew I was here but Noah.

"Room service," a woman called.

"Wrong room," I yelled without getting off the bed.

"Ms. Fitzgerald?" she called again.

I sighed and shut my laptop and walked to the door. I opened it to see a woman holding a bottle of Dom Pérignon chilling in a bucket of ice. "I didn't order that," I said. Champagne for one felt a little lame, and besides, I would've ordered something much cheaper.

She smiled, but ignored me and walked into my room, setting the ice bucket on the small table by the sliding glass doors. She handed me a card: *Olivia, sorry for the delay, still working through the translation. Let's meet again tomorrow. I'll send a car in the morning. So excited to work on this project with you. You're amazing! Cheers!—A*

"Shall I open it for you?" the woman asked as I looked up from the note.

I nodded and reread the note again. Instead of sending an email about the delay, like any normal person would've, Ash sent me a bottle of champagne. A very expensive bottle of champagne. Or was this just his eccentric wealthy person's way of giving me an official offer to work together? Whatever test he'd been putting me through these past two days, had I passed? *You're amazing.*

My face felt hot as the woman handed me a glass half-full with bubbly and asked me if I needed anything else. I realized I was probably supposed to tip her and quickly rummaged through my purse, embarrassingly coming up with only a one-dollar bill and a few quarters, which I shoved into her hand with a mumbled apology.

After she left, I went out onto the balcony and sipped the champagne. It was smoother than the cheap stuff I'd normally drink, and I reveled in the velvety feel of it against my tongue.

Dude always gave me the creeps. The Reddit poster popped back into my head.

But then I took another sip of the champagne, soaked in the beautiful roar of the ocean in front of me. Ash's world was unusual, sure, but expensive champagne and an interesting story about a wealthy wife in the 1930s? Well, maybe I needed to stop overthinking and enjoy wherever this new project would lead.

Excerpt from *The Wife*

"What are you doing in here?"

He walks into my room without even knocking, loosening his tie and frowning at me from just past the doorway. My room is his room. I am his. A possession isn't supposed to feel, so why am I always so sad?

I stand up from my desk, glance out the window. It has suddenly grown dark. The entire afternoon spun away from me, and now it's impossibly already night.

What am I doing?

I'm writing again. That's what I'm doing, and it's glorious. Freeing. Words tumble from my head, down my arm, through to my fingertips, gracing the blank paper in front of me. One after another, building into sentences, paragraphs, meaning. It has been so long that at first, I'd forgotten this hypnotic feeling. Forgotten the magnetism of words.

I was cleaning a few weeks ago when I came across the old box of my things, high up on the closet shelf. My story from long ago was tucked inside. What happened to a wife when her husband abandoned her, moved on to a new young woman? Reading it again, it almost felt like a premonition.

Writing is a memory too. A balm. Words belonged to me once, gave me power. And maybe they will again. I have a story to tell, and now it is mine, all of it.

"Are you writing about me?" he asks, grinning. He pulls off his tie, throws it down, then walks across the room toward me. He spins me around and wraps me in a hug from behind. Too tight. It suffocates.

I try to squirm a little out of his grasp, but he won't let go. He never lets go.

"Everything isn't about you," I say emphatically. But of course, I am writing about him.

He laughs and squeezes me tighter. He doesn't believe me. Everything is about him. He's the sun, and I simply exist to orbit around him. Though if I dare get too close, I'll burn up, burn out. That's exactly what I'm writing about.

He finally loosens his grip, but runs his hands up my stomach, resting his palms on my breasts, stroking softly with his thumbs through the fabric of my dress. He kisses my earlobe. "Come on," he whispers. "I'll inspire you."

"Let me finish what I'm working on." I reach for his hands and move them off my breasts, and then he finally takes a few steps away from me. I turn to face him and his cheeks are red with annoyance. Or anger. The sun burns too hot. Even he can't stand it himself.

"Just give me another half hour," I finally say. "I was in the middle of a thought when you walked in. Please?"

He sighs, but finally concedes with a nod, and I hate myself for sounding like I'm begging him for this time.

And maybe, even then, I already understand. I do not have it in me to play this game forever. If it hasn't happened yet, certainly it will soon enough. He'll tire of me, rid himself of me, someday.

The wife is a temporary job, with a temporary title. You can't dance with the sun forever, without eventually bursting into flames.

TEN

I woke up the next morning, my head throbbing, sunlight streaming in through a break in the curtains. I hadn't closed them all the way when I'd stumbled into bed last night, having drunk most of the bottle of Dom Pérignon out on the balcony. (I couldn't stand it going to waste.) But my pulsing headache told me that had been a mistake.

I rubbed my temples, sat up, and checked my phone. It was 9:30 a.m.—with the help of too much champagne I'd finally adjusted to Pacific time. I saw Ash had texted me two hours ago, telling me Nate would pick me up at ten. I jumped out of bed too quickly, and my head reacted with a more intense ache. I groaned and fished around in my purse for an ibuprofen, swallowing it down dry before stumbling into the shower.

I knew I needed to rush, but the warm water felt too nice, and I stood under it, letting it wash over me as I tried to get my head together. After the champagne last night, I'd returned to Reddit, and had fallen asleep after scrolling through the replies about the Angelica Asherwood "sighting." There were a lot of theories, ranging from Angelica faking her death to

Ash poisoning her and hiding her away in his mansion to Ash murdering her and covering it up with the accident. A little tipsy and half dreaming, I'd thought about the woman standing on Ash's balcony, and my last thought before falling asleep was whether anything on Reddit could be anywhere close to truth. Was it possible that Angelica was the woman I saw?

In the shower, the steam permeated my head, and I could suddenly think clearly. That all felt ridiculous. Ash was grieving, that much was clear. His wife had died last year in an accident. People posted crazy shit on Reddit all the time, and the woman I saw could've been anyone—a housekeeper, a girlfriend, a one-night stand. Thinking of those last two options annoyed me, though I knew they shouldn't. Ash and I were going to work on a book together—our relationship was purely professional.

So I couldn't really explain what I did next, as the warm water ran across my body, and my fingers traced it, down my chest, my stomach. I closed my eyes, and imagined they were his hands, that it was Ash who was touching me as my finger spiraled in between my legs.

"You got my champagne?" Ash asked as I walked inside his house an hour later and he motioned for me to come sit down on the sofa across from the floor-to-ceiling views of the ocean.

"I did. It was very kind, thank you." I took a seat on the cool white leather and lifted my sunglasses on top of my head. Not because I wanted to, but because it seemed rude not to. I squinted and tried not to grimace at the sunlight reflecting off the water, streaming in through the giant wall of windows.

He smiled, clearly pleased with his thoughtfulness. And I felt that electricity again that I'd felt the first time I'd walked in here, the first time I'd met him. I swallowed back embarrassment thinking about my moment, or whatever it was, in the shower, and I leaned forward and crossed my legs.

But he'd turned his attention away from me, as he was pulling a spiral-bound notebook off the glass end table next to him. "I have the translation so far right here," he said. "I guess I should've mentioned I handwrote it. Last night, after you left, I was going to scan it in and email it like I'd promised, but... I don't know. I thought it made more sense if we went over what I have today together in person."

I nodded, still unsure whether the champagne was an apology or a promise. Or an invitation. "Sure, can I see it?" I held my hands out, but Ash hesitated for a moment.

"There's not that much yet. I have to work through the rest of the translation. But you can get a sense from this... I hope you can..." He still clutched the notebook, not letting go.

"Ash," I said his name softly and leaned forward and put my hand on the notebook. For a few seconds we held on to it together, and I swore it felt hot, like even Ash's fingers were electric. But then he smiled sheepishly and let go.

I opened the notebook, and scanned through, anticipating it would be all filled. But only the first two pages were written on, in neat block letters. I flipped again in case I missed something. But nope, just two pages.

Last night I dreamt I went to Malibu again...

"Malibu?" I questioned, looking up after the first line.

"Grandfather had an estate up at Malibu Lake. He and Grandmother Emilia lived there for years. Until it burned down."

Burned down. Of course it did. Just like Manderley in the opening pages of *Rebecca*.

I went back to the notebook to read the rest. It was so short, there wasn't enough here for me to really tell much, except that it read similarly to how I remembered the beginning of

Rebecca. Emilia described her dream of being back at the estate, her memory of her time there. But then it just stopped.

Two pages? What was I supposed to do with this, exactly?

I cleared my throat and shut the notebook. "I'll definitely need to see the rest, the whole translation."

"Of course, absolutely."

I felt something strange creeping in my stomach, thinking about exactly what I was going to write for Ash. We couldn't just accuse Daphne du Maurier of plagiarism. Or at least, I would need much more compelling evidence than two hand-written pages Ash said he had translated himself. "And we have to discuss exactly what kind of book it is you want me to write. I think we have to be careful," I said, hoping my honesty wasn't too much. "Daphne du Maurier was a beloved literary figure. *Rebecca* is a classic. Trust me, from personal experience. Reviewers hated *Becky* because they thought my modern-day retelling didn't hold up."

"I strongly disagree," Ash said quickly.

I laughed a little. "Well, thanks. But my point is, I think that we need to approach this delicately."

Ash shrugged, and it occurred to me that maybe he'd never had to approach anything delicately in his entire life. What would it have been like to have been born and raised amidst so much money and fame and endless opportunity? I grew up in suburban Connecticut, in an upper-middle-class household. My dad was a lawyer who made a good enough living that my mom quit being a lawyer after I was born to stay at home with me and Suzy. We had everything we needed, or at least, we thought we did before she died. But I knew that was a far cry from how Ash had grown up, how he lived his life now.

"I guess I understand what you're saying," Ash finally said. "But being careful isn't really my specialty." He paused for a moment, then added, "I don't think I mentioned it last night, but I sent her journals out to get them authenticated."

He hadn't mentioned it last night, nor had he mentioned he'd only translated the smallest portion of them. "That's good," I said, because authenticating them at least felt like a start. "But also, do you know if your grandmother had any connection to Daphne du Maurier? If she wrote *Rebecca* first, as you believe, how could Daphne possibly have seen it to steal it?" Ash frowned, and I wondered if I was unintentionally sabotaging our whole project by asking so many questions. "I mean," I quickly added, "what exactly is the story you want me to write? Is it your grandmother's life story, that somehow weaves together with Daphne du Maurier's, or is it more a novel based on her life, that's something like another *Rebecca* retelling itself?"

He nodded slowly. "See, this is exactly why I knew you were the right person to write this."

"But I don't have any of the answers," I said.

"You're going to figure it all out, though." He spoke with the easy confidence of someone who'd probably never failed at anything in his life. I didn't feel so certain, but for fifty thousand dollars I was going to try my best to figure something out. "Hey, I should get the authentication back tomorrow, but if you're free for the rest of the day, we could get out of here. I could show you around Malibu a little bit. Do you want go for a hike?"

Hiking felt akin to running, which, after Jack moved out last fall, I'd tried to take up as a hobby. It lasted briefly, a whole week, until I admitted to myself that I hated running more than I hated being in my apartment all alone.

"Malibu has the best hiking," Ash added.

I looked down at the cute red flats on my feet now—definitely not hiking shoes. I thought again about my moment in the shower, and I wondered if spending the whole day with Ash, not specifically working on the writing project, was really the best idea. "I don't have the right shoes," I finally said, my voice faltering a little.

"What size are you?" Ash scrolled through something on his phone. "I'll have a pair of hiking boots and some socks messengered up from the store warehouse. They'll be here in forty-five minutes."

"I… I…really…you don't have to go to all that trouble…"

He waved away my protests with a small shake of his head, clearly not about to take no for an answer. "It's nothing, just tell me your size."

"Seven and a half," I finally relented. "But I have to admit, I'm not much of a hiker." I laughed weakly.

"Ahhh." He laughed too, a big, infectious laugh that crinkled around his eyes and reminded me again why he was *People*'s Sexiest Man Alive. *Twice.* "Well, that's because you've never gone hiking with me."

ELEVEN

An hour later, I had my new Asherwood Collection™ hiking boots on and laced up and was, against my better judgment on many fronts, following Ash up a hiking trail just across the Pacific Coast Highway from his house. It was seventy degrees and partly cloudy—perfect hiking weather, and Ash had promised—as we'd walked past his outdoor kitchen, pool, pool house, and tennis court to get to his own private underpass to the trail—that it would not be too difficult of a hike either. Though, twenty minutes in, I was struggling to keep up with him. The trail felt *difficult* to me. It was steep, a little rocky, and I was pretty sure I hated hiking as much as running, if not more. At least running I wasn't worried about sliding down a mountain and dying.

Ash stopped and turned around, suddenly noticing I was more than a few steps behind him. "You doing okay, Olivia?" he called out.

I nodded, though I could feel my face was bright red and hot, and I was sweating enough to look like I was definitely *not* doing okay.

He smiled easily as he stepped back down a few rocks toward me. "It's worth it at the top, promise," he said. I was staring at his gorgeous face, not my own feet, and as I took the next step, I teetered. Ash quickly grabbed onto both my arms, steadying me. "You're okay," he said, a statement, not a question, as he held on to me tightly.

But I was far from *okay*, this close to him, with his hands on my arms like this. I was breathing so hard now, my chest shook, almost close enough to touch his. But not quite. I looked up and our eyes locked for a minute—his were a piercing radiant sky-blue in this light. So bright, I wondered if they could possibly be real or were, more likely, colored contacts.

He dropped his gaze first, and slowly let go of my arms, taking my hand in his instead. "Come on, it's just a little farther to the top. I'll slow down and help you out. I didn't mean to go so fast."

I felt kind of silly needing his hand, but I didn't exactly want to let go either, so I held on, and accepted his help getting from rock to rock, climbing the trail as it got even steeper, windier, until finally we reached a clearing, a large flat cliff. Ash walked toward the edge to look out, and even though I didn't need his help anymore, he didn't let go of my hand.

From here we could see the whole wide Pacific Ocean, the curved coastline, and then the city far enough in the distance to look like an imaginary world, filled with toy buildings. "I love it up here. It makes me remember how small I am," Ash said. "How much more is out there, beyond me. It gets me out of my head, you know?"

Maybe I did know. Inside my apartment in Boston, it had felt for months like I was slowly dying inside, like the walls themselves would surely suffocate me if I didn't get out of there. But I did. And here I was. "It's beautiful up here," I agreed.

"Worth the hike, right?" He grinned.

I nodded. And the truth was, I'd actually forgotten to hate hiking once I was holding on to him.

"I came up here every day after she died. For weeks. I just sat up here and stared at the ocean."

"Did it help?" I asked softly. But as I stared out now, I felt a calm wash over me, and I understood that it had. It must have.

"Sure, as much as anything could, I guess."

"I'm so sorry," I said. "I can't even imagine."

"You're not married?" he asked. I shook my head. "Engaged?"

"Nope. Completely unattached," I said, unable to hold in a giant sigh.

"Ah, so there's a story there."

"Not really," I said. He raised his eyebrows. "I dated someone, lived with him, since college—for nine years! And six months ago, he decided he was done, just like that, and moved out."

"Poor Olivia," he said, and I couldn't tell from his tone whether he was serious or being facetious, but then I looked up, and his face looked earnest.

"It's fine," I said quickly, and as I said it, I realized it actually was. I hadn't thought about Jack the whole time I was here, except for texting him about feeding Oscar. *Oh, Oscar.* I hadn't thought about him either. I wondered if Jack had remembered to feed him or if Oscar had gone the way of his friends and was floating on the top of the tank.

"Hey," Ash said, bringing me back here. "If you don't have any plans tonight, I bought fresh shrimp at the seafood market this morning. I was going to try a fra diavolo, and it's really no fun to try recipes alone."

I hesitated, wanting to say yes, knowing I probably shouldn't. We couldn't really get more work done on his project until he got the journals back from the authenticator, and what were we doing together if we weren't working?

"I think it's good we're getting to know each other," Ash added, as if reading my mind. "It'll help with the project."

"Sure," I said, and even as the words escaped my lips, I already knew I might regret them later. "I'd love to join you for dinner."

TWELVE

I was a sweaty mess by the time we got back to Ash's house, and as if he had already anticipated that this would happen, that I would both agree to hike with him and agree to stay for dinner, he told me he'd had some clean clothes sent up from the Asherwood warehouse for me as well. "I told Clara to put them on the bed in the guest room," he told me as we walked back inside his house.

"Clara?" I asked him.

"My housekeeper," he clarified. Of course he had a house-keeper. Maybe she was the woman I'd seen on the balcony? "She's actually taking the next few days off." Ash was still talking. "But she promised to get that room cleaned up before she left, just in case you wanted to use it." He said it all so easily, it was clear he'd calculated this entire day before I'd even left my hotel this morning, so certain I would just agree to all of it. That I would do anything he asked me to. "Feel free to use the shower back there if you'd like," he added. "Dinner at six?"

I glanced at my phone. It was almost five. I'd skipped both

breakfast and lunch and had probably burned more calories on that hike than I had all last month combined. But I followed him back down a long hallway to the guest room, thanked him, and then walked inside and shut the door behind me.

There was a different air to this room than the rest of the house. The common rooms were cold and masculine, gleaming white edges, marble and slate and stone finishes. This room had rich, dark hardwood floors, cream-colored walls, a large king-sized bed draped in a pale blue comforter, and lacy shams on the king-sized pillows. There was a feminine sort of sense to this room that the rest of the house (or the parts I'd seen so far) seemed to lack. I spun around slowly, taking it in. A large portrait hung above the fireplace across from the bed: a woman with wild auburn hair, bright green eyes, pink cheeks, and bright red lips. I didn't know her, but I knew who she was immediately: *Angelica*.

I sat on the edge of the bed and stared at her for a moment. Ash had called this the guest room, but her presence felt overwhelming here, an odd contrast to the rest of the house, where it felt she'd been erased. The decor, this painting. This was *her* space. I stared at her bright green painted eyes. There was an intensity to them, even in this painting, and her look penetrated me. Somehow, I felt she was glaring at me. Telling me I wasn't good enough, pretty enough, glamorous enough, to even be in this room at all.

I laughed, a quiet nervous laugh, and looked away. Hunger must be making me delirious. I rifled through my purse and found the protein bar I'd stuffed in there for the flight and had never eaten. I pulled it out, devoured it now, forcing my gaze away from the fireplace and the painting, toward the balcony and the Pacific Ocean instead.

But something caught my eye on the nightstand next to the bed: a stack of books. They were turned sideways, so I could only see the edge of one of the spines, the word *du. du*

It feels funny to read that, sitting right here, on the beach in Malibu, letting the cool water lap my toes as I pop a piece of warm halibut in my mouth.

These pages are fiction, but they aren't too.

I stare off at the water, and it's dark and beautiful. But even here in this moment, I understand I will leave this place someday soon. That whenever I return again, it will be as a stranger, or as a ghost of the woman I am now.

"What are you doing down here, all by yourself?" My cousin's voice interrupts my sudden melancholy, and I look up. She stands behind me, hands on her tiny hips, frowning.

"You found me," I say. I gather up my pages and pat the spot on the hard sand next to me. "Have a seat."

But she doesn't move for a moment. "Don't you have to get ready?" Her frown settles, illuminating tiny crow's feet.

Ready. Of course. There's a party tonight at the house. I can't even remember what it's for and have put it out of my mind until right now. I sigh.

"I laid your dress out on your bed," she says. "And then I couldn't find you anywhere. I've been walking the beach for thirty minutes!"

My poor cousin, she's a sweetheart. We were best friends growing up, she was a bridesmaid in my wedding, and then afterward she just stayed, moved out here to help me. I have a budget for staff, in my role as the wife—it's a lot of work being married to such a rich man. Who can do it all on her own? Who would want to? Why not pay my cousin, whom I love dearly, to work for me when I long for her companionship anyway?

I pat the spot next to me on the sand again. "Come on, sit for a little bit. We have time." When we were younger, we used to sit and talk for hours, just the two of us. But now it grates on me how even when we're alone, all we talk and worry about is him.

She frowns again, but I keep staring at her, and finally she relents and sits down. "Are you all right?" she asks me. I offer her a bite of fish from my fork, but she shakes her head, gently refusing it.

"I'm fine," I say.

"You can't skip this party," she admonishes me, and suddenly, I don't like her tone. Yes, I skipped the last one to write, and yes, my husband was livid.

"I just wanted some fresh air and some lunch. Is there anything wrong with that?" My words come out snappish, even though my annoyance isn't really directed at her, but at these godforsaken parties that are supposed to be my entire life.

Then she seems to suddenly notice my stack of pages, and her expression softens. She points to them. "Aren't you ever going to let me read it?"

She knows that I've been writing. I've told her how there has long been a novel inside of me, how it has been finally working its way out after so many years. She forgives me for my distance in a way my husband can't, or won't. She tells me she understands it, envies it even, what it must feel like to have creativity in your soul, words in your blood, a private space all your own.

I shake my head in response to her question, though. My words feel too raw for me to show her yet, too fresh. Once I let them go, once I let anyone else see them, even her, they won't belong to me anymore. They'll become something else. I'll become someone else. And worse, what if she hates them? I shuffle the large stack of paper back into my messenger bag.

"Don't you trust me?" She nudges me with her shoulder, half joking, half hurt.

But I'm not in the mood to placate her. Or to joke around. "Maybe I don't," I rebuff her, standing and putting my bag over my shoulder.

Maybe I shouldn't trust anyone anymore.

FOURTEEN

I woke up early the next morning and took a long, quiet stroll on the beach. As I walked in the sand, staring off at the gray mist encapsulating the water, I grew more determined to focus on work, on the project today. And first things first. I needed to do my own research.

I decided to take a Lyft to the closest public library to see what I could I find out about the Asherwoods' history, from any old press they may have archived in this area. Ash had promised he'd have his grandmother's journals back later this afternoon and had arranged for Nate to pick me up around five. In the meantime, I had the whole day to myself and wanted to put it to good use.

According to the biography I'd read on the plane, Emilia Asherwood had died in 1942, but my online research on Newspapers.com last night hadn't turned up much more than Ash's dad's birth announcement in 1939, and then Emilia's obituary two and a half years later, which had appeared in both the *New York* and *LA Times*. It read like an entry from the society pages, noting the family's fame and fortune more than anything substantial about Emilia herself. On my way to the library now, I wasn't sure what I was looking for exactly. But there had to be something else out there about her. *Something real.*

I stepped out of the Lyft, and the library itself was cute, a small older one-story building that reminded me a little of my childhood library back in Connecticut. Noah had designated Malibu as *fancy*, but I'd noticed that was only half-true. Sure, the mansions and estates and five-star restaurants sat on the sprawling cliffside coast, but just across the four-lane Pacific Coast Highway, the Malibu leading into the hills felt older, a little more rustic, with the charm of a small old-fashioned New England town. This library felt more bucolic than fancy.

I walked inside and inhaled the smell of old books, feeling more at home here than I had at any point since I'd arrived in Malibu. Libraries were libraries anywhere, and I smiled as I approached the reference desk and asked the librarian for help finding and accessing any smaller local California newspaper archives. According to her obituary, Emilia had died at Malibu Lake. I hoped there would be something here the librarian could help me with, some clues as to who Emilia was.

Vera, as her name tag told me, frowned as she looked at me over her bright pink readers. "Malibu Lake in late 1930s, early 1940s? What about it exactly?"

"I want to see if I can find anything on Emilia Asherwood. I think she lived here during that time, and died at the lake," I clarified.

"Ah." She nodded. "Are you working with that other woman?"

"What other woman?"

"The filmmaker."

Filmmaker? I shook my head. "No. I'm not working with

anyone. A filmmaker was here recently?" Did Ash already have a movie deal that he'd failed to mention to me?

"Well, not that recently," she clarified. "Maybe…a month ago."

A month ago? Had Ash contacted a filmmaker first, before he had his manager call Charley? If so, it felt like an important point he'd intentionally left out in our discussions of the project thus far. "I'm not working with her," I said to Vera. "But if you could show me anything you showed her, that would be a big help."

She frowned again. "I'm afraid I can't," she said.

"I'm not a filmmaker," I tried. "But I am writer, and I'm working on a book…" My voice trailed off as the words I was saying hit me. It felt both good and weird to say them out loud after so long, to believe that maybe they were true. I *am* a writer. I *am* working on a book.

"Oh, hon, I'd love to help you. I really would." She smiled apologetically now. "But what I'm saying is, I really can't. She stole it all."

"What?" I shook my head, confused.

"The filmmaker. She took every piece we had in the archives on the Asherwoods, and she never brought it back."

FIFTEEN

I spent the rest of the afternoon in the library's quiet back room reading a biography of Daphne du Maurier that Vera pointed me to once I'd gotten over the initial shock of everything about Emilia being stolen.

I hoped that within the pages of Daphne's life, there might be some clue about Emilia's too. And I sketched out a timeline of Daphne, wondering if I could find any intersection with Emilia—Daphne's birth in London in 1907, her time in Meudon, France, at finishing school in 1925, her marriage to Frederick Browning in 1932, her time isolated in Egypt with him where she first started writing *Rebecca*, and later, her life in Cornwell, at the Menabilly estate, which many said inspired Manderley.

I wasn't sure how or if Emilia fit in to any of that yet, and a few hours later, walking back into Ash's glass estate, random facts about Daphne still swam around in my head. But what I really wanted to know was more about the filmmaker who'd stolen the library's archives on Emilia.

Before I could say a word, though, Ash grabbed my hands.

My arms coursed with a warmth that quickly spread up my shoulders to my face. Suddenly everything I wanted to say vanished from my mind, and instead I could only muster, "What's going on?"

"I have something to show you." His voice was effusive, and he didn't let go of my hands. He led me out onto the veranda, still holding on to me. I considered that *I* could let go, simply follow a safe distance behind him in a calm and professional manner. But I didn't exactly want to. As much as Ash's attention and closeness unsettled me, I was beginning to understand that maybe it thrilled me even more.

I glanced at the wide plank table as he led me outside, expecting to see his grandmother's journals laid out there. But the table was set for dinner, there was no sign of the journals, and Ash kept on holding my hands, pulling me all the way to the veranda railing before finally letting go and pointing out to the water in front of us.

"I don't understand," I said. It occurred to me I'd already said this today, and several times this week. Everything in Ash's wake felt incomprehensible, and yet here I was, feeling strangely more drawn to him than annoyed by it.

He put a finger to his lips to quiet me and pointed straight ahead of us again to the water.

The Pacific Ocean was a pearlescent blue-gray, shimmering in the late-day sun. It looked more sparkly than it had this morning when I'd walked along the beach before the early morning fog had lifted, but it was otherwise unremarkable.

Then suddenly the water rippled, and a massive gray arch rose from the surface. "Is that...a whale?" I whispered, as if speaking any louder might disturb it.

Ash nodded. "They're migrating. They come through on their way back from the artic to Mexico every winter. They're late this year."

"They waited for me," I joked.

"Well worth the wait," Ash said softly. His words dropped,

like pebbles rippling the water, and I felt them penetrating my skin. That heat. That electricity. Proof that I wasn't just imagining that *the sexiest man alive* had noticed me for something other than my writing.

The whale rose again—two of them now. A hump, then a giant tail. Then a second hump. "'There she blows,'" I said. "'A hump like a snow-hill.'" Ash tilted his head and looked at me. "Sorry." I shrugged. "English major humor. It's a line from *Moby Dick*," I clarified. "My most hated classic that I had to write a paper on in college. That line just popped into my head."

"Isn't it blasphemy for a writer to hate *Moby Dick*?" Ash's eyes crinkled, and his voice was light.

"Pretty much," I said. "But seriously, have you read it?" He laughed and shook his head. "Wouldn't recommend."

"You're funny," he said lightly. "I wasn't expecting that before we met. But I like that about you, Olivia."

I laughed off his comment, unwilling to fully acknowledge it. Humor, as Noah always used to say in college, was my defense mechanism. And it was true, that I was always laughing right up until the moment when I started crying.

But I did not want to discuss any of this with Ash, so I changed the subject. "We should get to work, huh? I'm only here for a few more days, and I want to make sure I have everything I need before I head back to Boston."

He nodded, but didn't move away from the edge of the veranda, and neither did I. Instead, he leaned his head down closer to mine, so when he spoke again his breath hit my earlobe. "But this is so nice," he said. "Let's just stay like this. For a little while longer."

I shivered as the wind blew off the water, and his warm breath lingered against my neck. It had been a really long time since anyone had *wanted* to be this close to me. He was right. *It was nice.* So I didn't move. I just stood there with him, watching the whales.

★ ★ ★

It was dark, and I was freezing by the time we went back inside.

"Olivia, your lips are blue!" Ash exclaimed as we walked into the full light of the glass chandelier that hung near his grand piano. "I'll get you a sweater."

He jogged away, and I put my fingers up to my lips to touch them. I was pretty sure he was exaggerating about them being blue, but I really was cold. Thinking about Ash's eyes on my lips instantly made me feel a little warmer, though, and I allowed myself to revel in that while I waited for him to return.

He was back a few minutes later, and he wrapped me in a thick beige sweater. I wasn't sure if he'd had it sent up from the Asherwood warehouse on the off chance I'd get cold, or if it was Angelica's. Probably Angelica's. I shivered a little at that thought, and he rubbed my arms. "Poor Olivia. Why did you let me keep you outside so long?"

"No…it was my fault… I should've dressed warmer," I stammered. My head was freezing too. My words tumbled out thick and muddled. Every question I had, every professional thought that was in my head before I'd arrived had escaped me, and now, as Ash rubbed my arms, everything was very far away but the feeling of him. This close to me.

What is wrong with me?

I pulled out of his grasp, took a giant step back, and exhaled. "The journals." I finally found the words. "Your grandmother's journals. We were going to go over them tonight."

He averted his eyes from me. *Finally.* And he sighed. "Unfortunately, they got held up at the authenticator's, and I didn't get them back today."

Now that he'd stopped looking at me, my head cleared, and I remembered everything I should've been thinking about all along: Vera. The filmmaker. The stolen archives. Fifty thousand dollars. If I was going to get paid, I was going to have to ask all my questions. And get all the answers too.

"Sorry." Ash was still talking. "I meant to tell you about the authenticator right when you got here, but then I had just seen the whales, and…"

I held up my hand. "No need to apologize. The whales were amazing." He shot me a half smile that made me draw in my breath. I exhaled slowly, then continued, "But I tried to dig around a little on my own today, and I had some other questions for you. Do you mind?"

"Please, come sit down." He pointed to the two couches in front of us, and I walked to one at a safe distance ahead of him. He sat across from me on the other one. "Whatever questions you have, Olivia, ask away."

I told him about my trip to the library, about what Vera had said about the filmmaker stealing all the archives a month or so ago. "Is she someone you're working with too?" I asked, unable to keep the annoyance—or was it jealousy?—from creeping into my voice. Not that I had the right to feel that way, having only known Ash and this story for a few days myself. But even in this short amount of time, Ash had the ability to eclipse all my other, more rational feelings.

He frowned, shook his head. "No, Olivia, you are the only one I've talked to about any of this." He sighed and ran his fingers through his hair, and it was clear my question, my doubt, had upset him.

I wanted to reach out and hold on to him, to apologize with my fingers running through the coarse texture of his hair. My fingers twitched a little, and I balled my hands into fists.

"Probably paparazzi," he finally continued. "Ever since the…well, you know. The accident…" He looked up and met my eyes. His eyes were watery now, but no less shockingly blue. I nodded to show him I understood. "They've been after everything they could find about us. I haven't done any interviews. I just can't talk about it. And that makes them all the more interested." His voice broke a little, and he looked away, down at the floor.

"I'm sorry," I said. "It's just…" It's just that none of that made any sense. Why would the paparazzi have wanted information on Ash's grandmother, and furthermore, why would they have stolen it? The story he was talking about was Angelica, her accident, her relationship with Ash. What did any of that have to do with something that had happened in the 1940s to his grandmother? "It's just…" I tried again, but I couldn't figure out what to say that didn't sound accusatory.

"Just what?" Ash lifted his head, looked at me again. Suddenly he wasn't *the sexiest man alive*, but just a man. Just a really sad, beautiful, broken man, and I couldn't help myself. I stood up, walked the few steps to his couch, and sat down next to him. I put my hand on his hand. His skin was warm, and he turned his hand over, clutched my hand in his palm, and squeezed it softly, like suddenly he needed me. I was his lifeline.

"I didn't mean to upset you," I said. It was hard to speak, hard to think sitting that close to him, holding his hand like that.

"Olivia." He said my name softly, a whisper, a song. "Why would they steal it? Why did they have to steal it?"

The image of the bold Sharpied word, **THIEF**, came back to me now, and I wondered again if I'd imagined it. "I saw your copy of *Becky* in the guest room yesterday," I said softly.

"What?" He tilted his head, like the sudden subject change confused him.

"On the nightstand in there, my book." My voice croaked out, uncertain.

"No, your book is over here." He let go of my hand and pointed to the large white bookshelves framing his fireplace, just across the room. "I keep it in this front room, with all my most loved books." He stood and strode over to the shelves, scanning them, until he pulled what was unmistakably my bright blue book off one of the shelves. "See, it's right here!"

He walked back to me, held it out, and I took it, flipping anxiously to the title page, feeling my heart pulse against my rib cage as I waited to be assaulted by that one tiny, weighted word again. But then, it was just a normal, clean title page, nothing written on it at all aside from what was printed there. What was wrong with me? Had I really imagined that whole thing?

He was staring at me, his head cocked to the side with a half smile on his face, and I couldn't tell if he thought I was crazy or amusing. What had he said about me earlier, that he liked that I was *funny*? Did he think I was being funny now? I opened my mouth to explain that the long hike and my hunger must've made me dream something up yesterday. But I couldn't manage to say anything at all. Doubt rose up inside of me, and I didn't like the feeling of it. I couldn't trust myself in this house, and I suddenly wanted to get out of here.

"I should go." I stood and handed him back the book.

"No, wait, not yet."

"It's getting late," I said. "I'll come back tomorrow." But I had this weird feeling that I shouldn't come back. That I should get on the first flight back to Boston instead. That this strange red-hot doubt wouldn't subside until I got far enough from Ash that I couldn't remember the perfect shape of his face up close or the way my skin warmed when he was near me.

"Well, you at least have to sign this for me first," he said, handing me back his copy of *Becky*, reopened to the clean title page.

I relented and reached for my purse. My hands shook as I fished around for a pen.

"And Olivia." Ash leaned down closer, so his breath hit the back of my neck as he said my name. "Anything you need, anything you want to know, just ask me, okay? You don't have to worry about the library or any stolen archives. All you have to do is ask me for the truth."

SIXTEEN

I felt restless when I got back to my hotel. Away from Ash, my head cleared again, and I replayed the scenes back at his house over and over again in my mind. *All you have to do is ask me for the truth,* he'd said, just before I left. But *the truth* felt so ethereal. I had more questions than answers. Something wasn't right, something was off, but I couldn't put my finger on what it was, or whether it was just my writer brain over-thinking again, working up stories that didn't exist.

My stomach growled and I realized I'd never eaten dinner, so I ordered a room service hamburger and the cheapest bottle of wine on the menu, a still somewhat pricey $60 merlot (a big expense, considering I had barely any money in my bank account). I tried to console myself with the thought of the fifty thousand dollars I'd get for writing Ash's book, but that felt ethereal too. I wasn't sure I'd ever figure out what I was supposed to write, much less see any of that money.

But once my food and wine came, I signed the tab, pushed my money worries aside, and I took it all out on the balcony. I shivered from the dampness of the evening fog, and realized

I was still in the sweater Ash gave me. I wrapped it tighter around myself, tucked my cheek in the shoulder, letting it rub my skin and inhaling the lingering smoky cedarwood scent of him. I closed my eyes, breathed deeply, thought about the feel of Ash standing so close to me out on his veranda as we watched the whales… God, what was wrong with me?

I poured a big glass of wine and sipped it down too quickly, then greedily inhaled my burger, and poured another glass, drinking this second one a little slower. I checked my email and saw I had one from Charley, asking me how things were going out in Malibu with Ash. I'd had enough wine at that point to send back a somewhat honest reply: Okay. Maybe? But everything is a little weird to be honest.

Five minutes later my phone rang; Charley's name popped up on my screen. I was shocked. It was almost midnight in New York.

"What's a little weird?" she asked when I picked up, forgoing hellos.

I hadn't expected a phone call, and the two glasses of wine made it even more challenging to put into words what felt off. Wind blew across the water, hitting my face, and I wrapped the sweater around me a little tighter. The cedarwood smell wafted, and I warmed. "You're up late," I finally said. "You didn't have to call me."

"No, believe me. I've been dying to know what's going on out there. Henry Asherwood, what's he like? What's his story? What's weird about it?"

Charley had also signed an NDA to bring me the project and collect her eventual 15 percent, and I realized I could actually talk to her without violating the agreement I'd signed. I told her about what Ash had told me, about his grandmother living the true story of *Rebecca*, about her French journals that were late coming back from the authenticator, about how I'd seen the translation of exactly two pages, and then the librarian's story about a filmmaker stealing everything about Emilia from the archives. I left out the part about the copy of *Becky* I'd maybe imagined in the guest room, about the sweater I was wearing right now, and about the whale watching and the hike I'd gone on with Ash, though I supposed maybe those were the weirdest and most interesting parts.

"Hmm," Charley said now. "So that's why he wanted to hire you. *Becky*, huh?" The incredulity in her tone told me that she, like me, could not believe someone else had actually read *Becky*. *Thanks a lot, Charley.* "But what kind of book are you going to write for him?" She was still talking. "A memoir? A novel?"

"Exactly," I said. "I have no idea."

She was quiet for a moment on the other end of the line, and then she said, "Well, who the fuck cares? You'll figure something out. We'll just pitch it as fiction based on a true story, and then you can write whatever you want. We don't even have to use the Olivia Fitzgerald name. You can ghost-write it with a different pseudonym."

None of that made me feel any better. "But there's something I can't put my finger on, Charley. Something just…feels off about this whole story. I just got back from visiting with Ash at his house, and—"

"Ash?" Charley cut me off. "And oh my god, his house! What is that like?"

I laughed a little. "Pretty much what you'd expect. A huge glass mansion on the edge of a cliff, overlooking the Pacific Ocean," I said.

She sighed. "And tell me, Olivia, is he super fucking hot in person?"

I closed my eyes for a second. Charley and I did not have this kind of relationship, and I suddenly wished I'd waited until morning to reply to her email, sober, when I would've surely lied and told her everything was *great* and that I was already hard at work writing *the world's greatest book*. She'd met Jack exactly once, at my book launch party for *All the Little Lights*, and I couldn't even remember now whether I'd told her he'd moved out. Our conversations were strictly about work. Up until now, anyway.

"He is, right?" she prompted me now.

"I mean…yes?" It was undeniably factual.

"Of course he is." She sighed a little. "But he's probably an ass?"

I rubbed the wool of the sweater, feeling the scratchy texture in between my fingers. "He's not. He's actually really nice." And a little intoxicating. *No, a lot intoxicating.* I pushed the thought away. Now that I had Charley on the phone, I really needed to pick her brain. "But you know what else is weird?" I said, trying to bring the subject back around. "People on Reddit think his wife is still alive. That she faked her death or something."

"People on Reddit think Jesus Christ is still alive." Charley cackled. She was quiet for a minute. Then she added, "You know, she was rumored to have been shopping a book proposal before she died."

"Angelica?" I thought about the looming painting of her in Ash's guest room, and even saying her name felt uncomfortable. Another breeze blew across the water, and I felt chilled all over again.

"Of course, what billionaire's wife *isn't* shopping a book proposal?" Charley sighed. "It probably would've been a juicy tell-all."

I remembered some of the comments on Reddit, theorizing Ash had poisoned Angelica and was currently hiding her away or worse, that he'd murdered her. "What are you saying? Do you think her death was suspicious?"

Charley laughed, a big boisterous laugh that reverberated in my ear. I moved the phone away a little until she stopped.

"This feels very meta, doesn't it? Gorgeous widower, big house on the water, rumors about his wife's death."

Is that what had been bothering me, what I couldn't quite put into words? I'd practically stepped inside my own personal retelling of *Rebecca*, hadn't I? And I was supposed to be writing some sort of story about Emilia Asherwood and *Rebecca*, after I'd already written my own *Rebecca* retelling. Charley was right. Extremely meta.

"Just don't marry the guy and get any more obsessed with her, okay, Olivia?" She laughed again. She was obviously joking. "But seriously," she added, her voice stoic now. "Take a breath. You've got this. Go through his grandmother's journals tomorrow. Take a lot of pictures and notes. Then go back to Boston and write a draft. I'm going to sell the shit out of this and make everyone a ton of money."

God, she made it sound so easy. Like all my doubts and worries were whispers, not screams.

After we hung up, I sat out on the balcony and drank the rest of the bottle of wine, until finally, I felt numb, my doubts withered, Charley's words distant, and then I stumbled into bed. All I could think about as I drifted to sleep was the feel of Ash holding on to me, standing on the edge of his veranda.

SEVENTEEN

"Okay, bad news," Ash said as he let me into his house the next morning. I walked into the living room, still wearing my sunglasses. The entire bottle of merlot had been a bad choice, and my head throbbed. But this was going to be my last full day in Malibu, and I needed to get to work so Charley could, as she put it, *sell the shit* out of this book. "The authenticator FedExed the journals back, and they seem to have been held up in transit."

"Seriously?" I sighed and sat down on the couch, gingerly moving my sunglasses to the top of my head. I winced at the morning light coming in through the windows, reflecting off the water.

"I thought we could take a field trip today instead."

"Ash." I said his name as sternly as I could muster it. "No more whales. This is my last day here, and I have so many questions still."

"I know," he said. "I thought I could take you to Malibu Lake, show you where my grandmother lived. And died," he added softly. "How does that sound?"

I nodded. I actually really liked that idea. I was a visceral writer. I needed to feel the ground beneath my feet, rub the soil between my fingers. Smell and feel the air on my skin.

"Do you want some coffee first?" Ash asked. "You look exhausted."

I'd had two cups of coffee in my room before I left, and now I was in that strange state of feeling both jittery and hungover at once. And I didn't want to linger here—the clock was ticking. "No, I'm good," I said, hoping I sounded more convincing than I felt. "Let's go get to work."

Ash led me into his six-car garage, and then to a black Porsche, telling me he'd given Nate the day off as he wanted to drive us himself. He opened the passenger door for me before running around to start the car. I buckled myself in, pulled my sunglasses back down, and eased into the moment. I thought about how I might describe this to Charley next time I talked to her, me, *in the passenger seat of Ash's Porsche*, and weirdly, even being in the moment, it already felt surreal.

Ash pealed out of the garage, down his winding driveway, and out onto the Pacific Coast Highway, driving fast, in a way that felt almost surprisingly reckless. As we took the turns too quickly, I couldn't help but think again about Angelica. She'd died in a car accident in Malibu. You'd think that would've made Ash more cautious on this road. I gripped the door, and Ash glanced at me sideways, noticing. He eased his foot on the brake and I exhaled as we slowed.

"Sorry," he said, sounding sheepish. "I don't drive myself all that often anymore, and when I do it's like this overpowering freedom hits me. I get carried away."

I nodded, like I understood, though how could I ever understand what it would be like to live a life like Ash's? "I haven't driven in a while either," I said. "I don't even have a car in Boston." That was putting it mildly. I didn't explain that I hadn't actually driven since my mom's accident. Like I forgot how to trust myself, and this big metal death trap I was supposedly licensed to operate, in the aftermath of what had happened to her. The few times we'd rented a car for things in the years since, Jack had always driven us. I was personally a big fan of rideshare, public transportation, and my own two feet.

"Ange hated my driving," Ash said suddenly, surprising me. Because it was the first time I'd heard him say her name this whole week. Not Angelica. *Ange*. "She refused to go with me. Said she only felt safe when she was driving." I chewed on my bottom lip, not sure what I was supposed to say. "I guess it's ironic, isn't it, that she was driving when she...?" His voice trailed off, and we were both silent for a few minutes. He turned onto Malibu Canyon Road and took it more slowly as we wound into the canyon.

"I'm sorry," I finally said.

He nodded. "She loved Malibu Lake. We used to come up here all the time. No one recognized us or followed us up here. Forty minutes from home and it felt like another world." He paused for a minute. "I haven't been back here since the night before the accident..."

I didn't know what to say. I wasn't sure if he was sad or grateful to be returning now, today. "We don't have to go if it's too much," I said softly.

But he shook his head. He kept driving, slowly sinking into the canyon, then rising, until the wide blue lake lay just up ahead.

The Asherwoods still owned a house overlooking the lake, though Ash clarified that it was not the same house his grandmother had lived in. That one, he reiterated, had burned down. His grandfather had rebuilt it and then remarried too. After his grandfather's death, Ash had kept the house as a weekend retreat for himself, and his grandfather's last housekeeper still lived there with Ash paying her to look after the house.

"She's too young to have known Grandmother," Ash said as he pulled down the long drive. "But I thought you might want to talk to her anyway. She knows all about the lore of my family, this house and the rebuild, and spent more hours with Grandfather than anyone in the end."

He turned off the car, and I looked at the house in front of us. It was large, though not excessively so like Ash's estate in Malibu. A two-story wood Craftsman, it felt like a compromise between a log cabin and a mansion.

"Is this where you grew up?" I asked Ash as we got out of the car, and I remembered what I read in the biography on the plane. That his grandfather had raised him.

"Partly. I went to boarding school in Vermont from twelve on. And then we summered in France." *Of course he did.* Ash cleared his throat, stopped for a moment, and stared at the house in front of us. "But my childhood memories are all right here, yeah. In this house, on this lake." He inhaled deeply. Tasting the air.

I did the same, wanting to remember this detail for however it might figure into our book later on. The air was crisp, redolent with the scent of pine and dampness only nearby water could bring. I understood already why Ash loved it so much up here, and maybe why Angelica had as well.

Ash opened the front door with a key, and I followed him inside the house, stopping in the two-story entryway. I looked up, and a large crystal chandelier hung high above my head. "Hello," Ash called out. "Mrs. Daniels, are you here?"

A few seconds later, a tiny middle-aged woman popped around the corner. "Oh, Ash, love, what a nice surprise." He bent down and wrapped her in an enormous hug. She embraced him for a moment, then stepped back and stood on her toes to put her hands on his cheeks. "Let me get a look at you. It's been too long."

I felt like an outsider witnessing their reunion. My face

instantly flushed, and just then, Mrs. Daniels seemed to notice me.

She frowned a little and turned back toward Ash. "Who's this?" she asked him, her voice taking on an accusatory tone.

"Oh, forgive me. This is the writer, Olivia Fitzgerald. I've hired her to write Grandmother Emilia's story, and we came up here to do some research."

She looked at me again, glancing down then up my face, seeming to pause on my mismatched eyes. I blinked and put my hands to my cheeks, self-conscious under her scrutiny.

If I'd trapped myself inside my own twisted *Rebecca* retelling, then I wondered if Mrs. Daniels was my *Mrs. Danvers*. The thought was so ridiculous that a laugh bubbled up inside of me and popped out sounding more like a rattled cough. I covered my mouth with my hand. "Excuse me."

Mrs. Danvers—no, *Mrs. Daniels*—was still frowning. Her forehead creased, and maybe she was older than I'd originally thought. Past middle age and closer to her twilight years.

"It's nice to meet you, Mrs. Daniels," I finally got the right words out. "Ash tells me you're the authority on this house and his grandparents. I'd love to ask a few questions."

Her frown eased a little bit, and now she eyed me more with skepticism than anything. "What kind of a writer are you? What have you written?" she demanded.

"The brilliant kind," Ash said, reaching around my shoulders with his arm, and giving me a squeeze. It was inappropriate, yet much appreciated. And I didn't pull away. "Do you have any of your delicious breakfast burritos on hand?" Ash said, dropping his arm to his side and turning back to Mrs. Daniels. She smiled at him, and clearly, she was just as in love with this man as every other living, breathing person in his orbit was.

"No, but I'll whip some up. Do you like breakfast burritos,

O-liv-i-a?" She pronounced every syllable of my name, making it sound hard and awkward.

"I do, thank you," I said.

She squinted at me one more time before spinning on her heel toward the kitchen. Ash shrugged a little at me, then called after her: "I'm going to take Olivia down to see the lake, and then we'll come back, and we can all chat over brunch?"

"Sure, give me about thirty minutes to cook the burritos, love." He smiled, and then she turned and said pointedly to me, "Olivia, watch where you're walking out there. It's rattler season."

"Are there really snakes?" I asked Ash as he walked quickly down the stony path from the house to the lake. I rushed to catch up with him, awkwardly staring at my feet as I ran, trying not to trip, or accidentally step on a snake. I was back in my cute red flats. Should've worn the Asherwood Collection™ hiking boots.

Ash stopped suddenly, and I almost bumped right into him. He held up his arms to catch me, and inadvertently hugged me. He held on to me for a second, until a nervous laugh escaped my throat, and I quickly took a step back. "Sorry, looking at my feet. Snakes," I mumbled.

"There might be snakes," Ash said. "But I've never seen them. And Mrs. Daniels has a wicked sense of humor." He smiled.

"So...that was a joke?"

He shrugged. Maybe he wasn't entirely sure, but he wasn't exactly worrying about snakes either. He held out his hand. "Come on. Walk with me. I'll watch out for the snakes for you."

I shouldn't take his hand. I knew I shouldn't take his hand. But he kept staring at me, holding out his hand, and then it almost felt rude *not* to.

His hand was warm, and I hadn't realized I was cold until my fingers touched his. He threaded his fingers with mine, as if it were no big deal, and we kept on walking, holding hands, toward the lake.

A few minutes later the path ended, and there in front of us was the water. Wide and bright and blue. Unlike the Pacific Ocean, the water was calm, and I could see from shore to shore. It would be impossible to get lost here the way you could at sea. I thought about Emilia, standing here, right at the edge of this very lake once, and then I realized that I wasn't sure how she died. The obituary hadn't mentioned it. I asked Ash now, as we stood staring off at the water.

"The fire," he said quietly. "Grandfather never wanted to talk about it much. But I know he made it out of the house, and she didn't, and that was a guilt he lived with for the rest of his life."

"That's really horrible," I said. "And she was so young." For some reason I'd had it in my head that she had drowned, in this lake. Burning up in the fire felt like the opposite of drowning. Or maybe in the end it was all the same—suffocating by water or by smoke was still suffocating. I felt chilled again, even holding on to Ash's warm hand.

"Everyone has forgotten about her," Ash said quietly. "My family has gotten so much press over the years for so many reasons. Several biographies, authorized, unauthorized. Grandmother Emilia is never more than a footnote, but maybe you can change that?"

I nodded and squeezed his hand gently. He squeezed back. And then, standing there with Ash, still staring out at the lake, I suddenly believed what Charley had said to me last night, that I was going to figure out how to tell Emilia's story.

Cooking breakfast burritos seemed to have put Mrs. Daniels in a better mood, because she was no longer frowning at me when we returned to her kitchen. She kindly handed me a plate, offered me a chair at the table. Ash walked to the large stainless steel fridge and then came back and sat down with a bottle of hot sauce. He doused his burrito in it, offered it to me, but I declined.

"I don't know how he eats it that way." Mrs. Daniels tsked and shook her head, but she was smiling. I could suddenly picture Ash sitting here as a little boy, a teenager, and I smiled too. She turned to me: "All right, Olivia Fitzgerald. Tell me, what kind of book are you going to write?"

I glanced at Ash, and he nodded a little as if to say it was okay to be forthright with her. "Ash found some of his grandmother's journals, and he's working on getting those translated and authenticated. So primarily, I'll be looking at those to tell her story. But can you tell me, do you have any idea if Emilia knew Daphne du Maurier?"

"Who?" She wrinkled her nose. Was it possible that nonreaders, nonwriters, wouldn't recognize Daphne's du Maurier's name? I'd first read *Rebecca* when I was fifteen, and then again in college. After my mother died, it was the book I lost myself in for comfort. No one could turn a sentence like Daphne du Maurier, and no character had ever stayed with me more than Rebecca de Winter. It felt inconceivable that there were other people in this world who didn't know du Maurier, who hadn't ever read *Rebecca*.

"Olivia, maybe you should ask her questions about the house," Ash interjected now, reaching for the hot sauce to sprinkle more on his burrito. "That's why we came up here, right?"

"Right," I said quickly. "The house." But I wasn't sure yet how—or if—this house played into Emilia's story, or the book Ash wanted me to write. "So...this one was rebuilt after a fire?" I asked, thinking about what Ash had mentioned earlier.

She nodded. "Exactly as the other one once was. Henry—

Ash's grandfather—used to say it had been replicated down to every last nail. Even little details, like those crown moldings—" She pointed to the moldings framing the picture window in the breakfast nook. "It's all exactly the same. So no one would ever be able to tell the difference. But him," she added.

A breeze blew in through the open picture window now, and I shivered a little, chilled again. How strange it must've been to lose his wife in a house fire, only to rebuild another exactly as it once was. And to continue to live on here, for the rest of his life, without her. My dad sold our childhood home nine months after my mom died. I had yet to visit him in his new house where he lived with Shawna, a point Suzy loved to harp on, every time she got me on the phone. But my dad also married Shawna only two years after our mom's accident, and while I understood, understanding and acceptance weren't exactly the same.

"When did he get remarried?" I asked both Ash and Mrs. Daniels now, glancing between them.

She was the one who answered first. "Quickly. Right, Ash?" He nodded in agreement. "Many said too quickly," Mrs. Daniels continued. "But Henry always did things his own way, didn't care what anyone else thought. That didn't mean he didn't love Emilia." She paused. "But by the time this house was rebuilt two years after the fire, he moved in with his new bride, Rose. They lived here together while he was still alive."

"I assume she was young, and she became obsessed with Emilia?" I laughed dryly. I was being facetious more than asking an actual question.

But Mrs. Daniels nodded, not picking up on my commentary on the *Rebecca* plot. Of course she wouldn't, since she'd never read it. But my writer brain couldn't help but make the comparison.

"Well, to tell you the truth," Mrs. Daniels continued, "we were all a little obsessed with Emilia's memory. Weren't we, Ash?" He nodded again as he finished off his burrito. "As you might imagine, the second Mrs. Asherwood—Rose—didn't love it when Henry used to say he could still feel Emilia's presence," Mrs. Daniels added softly.

"Like…a ghost?" I asked.

She chuckled, folded her hands in front of her. "Olivia, ghosts aren't real," she admonished me, twisting her fingers together, looping them in and out, as if considering whether she should say anything else. Then she finally said, "But when people leave us, they don't just disappear. They haunt us. I don't mean in supernatural ways, but in many tangible ones too. Do you understand what I'm saying?"

I didn't exactly, but I nodded anyway.

On the ride back, I was still thinking about what Mrs. Daniels said. That the people who are gone haunt us. In tangible ways.

I glanced at Ash, and his eyes were trained steadily on the road, which he was, thank goodness, taking more cautiously now. Was he thinking about what Mrs. Daniels had said too? Was that true for him with Angelica? *Ange*, as he'd called her? And what about for me, and my mother. It wasn't she who haunted me, but the things she had done, the broken pieces she'd left behind. This new man my father had become—someone else's husband, for goodness' sake—who I barely recognized now in the aftermath. Was that my continual haunting?

As I thought for a moment about my dad's second wife, Shawna, something else Mrs. Daniels said struck me: *The second Mrs. Asherwood* wasn't thrilled about Henry's obsession with Emilia. But Ash had told me that Emilia *was* the second Mrs. Asherwood. That his grandfather's first wife had even been named Rebecca, just like in du Maurier's novel.

"What about Rebecca?" I blurted out now.

"What about it?" Ash looked away from the road for a second to glance at me, and I noticed how downcast his face was. His eyes flickered with a darkness. It lasted only a second. Then he smiled, turned his focus back to the road.

"Not the book," I clarified. "Her. *Rebecca Asherwood*, your grandfather's first wife. You told me the other night that his first wife's name was Rebecca just like in du Maurier's book. But Mrs. Daniels just referred to the woman your grandfather married after Emilia as *the second Mrs. Asherwood*. Wouldn't she be the third? Emilia was the second. Rebecca was the first."

Ash nodded but didn't look away from the road this time. "Mrs. Daniels misspoke."

"So, what about her?" I pressed. "What happened to Rebecca Asherwood?"

Ash turned back onto the PCH and sped up, pulling us too fast around a turn. I felt the breakfast burrito rolling in my stomach, threatening to come back up, and I inhaled deeply, then slowly exhaled.

"What happened to her?" Ash finally said as he whipped around a bend. "The same thing that happened to her in du Maurier's novel."

Excerpt from *The Wife*

I can tell you the first moment I thought about fire.

It's a Thursday, just about 6:00 p.m., the sky the pearl-gray color of dusk.

I'd gone to the library to work on revising my novel—by then I'd learned it was easier to write out of the house. No questions, no interruptions. Just quiet, and all those books surrounding me; they were calming. It was heaven.

I walk inside the house, and it's completely dark. No one is home, not even my cousin, which feels strange. Because this morning before I left, she'd told me she'd prepare dinner. I'd told her not to bother. I'd planned to stay in the library until it closed at nine. But since when did she listen to me about this sort of thing? Every time I'd said that before, I'd come home and found dinner warming in the oven, her waiting for me in the kitchen. She was always taking care of me, even when I forgot to take care of myself. But not tonight.

I'd changed my mind today at 5:30, felt done for the day, and hungry. And now, walking through my quiet house, my stomach rumbles a little, and I'm disappointed she'd listened to me for once. I put my things down in my writing room, and then walk down the hallway to change.

It's funny, I notice at first the way the door to my bedroom is slightly ajar, and I'm positive I closed it this morning after I'd gotten dressed and ready for the day. I always do. The strangest thought comes over me, that someone has broken in. And now they're hiding in my bedroom, waiting for me to return. My husband still at work, my cousin gone...somewhere. An intruder, in my bedroom?

I'm paralyzed for a moment, unsure what to do. Should I call the police? But my husband hates bad press more than anything, and what if I'm wrong? My mind is so wrapped up in my novel, maybe I simply had forgotten to close the door this morning.

And so, I walk forward, edging my way softly toward the room. The danger feels so palpable that my heart thuds in my chest, making me feel alive in a way I haven't in this house in so very long.

I push on the door gently with my hand, and a soft white light spills out from inside. The bathroom light, or my night table light? I can't tell from here. How strange that a thief has come in here and turned on only one small light.

Then, I hear an unmistakable sound—a woman's small laugh followed by my husband's voice. Is that what you want? he demands, in that brash way he has of demanding everything.

The giggle again, and this time it's loud enough for me to recognize it. My cousin?

I understand exactly what's going on: she's in my bed, with my husband, and she's stark naked, on top of him.

And that's the first moment I think of it. There is only one way out of this life: I have to burn it all to the ground.

EIGHTEEN

Ash dropped me back at my hotel so I could pack, but he made me promise to come back to his house for dinner so we could strategize and talk next steps before I flew home tomorrow morning.

"I won't even subject you to my cooking," he joked, his demeanor light again by the time he pulled up in the circular drive of the inn. "My chef is coming this afternoon to prepare everything."

"You didn't have to go to any trouble," I said. But he laughed. Right. A chef was no trouble at all for someone like Ash.

Back in my room, I ignored my suitcase and the dirty clothes I'd strewn over the corner armchair. Instead, I grabbed my laptop and sat on the bed. I wasn't satisfied with Ash's answer in the car, and I googled Rebecca Asherwood.

Did you mean Rose Asherwood? Google asked me.

Nope.

I scrolled through the hits, looking for anything about Rebecca Asherwood, and though I was able to find things about Rose, about Henry, and even about Ash's parents,

Henry II and Betsy, I couldn't find one single thing about Henry's first wife, Rebecca.

Odd, but maybe not entirely remarkable. If she had died before Emilia married him in the 1930s, maybe that was long enough ago that any record of her might not have made it to the digital age, especially since it would've been before Henry Asherwood started his store chain, before he'd made a name for himself. Maybe Rebecca Asherwood had lived and died too far in the past, and maybe she was too obscure to come up in a simple internet search. But even as I explained it all away in my head, I didn't quite believe it.

I logged into Newspapers.com and hoped maybe I'd luck upon something there. Her obituary? A marriage announcement? But I typed her name in the search bar, and nothing came up there either.

Still, I couldn't stop thinking about what Ash had said in the car. What had happened to her was what had happened to Rebecca in du Maurier's novel. Was he being serious?

In the novel, Rebecca was murdered by her husband, Maxim. Sure, she had set him up to do it. And sure, it was questionable, in the end, whether it was truly a murder or more like suicide, since she'd goaded him into it, knowing she was about to die of cancer anyway. But nonetheless, I'd taken a firm stance when I'd written *Becky* that Maxim de Winter was indeed a murderer. Did that make Henry Asherwood a murderer too? Was that what Ash had been saying to me in the car? If he was talking about his own grandfather, how had he said it so casually?

But the internet had no answers about Rebecca Asherwood, and I thought again about Daphne du Maurier. I remembered reading an article when I wrote *Becky* about her possible real-life inspiration for her character of Rebecca de Winter, and I searched for it again now to refresh my memory.

There were several prevailing theories—none of which

were tied to Emilia or Rebecca Asherwood, of course. Aside from the claims of plagiarism, and the similarity to *Jane Eyre*, there was the theory I was personally most drawn to: Daphne had stumbled upon some old love letters to her husband from his ex-fiancé, a woman named Jan Ricardo. In the letters, back from when the two of them were together, Jan Ricardo signed her name with a flourishing *R*. Some scholars theorized that Daphne herself had become somewhat obsessed with Jan, with these letters, with her signature. The glamorous and flourishing *R* haunted her, and thus the character of Rebecca was born.

My phone dinged with a text, and I grabbed it, expecting Ash with something last minute about dinner. But no, it was Noah: You up for a quick beer at your hotel? I'm not too far…

Noah. When we'd said goodbye after coffee the other morning, I'd promised to meet him for a drink before I left. But I never texted him again. The past few days had gone so fast, and I'd gotten so caught up in Ash. I glanced at my watch. I had about two hours before he was coming back to pick me up for dinner, and I wasn't getting very far sitting here searching the internet. I closed my laptop and pushed thoughts of Jan Ricardo, Daphne du Maurier, and Rebecca Asherwood aside for now.

Sure, I texted Noah back. Meet you downstairs in 15 minutes?

As I waited in the hotel bar for Noah, I twisted a cocktail napkin in my fingers and thought about the last time the two of us had shared a drink together. It was right before my launch party for *All the Little Lights*.

Noah had come from LA, just for the launch, and we'd planned on a drink together before the party to celebrate the fact that I was actually becoming a bona fide *published author*. We were supposed to go, just the two of us, but on my way out of our apartment, Jack had suddenly insisted on coming along. And then he'd put on a huge possessive show in front of Noah, clinging to me in the booth, answering the questions Noah asked me. Which pissed Noah off, and rightly so. Jack was annoying me too, but I hadn't wanted to make a thing of it and ruin the entire night. My launch! Noah had frowned through that entire drink, casting angry looks at Jack.

Noah had been my person first. He was my college best friend and writing critique partner before I'd ever met Jack during our senior year in a silly tennis class I had to take to fulfill my PE requirement. Jack and I had one thing in common—we were both terrible tennis players. But Jack was—objectively speaking—extremely gorgeous.

After my mom died January of our senior year, Noah helped me not fail out of our senior writing seminar, while Jack distracted me with sex. Noah thought Jack was using me. Jack thought Noah was jealous. It was all a recipe for disaster, and in the end maybe Noah had been right all along. Not that Jack was using me, per se, but that I hadn't exactly been in the right emotional state to jump into a serious relationship, fueled by little more than good sex with a hot guy whose common ground with me was bad hand-eye coordination. I wondered now what it said about me that I'd stayed with him for so long, even after we basically stopped having all but the very occasional sex. What did it say about me that I didn't even consider how messed up our relationship had been until right now?

"Hey, Livvy." Noah's voice interrupted my thoughts, and I felt his warm hand on my shoulder. I stood and gave him a hug, and I suddenly felt the urge to apologize or to thank him, or to just stay here in this hug with him and forget everything and everyone else. I was so glad he'd texted tonight, that he was here with me right now. And I hoped we would keep talking again, even after I went back to Boston. But I couldn't bring myself to say any of that out loud. So much time had passed since we were close, really, truly close, that it almost felt wrong to get my hopes up. I just wanted to stay here, holding on to him, right in this moment.

But he let go first and sat down across from me.

"Thanks for coming all the way up here," I said. "I wish I'd had more time to see you this week."

"Me too." He smiled and flipped through the drink menu. "Did you order anything yet?"

I shook my head. "I was waiting for you."

"Do you still drink Corona with lime?"

"Not since college." I laughed. In the years since, I always chose wine, maybe an occasional cocktail. But Noah and I had spent many nights drinking Coronas on the beat-up couch in my college studio apartment, working on our short stories for class, quoting the old adage to each other, *write drunk, edit sober.* Though the truth was, we'd often edited over beers too.

"Well, for old times' sake then," Noah said, and he smiled a little like he was also thinking of those nights. "We'll both get one?"

A few minutes later we had our very nostalgic beer in front of us. I twisted the lime into mine, Noah did the same, and we clinked bottles.

"So how's your write-for-hire project going?" Noah asked as he took a sip.

"Good," I said quickly, thinking again about Charley's enthusiasm. But *good*—that one tiny word—felt like an enormous lie when I said it out loud to Noah. "I mean... I don't know," I stammered. "It's honestly all a little weird. Charley thinks I'll pull it together, but..." I let my voice trail off, and I shrugged and sipped my Corona. God, the taste of it made me remember how I felt sitting with Noah in my college apartment, warm and happy, tapping away on the keys of my cheap Chromebook, loving writing and my best friend

so much I was pretty sure I'd die without either one of them.
And yet, somehow here I was. Still breathing.

"I'm a good listener," Noah said. His face softened a little,
and for a minute, he looked younger again. Like I remembered him looking in college.

I nodded, took another sip of my beer, but didn't say anything. I chewed on my bottom lip.

"I know, I know," Noah said. "You signed an NDA. But
you know I wouldn't repeat anything you tell me."

I hesitated for a second. Once upon a time, Noah was my
person, and I would've trusted him implicitly. But one Corona
in a hotel bar didn't make up for five years of barely speaking to each other after he stormed out of my book party. I
couldn't do anything now that might jeopardize this project,
my fifty thousand, or the resurrection of my writing career
that I so desperately longed for. I smiled at him. "No, it's all
fine, really. I'll go back to Boston, figure out what to write.
Charley thinks she can sell it. It'll all work out."

Noah leaned across the table, grabbed my hands in his, and
held on to me for a minute. "Just be careful, okay, Livvy?
There are some rich creeps in Malibu."

I chuckled a little and rubbed my fingers across his knuckles. His hands were different—older, rougher, and stronger
too. Ash was certainly eccentric, and I'd yet to pin down exactly what he wanted from me, but he wasn't a creep. At least,
I didn't think he was.

"You're sweet to worry, Noah," I finally said. "But you
don't have to. I have everything under control."

NINETEEN

The beer buzz had worn off by the time Ash picked me up an hour later, but the feeling of melancholy that hit me when Noah gave me one last hug and whispered goodbye into my hair hadn't quite faded yet. I got into Ash's car feeling a little sad, a little tired, and a lot concerned about what exactly I was going to write when I returned to Boston.

I was only half paying attention, so I didn't notice that Ash had driven past the turn for his house until I looked up, and suddenly we were on an unfamiliar stretch of the PCH. "We're not having dinner at your house?" I asked.

"It's such a nice night, I thought we could have drinks on my yacht first."

Drinks on his yacht sounded nothing like discussing next steps for our project. But Ash had already pulled into the lot of the marina and was parking the car. He got out, ran around, and opened the passenger door for me. And he was right: it really was a beautiful night. Still a balmy seventy degrees just before dusk, and as he opened my door, the salty damp air hit my face, and I inhaled the scent of the water.

I stepped out of the car and followed Ash down the long dock until he stopped in front of the biggest, most spectacular boat in the entire row (of course it was). "She's a beauty, isn't she?" Ash said.

I thought about *Rebecca*. In Daphne du Maurier's book, Maxim de Winter's deception is revealed when Rebecca's boat washes up on the shore, her dead body inside. *Je Reviens* is the name of her boat—French for *I will return*. And she literally does as a ghost, in my retelling.

I looked at Ash's boat now, scanning for the name as I followed him around to the front, half expecting it to say *Je Reviens*. But instead, I saw the large blue letters across the bow: *Angelica*. I stopped walking for a moment and stared. Was it endearing or creepy that his yacht bore the name of his dead wife? I thought again about what Mrs. Daniels had said earlier, about the way the dead haunted us. Angelica really was still everywhere. A cool wind blew off the water—it was chillier here down the dock than back in the parking lot—and I shivered.

"Come on." Ash gently grabbed my arm and led me up the ramp to board the boat. "The sunset is spectacular from right here on the water. We don't want to miss it."

The sunset was also pretty spectacular from the veranda at Ash's house, but I kept my mouth shut and followed him down the long dock. He led me to the back of the boat, where a small table was set up by the railing, an ice bucket with champagne and two flutes in the middle. This looked like a scene from a rom-com, not a business discussion on a write-for-hire project.

Ash pulled out a chair for me, I sat, and then he reached inside a nearby basket, pulling out a light plaid blanket. "You look cold. It gets chilly out here on the water," he said, gently draping the blanket across my back, tucking it around my shoulders, letting his hands linger on my arms for an extra moment. I stayed perfectly still, waiting for him to move his hands but not exactly wanting him to rush either.

A cold breeze gusted off the water as he finally let go and sat down across from me, but I was no longer chilled. The blanket and his warm hands had taken care of that. I pulled my sunglasses down from the top of my head and stared off at the nearly blinding orange-yellow glow on the horizon, as Ash popped the champagne.

I could already tell he was right, that the sunset would be stunning, even better here than from his house. We were closer to it now than up on the cliff. The sun would glow hotter, brighter, burning up the water. *Spectacular.* Like Ash himself.

"I wanted to toast our partnership," Ash said as he poured the champagne. "My manager will send a contract over to your agent tomorrow to make it all official." He handed me a glass, his fingertips inadvertently brushing against mine, and his words buzzed past me.

Focus. Contract. Emilia Asherwood. Fifty thousand dollars. *Rebecca.*

"Cheers," Ash said, clinking his glass to mine.

"Cheers," I murmured, but took only the smallest sip before setting my glass down on the table. *Focus.* "Ash," I said, pulling my notepad and pen from my bag. "I'm really excited to toast our partnership. But I'm still not clear on exactly what our project is. We should figure that out tonight. Okay?"

He drank his champagne down a little as he stared off at the water but didn't say anything for a few minutes.

I sighed and chewed on the cap of my pen, thinking about what I needed to get from him most tonight: direction. Where did our book really start? What was it really about? I needed at least that much to go back to Boston and make a true start on this manuscript.

"Don't go home," he said abruptly. His voice was so soft,

it almost got swallowed up in the sound of the waves crashing against the side of the yacht.

I wasn't sure I'd heard him correctly. "What?"

"Don't. Go. Home." Then he looked back at me, smiled easily, and added, "Yet."

"But…my flight's tomorrow night. And I have to check out of my hotel before noon." The front desk had even called earlier to confirm I'd be out in time, as the entire place was booked starting tomorrow for a wedding.

"I have a guest room in my house. A whole guest wing. You can stay there."

I thought about the room I'd showered and changed in after our hike, the huge eerie portrait of Angelica hanging above the fireplace, the copy of my book on the nightstand that perhaps I'd imagined. Ash wanted me to stay. With him? *There?*

"I'll pay to change your flight," he added. "At least stay a few more days, until I get the journals back from FedEx. I'm not ready for you to leave yet." His voice softened on that last part, and he suddenly looked up again. His eyes caught mine, their blues particularly vivid in the yellow-and-orange glimmer of the falling sun. "I mean, I think we have a lot more work to do, like you just said."

That was very true. We had a lot left to figure out. And it was only going to become more challenging the farther away I was from Ash and his familial history. But the thought of essentially moving into his house, being that *close* to him twenty-four hours a day, felt somehow both dangerous and exciting. A disaster disguised as a brilliant plan. "I wouldn't want to impose on you," I said, choosing my words carefully. "I'm sure you have things to get back to here, and I have…" What exactly did I have in Boston? A cold apartment so quiet it made me crazy? Oscar, who may or may not be dead by now. The icy gray sludge of the New England March snow hanging on too late.

Ash shook his head. "You are my primary focus right now."

My face warmed, and I put my champagne down to cool my cheeks with the backs of my hands.

"I mean, this project. Our book," he clarified. "I want you to stay. It's not an imposition at all, I promise. And it would be silly for you to pay for another hotel when I have the room. And besides, LA LIT is on Friday night! You have to stay a few more days to go to that with me."

Excitement vibrated through me at his invitation. LA LIT was only the biggest literary gala of the year, which I would normally kill to go to. So how could I say no? To LA LIT. To any of it? My heart pounding recklessly against my rib cage didn't feel like a real reason. "Just through the end of the week," I finally relented. "I'd love to go to LA LIT. And we'll work on the project between now and then," I added.

"Good," Ash said. "It's settled then." He picked up the bottle of champagne and poured more into my glass.

I held my hand up to stop him. "I shouldn't have any more." I picked up my notepad, reminding him that we were supposed to be working.

"You should," he said easily, and topped off my glass a little more. "Please. Enjoy the champagne. Enjoy the view. Let's just relax tonight, and tomorrow, we'll get back to work."

TWENTY

I emailed Charley the next morning, to let her know I'd extended my trip for a few more days. But I purposefully left out the part about staying in Ash's guest wing, not wanting her to immediately call me to *discuss*. (Yes, Ash was extremely hot, but no, that wasn't why I was staying. *It most definitely was not*.) I kept the email as innocuous as possible, told her I'd call her once I got back to Boston next week to talk about a game plan, and left it at that.

I thought about texting Noah to tell him I was staying a little longer too. But my finger hovered over my texts with him, and I couldn't bring myself to actually type anything. We'd already said goodbye yesterday and had promised to keep in better touch. I was only staying a few more days, and I was going to be completely focused on pulling this project with Ash together. I wouldn't have time to see Noah again anyway.

Instead, I scrolled to Jack, and texted him and asked him to keep feeding Oscar. I'd hardly pressed Send on the text when my phone rang, jolting me with the unexpected chimes of Jack's ringtone.

"Shit," he said when I picked up, forgoing hellos. "I might have killed your fish."

I took a deep breath. Jack's voice sounded so distant but familiar too. It was mine, and not mine at all. Like that weird feeling I got once both of my books were finally out in the world. There was a time I'd known them so intimately that the characters would haunt me in my dreams. But then, by the time I did my first bookstore reading, a year after finishing my last revision, I could barely even remember the minor characters' names.

"Liv? You still there?" Jack said.

I sighed. "Might have killed him?" I asked. "Or definitely killed him?"

"I forgot to go over there and feed it. I know I promised you I would, but I got caught up at the hospital, and it totally slipped my mind…" His voice trailed off. His excuses ran out of air. Didn't they always?

I felt tears welling up in my eyes. Ridiculous, stupid tears because Oscar was just a fish, and I'd already killed his fish brothers and sisters. Of course, I hadn't starved them to death from neglect. But dead was dead.

"I'm sorry, Liv. Say something, please?"

I didn't know what to say, and I could hear Jack breathing on the other end of the line. Jack always hated silences, so I wasn't surprised that he kept talking even when I didn't respond.

"I'll go over there right after my shift today and check," he said. "I promise. And fish can live a long time without food, right? Maybe he's okay."

I sighed again. "Sure," I finally said. "Maybe." Then I added, "If he's not dead, can you just feed him until I get back?"

"Yeah." He paused and it was quiet again, but neither one of us moved to end the call.

"Things are going well in LA with your research, I guess?" he asked.

I was suddenly tempted to tell him I would be spending the next few days at Ash's house, *with Ash*. Even Jack would recognize the name Henry Asherwood III and his status as one of the *sexiest men alive*. I pictured that vein on the side of Jack's neck that used to twitch with jealousy when I'd even mention Noah's name. I chewed on my bottom lip. Would Jack care at this point what I was doing, who I was staying with? And why was I curious if he did?

"Liv?" he prompted again.

I finally forced myself to speak. "Yeah. Everything is great here. Text me later about Oscar, okay?"

And then I pressed the screen to end the call before he, or I, could say anything else.

Nate was back at work today, and he was waiting for me in the circular drive of the hotel after I checked out. He leaned easily against the passenger door of the Tesla, dressed in a sleek black suit and aviator glasses. I stared at him for a second before he noticed me and reached for my suitcase. "This is all your stuff?" he asked, eyeing my small carry-on roller bag skeptically. He opened the passenger door for me, then took my bag and wheeled it to the trunk.

"I'm only staying for a few more days," I said. "And I'm sure there's a laundry room I can use in that big house."

He nodded, pulled out his phone, sent a text, and then ran around to the driver's side. He glanced at his phone again as we both got into the car. "Ash is going to have some stuff sent up for you from the warehouse."

So, he was texting Ash about my laundry situation? My cheeks warmed at the sudden thought of Ash picking out things for me to wear. "He really doesn't have to do that. I just need a washing machine..." I stammered.

"Clara can take care of that for you. I'll leave your bag with her when we go in."

Clara. Ash's housekeeper. I guessed she was back from her few days off. "I don't want anyone to go to any trouble," I said.

But Nate didn't answer. And I held on tightly to the car door as he whipped around the curves leading to Ash's estate.

Ash walked out the front door as soon as we drove up, like he'd been watching out the window, excited for me to arrive. He strode easily toward the car and grabbed me in a hug as soon as I stepped out. By the time he let go, Nate—and my roller bag—had already disappeared. Before I even had another chance to argue about my laundry.

"I have something to show you," he said, taking my hand and leading me up the steps to his front door.

"The journals came back?" I asked, suddenly hopeful that I'd made the right decision by staying. When I thought about it, I wasn't sure how I could write this book, any book about Emilia, without actually seeing her journals myself. Even if my rudimentary French wouldn't allow me to fully grasp each and every word, I needed to see her handwriting, feel the texture of the pages, and run my fingers along the unfamiliar words that had once belonged to her.

Ash shook his head. "No, not yet. But I promise, you'll like this too." He led me into the house, still holding on to my hand, not letting go of me until we reached the couch. "Have a seat," he said.

I did, and then he sat down right next to me, close enough so our legs were touching. I was considering if I should move just a little when he leaned forward and pulled what looked like a photo album off the coffee table in front of us. "I was getting the guest wing ready for you, and then I remembered there was a whole other box in there, in addition to the journals." He held up the album now.

"Pictures?" I asked.

He nodded and handed over the album, leaning across me

to flip the cover open. It was hard to think with Ash that close, the cedarwood smell of him so intoxicating I could barely breathe, much less form sensical words.

Ash pointed to a black-and-white photograph of a young woman and man standing in front of what appeared to be Malibu Lake. "There's Grandmother Emilia with my grandfather."

Emilia was strikingly beautiful. That much I could tell even from the old grainy photograph. She was slight, and she wore a pale-colored sundress and floppy straw hat, but the brim didn't hide her wide, magnetic smile.

Ash flipped to the next page, and there she was in a canoe, holding the straw hat to her chest, her head tilted to the side, amusement bright on her face.

"Wow, she's gorgeous," I said. "We should include some of these in the book." Having never written anything like this before, I wasn't sure if that was something a publisher would want or not, but I could just imagine it now, a black-and-white cover with her stunning face.

"Yes," Ash said. "That's a great idea. People should know her name and her face. But what do you think of this one?" Ash flipped a few more pages, until he found what he was looking for: a younger Emilia, a freckled teenager with her hair in a braid, standing in a field of flowers. "She's in France here, where she grew up. Before she even met Grandfather." *France.* I thought again about Daphne's connections to France too.

"Daphne du Maurier attended finishing school in France as a teenager," I told Ash. "And her ancestors were also French like Emilia's. *du Maurier.*"

"*du Maurier,*" Ash repeated with what sounded to me like a perfect French accent.

"Daphne was actually obsessed with tracing her family history. She was raised being told her French ancestors were aristocrats who owned a glassblowing business, but then she went to France to research them as an adult, and she learned they were just workers there. Far from aristocracy, they fled to England to avoid debtors' prison. She wrote about it in *The Glass-Blowers*." I suddenly realized I sounded like an encyclopedia, and I stopped talking and pressed my lips together.

Ash laughed. "See, you *are* the du Maurier expert, aren't you?"

I shook my head. "I read up on her a little bit these past few days, wanting to find any connection to Emilia. I'm wondering if their paths could've crossed in France? If they could've gone to the same school, maybe?"

"Do you really think they knew each other in school, and that's when she stole the story?" He spoke now with a quiet urgency, a darkness that wasn't in his tone a moment ago. "Do you know how that could happen, Olivia?"

I thought about it for a moment. "No," I said truthfully. Even if they had known each other in school, by chance, Emilia would not have lived her own *Rebecca*-esque story yet. She wouldn't have known about Henry or Rebecca Asherwood back then. And I still knew nothing about Rebecca Asherwood. She felt oddly untraceable.

Ash sighed and slammed the photo album shut.

"Wait." I reached for the album, but he held on to it tightly, unwilling to relinquish it to me now. "What about Rebecca Asherwood?" The words tumbled out of my mouth without me really thinking them through.

"What about her?" His voice was gruffer now, and he shifted away from me.

Yet I couldn't stop myself. "Are there any pictures of her?"

"Why would I have that?" he snapped. An apology rose in my throat, but I swallowed it back. I had to ask questions to write this book. And half the point—no, more than half the point of *Rebecca*—was Rebecca herself. If Emilia had written something similar, Rebecca Asherwood seemed like she would have to be a major character in our story.

"Well," I said, trying to choose my words carefully. "If not in this album, maybe there's something still at the house at Malibu Lake—"

"That survived the fire?" he cut me off, and his frown creased even deeper.

Right. *The fire.* My cheeks flamed red again. "I... I..." I stumbled. "My writer's instinct is telling me I need to understand her to understand your grandmother's story. That's all," I finally sputtered out.

"Well, you don't." Ash quickly shot me down. "Just forget I even mentioned her." *Forget?* How could I?

His phone dinged with a text, and he grabbed it off the coffee table, suddenly engrossed in whatever it said. He put the photo album back down on the coffee table and started texting. "I have to go into work." He spoke curtly, efficiently, not even looking up from his phone.

"I'm sorry," I said, unsure how he'd turned from laughing five minutes ago to being so sullen. "I didn't mean to upset you."

But he didn't acknowledge my words or even look at me as he stood. "Go get settled in the guest room. Clara can help you with anything you need—she's in the kitchen. I'll be back later for dinner."

TWENTY-ONE

I recognized Clara the second I saw her standing there, wiping down Ash's marble kitchen island, her long wavy auburn hair falling across one cheek. The woman from the veranda that morning, the one I'd spied from the beach. Not Angelica's ghost, not Ash's lover. But Clara, Ash's live-in and very beautiful housekeeper.

I cleared my throat from the archway by the living room, and she put down the kitchen spray and looked up. "Oh!" she said. "You must be the writer. Ash could not stop going on about you at breakfast. Olive, right?"

I blushed. Again. God, I hated the way my body betrayed my continual embarrassment. I wished I could just look and act more confident. "Olivia," I corrected her, with as much poise as I could muster.

She shrugged and gave the counter another spritz. Whether I was *Olive* or *Olivia* didn't really make much difference to her. "I was off the last few days—went up to the Bay Area to visit my mom. Ash isn't big on cleaning up after himself. Men. Am I right?" She rolled her eyes conspiratorially, and I wanted to say that I was just the hired writer, that my place here was temporary, and that I knew next to nothing about Ash, not really. Clearly that was true from the way his mood had just turned on me on a dime.

But I bit my lip and simply nodded.

She stepped away from the counter and held the rag at her side. "Ash must be *really* taken with you to invite you to stay here." Annoyance crept into her voice now, and she stared at me as if waiting for me to say something in response. I wasn't sure exactly what. Between Ash just snapping at me and her not being very welcoming, I was already questioning my choice to stay here. But I wasn't about to tell her that.

"Well, we still have some work to get done before I start writing, and it'll just be easier this way…" My voice trailed off, the words sounding like a flimsy excuse for staying here, even to my own ears. They were the truth, though. Or at least the version of the truth we'd been admitting out loud.

Clara stared at me for another moment, scanning my face as if still trying to understand exactly why Ash invited *me* to stay *here*. "You know where the guest room is?" she finally asked. I nodded. "Can I get you anything?"

I shook my head. "I don't want to bother you. You seem busy. You won't even know I'm here."

"Nonsense," she said quickly. "You're Ash's guest. If you need anything, just ask."

"I'm good," I said.

"Not even a cup of coffee? I was about to brew some anyway." She smiled at me now, a genuine-seeming smile that made her bright green eyes crinkle a little, and I wondered if I'd mistaken her annoyance for mere curiosity. Maybe Ash truly didn't invite many people to stay here. I swallowed hard, not wanting to get caught up in the implications of exactly what that meant. It was too early in the morning for that.

And the truth was, I really could use some coffee. I hadn't

had time for a cup before I'd left the hotel. "Actually, coffee would be great, thanks," I said.

"Cream and sugar?" she asked.

I shook my head. "Just black is perfect."

She nodded. "Okay, go get yourself settled and I'll bring it back for you in a few minutes."

Ash's guest room was as I remembered it in my mind from the other day—the painted Angelica looming over the bed with her large watchful eyes—the soft colors of the walls and crisp whites of the linens feeling feminine and altogether out of place in this house. The nightstand was noticeably empty. And now the dresser was too. No du Maurier, no Sylvia Plath, and no Olivia Fitzgerald. No books at all.

I kicked off my shoes, lay down on the bed, and then stared up at Angelica. She was both achingly beautiful and terrifying, and I bet she never once blushed from embarrassment in her entire life. I wondered who'd painted her this way—if she had sat for this portrait inside this very house, or if it had been done by memory, or from a photograph, after she died. That thought chilled me a little and I shivered.

I was so fixated on the painting, on Angelica's haunting green eyes, that I didn't hear Clara enter the room. (Had she even knocked?) Until suddenly she said, "Olivia," as she was standing over me, and I nearly jumped out of my skin.

She laughed a little. "I'm sorry, I didn't mean to scare you. I thought you heard me come in." She put a steaming cup of coffee down on top of a coaster on the nightstand, and a small plate with what looked like a scone on it. "Just wanted to bring your coffee. And a scone in case you get hungry. Ash baked them last night. Raisin and…cardamom, I think?" She raised an eyebrow as she said it, and I thought about Ash's deliberation over the saffron the other night. I laughed a little. "Let me know if I can get you anything else, all right?"

"Thank you, I'm fine. I definitely don't want to bother you," I reiterated.

"Not at all," she said, but now her voice sounded tight.

The air in the room suddenly felt very still and hot, and I forced a smile. I remembered Nate taking my suitcase, saying *the housekeeper* would wash my clothes. "Oh, my suitcase, though. If you bring it in and let me know where the laundry room is—"

"I'll take care of that," she cut me off.

"You really don't have to. I can wash my own things." I felt strange, begging her to get my own clothes back.

"Nonsense," she said quickly. "Like I told you, you're Ash's guest." She offered me another tight-lipped smile. "I'll bring everything in when it's done."

Then she turned and left before I could argue about it anymore.

I stared at the empty doorway. It was just my dirty clothes. Why did I feel so weird about it? *Um, because it's kind of weird.* I could suddenly hear Noah's voice in my head, but I shook it off. Ash—and by extension Clara—was just trying to be nice.

I grabbed my notebook and pen from my bag and took a sip of the coffee Clara had left on the nightstand. It was black, strong, and bitter, exactly the way I liked it. Then I tried the scone—simultaneously spicy and sweet and unlike anything I'd tasted before. Unusual but intoxicating. Almost like Ash himself.

I pushed that thought away, and I considered the pictures of Emilia that Ash had shown me before he'd left.

Emilia was stunning, I wrote at the top of the blank page, doodling flower petals on the circle of the *g*.

Teenager in France? du Maurier connection?

No evidence of Rebecca left due to the fire...

Then it occurred to me, even if there wasn't anything left of Rebecca in the Malibu Lake house, there must be some record of the fire that had happened there. Henry Asherwood had, after all, already started making a name for himself by then when his house burned down. Emilia perished in the fire. That had to be news, and not just locally but nationally, if not globally.

I picked up my laptop and went back to Newspapers.com. I tried searching for *Malibu Lake, fire, 1942*, but *0 results* flashed back at me. Then I tried *Asherwood* and *fire* and *1942* and got only a newspaper ad in the *LA Times* for the Asherwood store from that year, touting a pair of fire opal earrings: *the perfect Christmas gift for that special woman in your life!* I tried *Asherwood* and *house fire* and *1942*, and again *0 results* blinked on my screen, taunting me.

It was one thing if the hard copy paper pieces of the Asherwoods and Emilia's death had been stolen from the Malibu library. But it felt like another altogether that no matter how many search words I tried, I couldn't find anything digitized on Newspapers.com either. Rebecca, the house fire, Emilia's life. How had it all vanished from the depths of the internet? I supposed someone as wealthy and powerful as Ash's grandfather might've paid someone to scrub it all. But then the question was, why? What didn't he want people to know about Emilia or the fire? And why, if Ash wanted so badly for others to know about his grandmother, was he avoiding so many of my questions?

I finished off my coffee and scone, shut my laptop, and put my empty cup and plate on the end table. I glanced up at Angelica again, and her eyes seemed to berate me now, as if my lack of understanding, or maybe even my incompetence as a writer, amused her. "What are you staring at?" I said. Then I covered my mouth with my hand, not quite believing I'd said it out loud.

Okay, I need to get a grip. I definitely should not be speaking to a painting of a dead woman.

I was suddenly very, very tired, and I wondered if Clara had brewed decaf. My eyes blinked closed, and it felt like so much effort to open them. Maybe if I just took a little nap, everything would make more sense when I woke up again. My body felt heavy, and I exhaled as I slid under the crisp white linens.

The last half thought I had before falling asleep was about something Ash had said earlier when I'd asked him if he had any photos, anything at all of Rebecca Asherwood. He had nothing, he'd said, because nothing would've survived the fire. But if Emilia Asherwood had died in that same fire, how exactly had her journals—and the photographs of her—made it out?

Excerpt from *The Wife*

I plan to set it on fire. Everything. Our entire life, every possession he owns. He deserves it after all, and in the days that follow, I imagine myself doing it. Imagine pouring gasoline over everything he loves, lighting the match, and running away toward the water, watching his entire life incinerate, hearing him scream.

It's a beautiful thought.

In fiction, it will make a brilliant scene. And I realize it'll fit perfectly with the story I've been trying to write all along. After all, my novel is the story of the wife, of what happens when she understands how her husband can discard her for a younger woman, just like that. Life imitating art imitating life. Is it truth or fiction? The line feels blurry between where one ends and the other begins.

I edit the first chapter of my novel to include a fire. My protagonist begins now by discarding the match, watching the destruction, watching the flames. I write each delicious and satisfying word, imagining the way they will destroy my husband when this is finally published, when he realizes this is all about him.

And then finally, with the heat of the fire, I feel it: my book is good enough to show to someone else. Not my cousin—I seethe with a secret hatred for her now. But there is a friend from school who works in publishing in New York. I call her and ask her if she'd be willing to read it, and she agrees. Is it because I'm his wife now? Or because she remembers my writing from school? Who can say? Either way I'm grateful for the connection.

Writing will be my way out. I won't be the wife any longer. I'll be a person, an author. Everyone will finally know my name because of the words I've written, not because of the man I'd married.

TWENTY-TWO

When I opened my eyes again, the room was dark. My head felt foggy, and I had no idea where I was, what day or time it was. I'd been dreaming, that I was back in my childhood bedroom in Connecticut, and my mother had been there, yelling at me to clean my room. *You always make such a mess! How will you ever be able to find what you're looking for?*

How would I ever find what I was looking for?

"Olivia?" His voice cut softly through the darkness now, and I felt his hand on my thigh through the blanket, gently shaking me. "Are you all right?"

Noah?

But then I suddenly smelled that intoxicating cedarwood smell of him, and I remembered where I was. Not with Noah. Ash. Ash's house. Ash's guest room. Ash's hand on my thigh, Ash's breath against my cheek.

I blinked to try and focus my eyes, and it was so very dark, except for the sliver of moonlight, a slit of white shining through the French doors, lighting up Angelica's eyes in such a way that they appeared to glow. It was night already? I'd slept the entire day? How was that even possible?

Ash said my name again: "Olivia." His voice sounded gentle, calm. Any trace of exasperation or annoyance from earlier was gone, and I wondered if he hadn't been angry at me after all, but caught up in whatever text he'd received from work. Or maybe he was feeling frustrated too? Even the gorgeous, powerful Ash couldn't make things that didn't exist appear from thin air.

I tried to sit up, but my head felt impossibly heavy. I put my hand to it and moaned a little.

"What's wrong?" He moved his hand from my leg to my forehead, felt it as if checking to see if I was feverish, then did the same on the back of my neck. His hand felt cool against my hot skin.

"I'm fine." I tried to sit up again, but my head was a brick, my mouth was dry, and I swallowed roughly.

"You're not fine," Ash said emphatically, gently pushing my shoulder back down. "Should I call my doctor?"

"No… I have some ibuprofen in my purse." The room was too dark for me to see where I'd put my purse down, and my head was too foggy to remember. "It's around here somewhere."

"I have some in my bathroom. Hold on. I'll be back in minute."

He stood, and as the bed released the weight of him, I suddenly felt desperately embarrassed. Why couldn't I have gotten sick on my own, back at my hotel? Why did it have to be here, in front of him, today? I thought about my mom's voice from my dream, tears stung my eyes, and I felt like such a child.

I pressed my hand back to my forehead, and my skin felt cool, clammy to the touch. I didn't think I had a fever? My headache felt more like a hangover, or migraine, than the flu, and something felt familiar about this feeling, this heaviness in my body. Then I realized what it was.

I'd felt something similar once before; I'd woken up like this, in college. But that time, Noah really was there. Noah pulled me out of bed to the bathroom to vomit. Noah brought me a glass of water on the cold tile floor.

But I definitely hadn't taken any narcotics today. That was a one-time mistake, those pills falling down my throat, so thick with grief it had been hard to swallow. But I'd forced myself to. All with the stupid, stupid belief that if I took what my mother had, even just once, maybe I could understand her, what had happened to her.

All I'd succeeded in doing that night was drugging myself into a stupor and scaring the shit out of myself and Noah. I'd promised Noah I'd never, ever do that again. And I'd kept my promise. So why did I feel this way now?

Clara's coffee? I'd happily drained the mug, inhaling its delicious taste. I was feeling fine just before that. Had she put something in there? The thought was so ridiculous that I laughed out loud. Or, no, maybe it was the scone, the cardamom. Was it possible I was allergic? I glanced at the night table, but the mug and the plate were both gone.

I pressed my hand to my aching forehead. My lack of sleep this week had caught up to me, and more likely I'd caught a virus. I was currently experiencing a classic case of what Jack used to refer to as "writer brain." By which he meant I had the inherent knack to make everything dramatic, to turn even the most mundane happenings into a story. It was why, he'd told me not so kindly, I was a great writer, but not the easiest person to live with. *Jack.* I remembered again about poor Oscar and wondered if Jack had ever texted me his fate, but I had no idea where I'd put my phone, and my head hurt too much to search for it.

"Here you go. Can you sit up?" Ash strode back into the

room with a glass of water in one hand, a pill bottle in the other. He put the water on the nightstand, shook two pills out into the palm of his hand, then put them in my hand.

I stared at them, but it was too dark for me to really see them or to read the bottle, and I hesitated for a second.

"Just ibuprofen, I swear," Ash said, laughing easily. He moved the bottle closer to my face. I squinted but still couldn't make out what it said in the dark. "I mean, if you want something better, I can call someone, but I don't have anything in the house." He laughed again, like he was joking, but also, I felt pretty sure if I told him I wanted *something better*, he'd whip out his phone and make it happen.

"No, no. Ibuprofen is good." *Turn the writer brain off, Olivia.*

I threw the pills in my mouth, he handed me the glass of water, and I swallowed them with one quick swig. "I'll be fine in the morning," I said, hating the way my voice wobbled as the words tumbled out now. "I need to sleep off whatever this is. Probably just a short-lived bug."

Ash sat down on the edge of the bed, reached up, and stroked my hair off my forehead, tucking it behind my ears. "Poor Olivia," he said softly. "I invited you to stay here, abandoned you all afternoon to go in to work, and now you're sick."

"It's fine. I'm fine," I said, my voice coming out hoarse. "You shouldn't get too close. I don't want to get you sick."

He shook his head, then leaned in a little closer. "I don't feel right leaving you alone. And I never get sick. I'm not worried." He stroked my forehead softly with his thumb. "I'll stay here, just until you fall asleep. Unless you want me to go?"

His thumb traced my forehead, and the ache eased. In the sliver of moonlight now, I could see the outline of his broad shoulders, his strong arms. He'd dressed up to go in to work, but had loosened his tie, unbuttoned the top button of his shirt, and I thought about Charley asking me if he was *super fucking hot*. Yes. "Stay," I whispered.

And then I leaned back against the pillow and closed my eyes.

When I opened my eyes again, pale gray light floated in through the French doors. It must be early morning, dawn. The room was empty; Ash was gone. Had he really been here at all, or had I dreamt him here?

The glass of water he'd brought me last night still sat on the nightstand, and I sat up and drank it all, but even that didn't quench my thirst. I got up carefully. My headache had dulled into a mild ache, but the room spun as I stood. I took a minute to get my balance before I walked into the bathroom, filled the glass with water at the sink and drank it down again.

I leaned against the vanity and looked at myself in the mirror. God, I was a mess. My hair was tangled and matted. Even though I'd slept so long, my eyes were ringed with dark circles, and my cheeks were pale. My forehead looked damp with sweat still. I thought about Ash's thumb gently stroking it last night as I fell asleep, and I felt mortified he'd seen me this way.

I jumped in the shower, trying to scrub my embarrassment away. I relaxed under the hot water and the steam, and it wasn't until halfway through shampooing my hair that I remembered my suitcase, my laundry, and the fact that I had nothing clean to wear when I stepped out.

Luckily there were several thick towels hanging over the tub. I wrapped one around my body, one around my hair, and then stepped back into the guest room, nearly walking straight into Ash.

He caught my elbows in his hands, stared at me for a few seconds, and then smiled. "You're feeling better?" I nodded and tugged the towel a little tighter around my chest so it wouldn't slip down. "Sorry, I knocked, but when you didn't answer, I was worried." He didn't sound sorry. He sounded... amused.

"Clothes?" I managed to choke the word out.

"Clara hung the things I had sent up for you from the warehouse in the closet. I think your clothes are still in the laundry room. I can have her bring them up now?"

I shook my head. "No, I'll get them myself. Just let me get dressed..."

"Oh, right." He laughed and let go of my elbows, like he'd forgotten he was touching me this whole time. I had not. How could I? "Sorry, I'll give you some privacy. Meet me in the kitchen for breakfast when you're ready?"

I found the closet after he left—a door that led to a large walk-in just off the bathroom. A row of soft V-neck tees hung in front of me, and a stack of sweaters sat on the shelf next to a few different styles of jeans in a size eight. (Was it weird that he knew my size or was it a lucky guess?) There was a row of boots on the floor—black, brown, zip-up, lace-up. It was too much, and all I really needed was a washing machine! But the Asherwood life was one of excess, wasn't it? I thought about Emilia again, remembering now my very last thought about her from yesterday. *How had her journals and photographs survived the fire when she had not?*

I got dressed in a gray tee and the top pair of jeans, which fit remarkably well. I threw a black sweater on top and stayed barefoot for now. I had four pairs of flats stuffed into my suitcase, which I hoped to retrieve myself shortly. Unfortunately, my suitcase also contained my makeup bag and my brush. So I finger-combed my curls, pinched my cheeks, and searched for my purse, which I finally located under a pillow on the plush chair by the French doors. I found an old lip balm at the bottom, which I ran across my dry, cracked lips, and then noticed my phone sticking out of the front pocket. I'd put it on silent yesterday in the car with Nate and must've never taken it off, because now I saw I had four missed calls from Jack last night, followed by a series of five worried texts from Noah going from midnight to about 4:00 a.m.

Jack called me. Said you're still in LA and he can't get ahold of you. I told him you went back to Boston, but he insisted you didn't. You okay?

Livvvy, text me back. I'm worried.

Okay, I can't sleep. Where are you? Seriously, should I call the police?

You're fine and just ignoring Jack since you broke up, right?

Livvy!!!

I knew it was wrong to feel somewhat satisfied, thinking about Jack worrying about me. But poor Noah, I'd made him worry too. I texted him back first.

I'm so, so sorry. I'm fine! Jack is right, I am staying in LA a few more days. I fell asleep really early and just seeing all your texts now. I think I caught a little bug. Much better today.

As soon as I sent the text, my phone started ringing with a FaceTime call.

"I needed proof of life," Noah said when my camera popped on.

I laughed and noticed I still looked a little pale on the phone screen. "I'm really sorry you were worried." It had been a long time since anyone had paid that much attention to my whereabouts. But I really did feel bad.

"Wow, your hotel room is reaaally nice," Noah said. My camera captured the French doors with the balcony and ocean in the frame behind me. I didn't correct him, not wanting to explain where I actually was. "But if you were sick, you should've texted me. The deli down the street from my apartment makes the best matzo ball soup. Like better than my grandma's—don't ever tell her I said that or she would kick my ass. I would've brought you some."

I laughed again. I'd visited Noah one summer during college at his family's house in upstate New York, and even now I remembered what a riot his grandma was. I was glad to hear she was still alive and in ass-kicking shape. "I just needed to sleep," I said. "I'm fine today, really."

"All right, well then, meet me later. You owe me a drink now."

"I'll, um…"

"Breakfast!" I heard Ash's voice calling in the distance.

"Who was that?" Noah asked.

"I…uh…the TV," I lied quickly. "Look, I have to go get to work, but I'll text you later if I can get away in time for a drink and I'm not too exhausted." Noah frowned, so I added, "But I'll definitely buy you a drink before I go back to Boston. I promise."

He nodded, but he was still frowning a little. I wasn't sure if it was because of Ash's voice and my lame excuse, or the fact that I pretty much said I couldn't see him later. "Oh, and Livvy—Jack told me when I got ahold of you to tell you *thumbs down on Oscar.* That mean anything to you?"

"Shit," I said. And then explained that Oscar was my fish who Jack had forgotten to feed.

Noah sighed. "Promise me the next guy you're with won't be another gorgeous self-centered dick."

I grimaced at Noah's spot-on description of Jack. And

though I couldn't bring myself to actually say it out loud, I understood now that Noah had been right about Jack all along.

"I'm serious, Livvy," Noah said, and his voice was softer, steadier, like he really was serious. "Promise me."

"I promise," I said, and only then did he drop it.

After we hung up, I considered texting Jack, letting him know I was fine. But then I thought about poor little Oscar, floating at the top of that large, beautiful tank, and I shoved my phone in my pocket.

TWENTY-THREE

Even though I was still drowsy, I turned down Clara's offer of coffee. "You sure?" Clara asked. "I heard you had a rough night." I nodded and smiled at her politely.

Jack was definitely an asshole. But he was also generally right about my writer brain, and I was 99 percent sure whatever had happened to me last night had nothing to do with Clara's coffee. But I still wasn't taking any chances.

Clara turned and shrugged at Ash, as if to say, *oh well, I tried,* and left us alone in the kitchen.

"I'm making an espresso for myself," Ash said, moving easily around the giant complicated-looking (professional-grade, no doubt) machine that sat on the counter by his Sub-Zero fridge. "You want one too?"

"Okay," I relented. Because one, I really needed the caffeine, two, I was watching him make it with my own eyes, and three, I trusted him more than Clara.

I'd brought my notebook and pen from the guest room to breakfast, and I sat at a stool around the kitchen island while Ash made our drinks. I reviewed what I'd scribbled yesterday: *Emilia was stunning...du Maurier connection?... No evidence left due to fire.* I looked up, and Ash was walking across the kitchen, an espresso in hand. "Hey, I thought of a question for you yesterday before I got sick," I said.

Ash leaned across me, put the small white espresso cup down in front of me on a matching saucer. He stepped back and smiled at me, that wide, sexiest-man-alive grin. It was hard to breathe for a second, and I tried to push that intoxicating feeling away.

"Go ahead, ask away." He walked across the kitchen to grab his own espresso. He wore jeans and a soft fitted tee today, was barefoot, and looked altogether much more at ease than he had in that tie last night. "You're the only thing on my agenda today." He smiled and sat down across the island from me. "I told work not to contact me unless a literal bomb went off."

"God, I hope that doesn't happen."

"Yeah, you and me both." He took a sip of espresso and then leaned his elbows on the island and sighed. I wondered for the first time if he liked this life, running his grandfather's company, living in this big house all alone. Maybe it was the fact that he was so kind to me last night when I wasn't feeling good, but I felt this swell of compassion for him in my chest. Was an extravagant life a good life? Had it been for his grandmother? Angelica? "What did you want to ask me?" he prompted.

I cleared my throat. "The pictures you showed me yesterday. The journals you sent to the authenticator. How did that all survive the fire?" I spoke tentatively, remembering how annoyed he'd seemed yesterday when I'd asked about his grandfather's first wife, Rebecca.

"Ah." He nodded and smiled a little and took another sip of his drink. I exhaled, relieved that he didn't seem bothered by this line of questioning. "They weren't at the lake house. Grandmother Emilia spent summers up there, but they had another house too, out in the valley. Closer to our warehouse in Burbank. Easier for Grandfather to get to work."

"Wait, you've had the same warehouse for over ninety years?" I asked.

He nodded. "Well, sort of. In the same location. We tore the original one down about ten years ago when I first took over the company. I built one five times its size in its place. I've quadrupled profit margins since then too," he added.

"Impressive," I said.

"I'm boring you, aren't I?" He laughed.

"No, I was being serious! You are extremely impressive." Everything about him was. And not just his business acumen. As he was sitting this close to me across the island, I felt acutely aware of his stunning blue eyes, the way his perfect biceps filled out the sleeves of his fitted tee.

He smiled at me, and god, that smile. My skin warmed and every nerve ending in my body started to come alive again.

"I'm so glad to see you feeling better this morning," he said kindly. "I was worried about you last night."

So, weirdly, that now made three men who were worried about me last night. Well, two and a half, because I wasn't exactly sure Jack counted.

"Honestly, I'm so embarrassed." I thought again about his thumb softly stroking my forehead, how nice it had felt. "I know it was all completely unprofessional, and I'm really sorry about that," I added.

He reached across the counter, grabbed my hands. His touch instantly resonated with a small jolt through my body, and I shifted a little on the bar stool. "First of all, you have nothing to be embarrassed about. And second of all, I'm entrusting *my grandmother* to you. That's not professional. That's deeply personal." His voice softened on the word *personal*, but he kept his eyes trained very steadily on my face.

I knew I should look away. But I didn't. I couldn't.

His sexiest-man-alive grin lit up his face again. "Oh!" he exclaimed and suddenly dropped my hands. "I meant to tell you last night, but then you were sick. FedEx found the boxes in Albuquerque. They should be here tomorrow. We can go through her journals together when they get here, and I'll translate for you."

"That's great," I said.

But tomorrow still felt far away. I wasn't sure I could stay in this house, this close to Ash, for much longer and continue to keep things professional. I was barely hanging on to that as it was, after less than twenty-four hours here.

I finished off my espresso, feeling the caffeine already coursing through my veins. Between that and Ash sitting this close to me, I was fully awake and alive again. And ready to get to work. "Okay," I said, trying to sound decisive. "Since we're still waiting for the journals, how about today we go through your grandmother's timeline, make sure I have all the details right? And I'd also like to see if we can begin to outline the book you want me to write."

Ash nodded. "Sure. Like I told you, I'm all yours today. Use me however you like." *For the project. He definitely means for the project.* I bit my lip. "What are you thinking, in terms of how you want to tell the story?" he added.

"The more I think about it," I said to Ash, "the more I think I should just write Emilia's story, the story she tells about her life in the journals. Even if we can find a connection to Daphne du Maurier, I don't know that I see any way to include that."

He frowned, entwined his fingers on the counter in front of him and stared at them. "So, what...? We just let her get away with it then?"

"Ash," I said softly. "We can't just accuse Daphne du Maurier of plagiarism if there's no way to prove it. Besides, the thing about your grandmother's story that will bring readers to it is that she's *your* grandmother. We tell Emilia's story, and then we let readers draw their own conclusions."

"So, it's all right to steal, then, if no one can ever prove it?" The words practically hissed out of him, snakelike, scaring me a little.

"That's not what I'm saying." I felt annoyed at the way my voice shook as I spoke. Ash acted like we were friends, but anytime I asked him a real question or brought up a topic he didn't like, he became upset. We weren't friends, though. This was a job. A job I wanted to do well. I took a deep breath to steady myself. "Look, if you can show me some evidence, some real evidence, that your grandmother even knew Daphne, well, then we could start there."

"I think they did go to school together," he said quietly.

"In France?" I asked. "You can prove this?"

He nodded and looked down, quiet for a moment as if trying to decide how much he wanted to share with me.

"Ash," I prompted gently, but I felt my heart pounding at the possibility of answers, of *something*, after days of dead ends. "If you want me to write this book, you have to tell me everything."

He looked up again, and his features were softer. He had turned back into the kind, sweet guy who'd brought me ibuprofen last night. "Are you up for a drive now?"

"Another drive?" He was always moving, always changing the subject. "But what about Daphne? School in France…"

"You'll like this. I promise." He smiled again. "And bring your notebook. I'm taking you to find answers."

Ash refused to tell me exactly where we were going, saying it was a surprise. An hour later, he turned down the long drive of what appeared to be a vineyard in, what the road signage told me, was the town of *Ojai*.

"Are you taking me wine tasting?" It was still just 11:00

a.m.! And I was finally feeling close to normal and did not need any alcohol in my system.

He laughed. "No. But you honestly can't leave this town without having a glass of pinot noir. We can do that later before we go."

Before I could argue, we reached the end of the drive, and my eye caught on the large white sign: *Green Oaks Care Suites*. Okay, maybe we weren't at a vineyard, but at what appeared to be a nursing home.

I choked back a laugh. "Sorry, I'm an idiot. But in my defense, you wouldn't tell me where we were going, and this really does look like a vineyard from the main road. What's in this place?" I asked, pointing to the beautiful white building in front of us—it had large gothic columns, and looked more like a mansion than a hospital or facility.

"Not what," Ash said as he parked the car. "Who?"

"Okay." I was intrigued now. "Who?" I echoed.

"My Grammy."

"What?" I shook my head, confused. This could not be what Mrs. Daniels meant when she was talking about ghosts. "But isn't she...dead?"

"Not my *grandmother*, Emilia," he clarified. "My step-grandmother. The woman who raised me. Grammy Rose."

TWENTY-FOUR

If I'd paid more attention in my internet searches, I probably would've known that Rose Asherwood was still alive. But in my defense, the third Mrs. Asherwood had seemed completely disconnected from Emilia's story—after all, she'd married into the family *after* Emilia's death. I'd totally ignored even the very idea of her until now. Walking up the front steps to her nursing home with Ash, I felt both confused and disappointed with myself for feeling like I'd missed something big.

"I have to warn you," Ash said, holding his hand on the front door but not actually moving to open it yet. "She's ninety-three, and she has her good days and bad days. Sometimes she's completely lucid, and others, well…she doesn't even really know who I am."

I nodded. "But what's this visit for, exactly? She married your grandfather after Emilia's death, right? Do you want the book to be about Rose too?"

He let out a dry laugh. "God, no. She might be in a wheelchair now, but she would find a way to murder me with her bare hands if I let you write a book about her. She's an extremely private person. Like Ange was," he added, his voice suddenly turning quieter. "They understood each other." He looked lost for a moment, the expression on his face reminding me of a little boy who'd looked up and suddenly realized he'd accidentally let go of his mother's hand in the crowded supermarket.

"I'm sorry, Ash," I said.

He nodded and shot me a grateful smile. "Rose is the last person left. That's why I brought you here."

"Your last living relative?"

He shook his head. "The last person left who actually knew Emilia."

As I followed Ash back through the lavishly decorated halls, he explained that we were heading towards Rose's *suite*—that's what they were called here, *elder care suites*. And Rose and the other people who lived here (extremely wealthy people, I was certain) were *guests*, not *patients*. Rich people even grew old differently than the rest of us, didn't they?

Ash continued talking as we walked, telling me all about this place, something about the billionaire who'd founded it, but I nodded politely and tuned him out. Instead, my thoughts were on Rose, wondering just what her relationship with Emilia had been like.

My mother and Shawna had been good friends. Shawna's son, Bryan, had been in my third-grade class, and my mom and Shawna were both elected room mothers that year. Bryan and I never said two words to each other, for that year, or the rest of middle or high school. But my mom and Shawna went to yoga together once a week for ten years before my mom died. I always assumed my dad fell in love with Shawna when she came around to console him after my mom's death. Deep down—I was ashamed of this but I couldn't help myself—I hated Shawna simply for being there to take my mom's place.

"I thought you could ask Rose about Daphne du Maurier," Ash was saying now, and the mention of Daphne's name brought me back. He'd stopped walking too, and now we stood outside what I assumed was Rose's *suite*. "But like I said, she isn't always totally lucid." He spoke in a hushed voice now.

"Ask her about Daphne? How exactly did Rose know Emilia?" I whispered. "Were they school friends?" But I tried to do the math quickly in my head, and if Rose was ninety-three now, she'd have to be quite a bit younger than Emilia and Daphne.

"They're cousins," Ash said. Then he added, almost as an afterthought, "Grandfather only met Rose because of Emilia."

Well, that isn't weird at all. But I nodded, trying not to show my reaction on my face.

"Rose is younger, but they both grew up in the French countryside. I'm pretty sure they attended the same school in France—even if they weren't there at the same time."

Goose bumps prickled on my forearms, the thought of it, Rose and Emilia and Daphne all roaming the halls of the same French school, literally making my skin tingle. I rubbed my arms.

"It's cold in here." Ash leaned in closer to me and pulled the two sides of my sweater together, his hands hovering just below my chest. I felt like the opposite of cold with him standing so near, and I suddenly had to make an effort to breathe.

"I'm fine." I took a step back to give myself some space, so I could think. He raised his eyebrows a little. "Really," I added, trying very hard to sound *fine*.

Ash nodded, and he knocked softly on Rose's door, then turned the handle to enter without waiting for her response.

On the other side of the door, there was a plush carpeted living room filled with plump red velvet couches and large windows dressed with lavish velvet curtains. A very old woman with thinning white hair sat in a wheelchair—but she was dressed in a light blue Chanel suit and wore a fist-sized glittering blue stone around her neck, with matching smaller ones adorning her earlobes. She was literally dripping in expensive diamonds, in a nursing home. No, an *elder care guest suite.*

"Ashy!" she exclaimed. *Ashy?*

"Hey, Grammy." He strode easily over to her wheelchair, leaned in, and gingerly hugged her.

"Oh come on, give me a real hug. I'm ninety-three years old, but I'm not going to break."

He hugged her a little tighter, kissed the top of her head, and pulled back to look at her. "You doing okay?" Ash asked. She nodded. "Where's the girl I hired to help you?"

"I sent her to pick up lunch," Rose said. "I wanted a Big Mac and a Diet Coke."

"Grammy! I told you not to eat that stuff. It's not good for you."

"So?" She shrugged. "I'll eat what I please, and I'll die when I die."

I put my hand to my mouth to stifle a laugh at their interaction. It was funny to see, this woman who'd raised Ash, and, it seemed, still had the upper hand around him.

"Who's this?" She suddenly seemed to notice me standing by the doorway and now lifted a finger to point in my direction.

Ash grabbed my hand and pulled me toward the couch, where we both sat. He turned Rose's chair a little so she was directly facing us. "Grammy, this is Olivia Fitzgerald. She's a writer I hired."

Her dark-brown penciled eyebrows shot up. "Writer?"

I glanced at Ash, and he nodded slightly. "Ash wants me to write a book about his grandmoth—about Emilia Asherwood," I clarified. "And he thought you might be able to talk to me about her and maybe about your time at finishing school in France."

She stared at Ash and frowned deeply. "Henry Asherwood III." *Uh-oh, his full name.* She was definitely not happy that

Ash had brought me here. "For one thing, you should've called first. You could give an old lady a heart attack dropping in like this."

"If the Big Mac doesn't do it first, huh?" Ash's tone was light, teasing. He was unfazed by her admonishment.

She swatted at his arm. "I'm serious. And for another thing, how dare you go stirring up more trouble for this family. After what you're doing to Angelica."

Her name was so unexpected, and followed by such a deep, long silence, that I swore I could hear the word *Angelica* reverberating against the gold-papered walls of the lavish parlor. I glanced at Ash, and his face had gone completely white. *What you're doing to Angelica?* What the hell did she mean by that? I thought back to the Reddit thread, all the conspiracy theories swirling. Ash poisoning her. Ash murdering her. Angelica still being alive.

"Grammy, you're forgetting yourself again," Ash finally said, speaking slowly, the way you might to a toddler, and I remembered what he said earlier about her going in and out of lucidness. "Ange was killed in a terrible car accident last year." The two of them locked eyes, stared at each other so steadily.

Ange was killed in a terrible car accident. Of course she was. Why was I even thinking about those crazy Reddit posts again?

I cleared my throat guiltily, feeling like I had to try and say...something to change the subject and bring things back around to Emilia. "I think Ash feels Emilia has been forgotten, and that's why he hired me to write about her." I spoke tentatively at first, hoping I wasn't saying the wrong thing. Rose nodded a little, which gave me the courage to continue. "I'd love to hear more about Emilia's story of being swept up by Henry Asherwood, marrying him so quickly, moving out here and getting wrapped up in his lifestyle..." I stopped talking for a moment, as I realized everything I was saying about Emilia possibly applied to Rose. And maybe even Angelica too. "But first I'm trying to figure out if Emilia had any connection to Daphne du Maurier. Ash thinks you all might've gone to the same school in France."

"*La fille Anglaise dans les rumeurs,*" Rose said softly, suddenly switching into what I assumed to be her native French.

"Rumors?" Ash asked.

"Daphne attended the same finishing school as us, yes. I didn't know her—she was years older than me, Emilia's age—but even in my year, we all knew *of* her. She was the English writer who'd once had an affair with a teacher. A woman teacher, mind you."

I'd read about this in the biography in the library the other day, that Daphne had left the school after the rumored affair. Later in life Daphne would also be rumored to be in love with Ellen Doubleday, the wife of her publisher. But in between, she married a man, Robert Browning, had several children with him, and even arguably became obsessed with his ex-fiancé Jan Ricardo, thus potentially inspiring her for *Rebecca*.

But it felt like a strange and altogether more exciting thing hearing this gossipy history from Rose, who'd lived adjacent to it, rather than simply reading about it in a book. It was the same kind of heart-pounding excitement I would get when I was writing a story, and I would suddenly figure out an elusive plot point. Maybe Rose was the answer to everything?

"Was Emilia close with Daphne, do you know?" I asked her. I was speaking quickly, my voice effusive. "And could they have stayed friends after school?"

Rose didn't say anything for a moment, but then she shook her head. "I don't know," she finally said. "But I don't think so? She never mentioned it."

Just like that, my heart plummeted in my chest, and I sighed. Maybe what I'd said to Ash earlier this morning was right. Maybe our book had nothing to do with Daphne du Maurier. Maybe the book we were supposed to write was just the story of Emilia, and in her story, Daphne going to the same finishing school was just a footnote.

We'd come all the way here. I really wanted *something* useful from Rose. "Could you talk to me about the Emilia you knew then? What was she like as a woman, a mother, a wife? I've had trouble finding anything real about her, anywhere."

Rose lowered her eyes, stared at her hands, twisted them in her lap. That's when I noticed the giant blue rock on her finger too. Damn, it had to be at least four karats.

"Grammy." Ash's voice was soft, pleading. "Won't you talk to Olivia, help her out? For me."

She looked up again, and now I noticed her eyes were a steely gray, the color of every morning in Malibu before the fog burned off across the water. "You want something real?" I nodded. She paused for a second, ran her fingers across the giant diamond of her ring. "Who do you think set the fire?"

"What do you mean?" Ash shook his head.

"Emilia wasn't well before she died. You want to write a book about her? About your family's skeletons? Well, there you go—Emilia killed herself and tried to kill your grandfather too. I guess there's a long history of *that* in this family."

The room was so silent for a moment, I could hear the breaths escaping Rose's chest in small gasps. A *long history* of what…? The Reddit post about Angelica rang through my head again. *No, no, no.*

"No." Ash finally spoke, softly. "The fire was deemed an accident."

An accident. Just like Angelica's death.

"And that can't be true," Ash added emphatically. "If it was, you would've told me this before now."

"Well, you never wanted to write a book about her before now," Rose snapped.

I had the sudden sense that our entire project, my money, the boost to my career, it was all in peril. But regardless of all that, there were so many questions running through my head that I wanted answers to now, about Emilia, about Angelica. And then, there was the ache I was feeling in my chest for Ash. In this moment, he wasn't a billionaire who had hired me to write about his family. He was just this sweet, beautiful man, who looked completely destroyed by Rose's one sentence.

"Big Mac's here!" A young red-haired woman bounded in through the door, holding a large grease-stained bag in one hand, a cardboard drink carrier in the other. She stopped suddenly when she noticed Ash. "Oh, Mr. Asherwood, I—I didn't know you were coming to visit today."

"That's because he didn't call first," Rose said coolly. "Mary Beth, honey, hand me that Diet Coke. I'm parched." She slowly extended a hand.

Mary Beth shrugged apologetically at Ash, and handed over the Diet Coke to Rose, twisting the paper off the top of straw and angling it closer to Rose's mouth.

"We never do this," she turned and said to Ash. "But Rose begged me today. I think maybe she needs the iron from the burger."

Nice try, Mary Beth. I felt reasonably certain Rose ate Big Macs for lunch most days.

"They can grill her a grass-fed burger in the kitchen. They stock Wagyu beef, for Christ's sake." Ash's voice came out just as icy with anger as Rose's had a moment earlier. "I don't pay you for this crap." He glared at Mary Beth, then raised his arm, and for a second, I thought he was going to snatch the greasy bag from her hand and throw it across the room in disgust. But then he seemed to notice me watching him, and he lowered his hand slowly again. "We'll go," he said quickly. "Clearly we're bothering you."

He grabbed my hand and pulled me to toward the door before I had a chance to say goodbye or anything else to Rose.

"Next time call first," Rose shouted after us.

Excerpt from *The Wife*

I'm with my cousin when I receive a call from my publishing friend in New York. It has been three months since that night I'd heard my cousin in my bedroom with him, and every interaction with her since has been painful. I can't tell her that I know. That I'd heard her. That I hate her.

Passive-aggressive is more my style, and so instead I pile on the work, give her impossible tasks. One day I send her on a wild goose chase for the perfect pair of pink pearl earrings to match a dress for an event, and then when she's gone, I go into her closet and poke tiny holes in all her favorite dresses. When she notices, I make a big to-do about moths getting in. Later, I do the same with my husband's silk ties.

Do I regret it, when she's kind to me? When I drink too much champagne, and I'm kneeling in front of the toilet the next morning? When she is there, holding my hair, rubbing my back. When she runs to the kitchen to fix me her hangover tonic that instantly soothes me. But no, even then, I do not regret it. She deserves all that and more.

Never mind her. Or my husband. Once I get my novel published, I'll leave him. Have my own life again, my own career too. My cousin can stay behind and be suffocated by his constant need for adoration, for affection. He can smother her, until she'll forget she's even a person in her own right. Let her be the second wife for all I care. I am getting out.

But then one morning, my cousin and I sit across from each other sipping coffee. My cousin is talking about a party later in the week, and I have half a mind to tell her just to go in my place. To say the thing out loud I've been thinking in my head for months. Just take my husband if you want him so badly, why don't you?

But I bite my tongue. And then the phone rings—my publishing friend calling from New York.

"I have to tell you something," she says, forgoing hellos. Her voice sounds grim, and my heart suddenly pauses, suspended in my chest.

"What's wrong?" I ask her. "Do you hate it? Is it that terrible?"

"No," she says. "No." Her voice softens. "It's not terrible at all."

"Then what is it? What's the problem?"

"The problem is," she says, "someone else has already written this book."

TWENTY-FIVE

"God, she's a piece of work," Ash said once we were back out in the parking lot. We reached his car, and he slapped his hands against the hood, out of anger or to emphasize his point.

"She's...feisty," I agreed. I folded my arms in front of my chest and had to squint to look directly at Ash. His frame was backlit by the bright midday sun, and if he weren't already gorgeous enough, there was something about him looking a little broken, and also glowing, that I could feel in a heated rush through my own body, from my stomach straight to my toes.

"Feisty is putting it mildly. She's a raging bitch." He ran his hand through his hair, messing up his curls, and then leaned against the frame of his car. "She always has been, for as long as I can remember. I'm sorry. I shouldn't have brought you here."

"No, I'm glad you did," I said, and he shot me a grateful half smile. "But the thing she said...about Emilia's mental health. Do you think there's any truth to that?"

Ash sighed. "I don't think so. But maybe?"

My initial reaction to Ash's story about Emilia writing *Rebecca* had been that Emilia had been writing fan fiction. Had Emilia long admired Daphne from a distance, starting back in school? Ash had said that fan fiction hadn't worked with the dates, but we didn't have anything back from the authenticator yet. Maybe the dates in her journal had been fiction too. Was it possible she'd written fan fiction to emulate her famous former classmate, or even burned down her own house in an attempt to emulate the ending of *Rebecca*?

I looked up, and Ash looked so forlorn leaning against his car that I couldn't bring myself to verbalize any of what I'd just been thinking. It felt like he'd been using this project, this time with me, this exploration of Emilia's story, to finally rise from his grief after Angelica's death. And here Rose had popped the delicate bubble of his excitement with one little terrifying sentence: *Your grandmother killed herself and tried to kill your grandfather too.*

I walked closer to him and put my hand on his arm. "It'll be okay," I said gently. "We'll figure it out. You said yourself, Rose isn't always lucid." Though even as I spoke, I felt reasonably sure that Rose had been at least somewhat coherent today. That what Rose had said had made almost more sense than anything else I'd heard about Emilia since I'd gotten to California.

"Do you think you could drive us back to Malibu?" Ash asked suddenly. He held out his key fob, dangling it in front of me.

I bit my lip, not sure how to explain to him that I hadn't driven since college, since before my mother's accident. *I couldn't drive!* I mean, technically, I could. I still had a valid license that I always renewed and used for ID. But the thought of driving Ash's Tesla on the terrifyingly packed freeway and windy roads back to Malibu, after not having driven anywhere in over nine years, absolutely scared the shit out of me.

The fear paralyzed me so much, I said nothing for a minute, and Ash took that as me agreeing. He gently reached for my hand, dropped his key fob in my palm, and walked around to get into the passenger seat.

"Wait, Ash." I finally found the words. "I can't… I've never driven a Tesla. I don't know how…" The lamest-sounding excuse fell out of me. Even I knew that these cars were supposed to practically drive themselves.

Ash laughed. "It's not that hard, I promise. I'll help you. Get in." He got in the passenger seat, and then I was just standing there in the sun, unable to move, clutching his key fob.

I couldn't do this.

"Olivia, come on," he called out for me.

Fuck. I had to do this.

I inhaled deeply, then exhaled, and slowly walked to the driver's side, opening the door and slipping into the seat. Ash was much taller than me, and the seat was so far back, my feet couldn't even reach the pedals. But I could barely process that, as the steering wheel loomed in front of me, taunting me.

"If you hit the second seat memory button, that was Ange's," Ash was saying now, not noticing the way my body was gripped with fear. "She was about your height. Go ahead," Ash prodded. "Don't be shy."

My hand shook so furiously as I hit the button, it knocked against the door. *Ange's seat. Ange's accident. My mother's accident.* "Now tap the brake, and it'll wake up the car." I heard what he said, but I couldn't make my foot actually move to do it. "Tap the brake," he repeated, his voice tinged with impatience now.

"Ash, I… I can't drive your car. I don't even have car insurance," I stammered.

"Don't worry," he said easily. "My insurance covers you." He smiled, and I remembered again that he was not a normal man. He was a billionaire who was used to being driven around by other people. No excuse I could give him right now was going to get me out of this.

I inhaled deeply again, trying to calm myself down, and then slowly moved my foot to tap the brake. The car screen came alive, and Ash smiled again. "You're good to go. Just use the gear shift to move into Reverse to back up." He reached for my hand and gently put it on top of the shifter.

My fingers rested there, sweating against the cool, smooth metal top. *Just move into Reverse.* Move the gear shift, look behind me, take my foot off the brake.

It wasn't that hard. I could do it. I knew how to do it. So why couldn't I get my hand to move?

"Olivia?" Ash's voice sounded like it was coming through water. "Olivia?"

"I can't!" I heard the words in my voice, but they felt like they came from somewhere else, far away. I yanked my hand off the gear shift like I was touching fire and it had just burned me. And I burst into tears. All-encompassing, embarrassing sobs that made my shoulders shake.

"Olivia, what's wrong? Are you hurt?" Ash's voice swam, ethereal, distant.

He must've gotten out of the car, because all of a sudden he was opening up my door, unbuckling my seat belt, pulling me out, like he was rescuing me a from a burning building. He held on to me and stroked my hair until my sobs subsided. And then he took a step back as if to examine me, running his hands slowly down my face, my arms, checking me for some invisible injury.

"I don't drive," I finally said when I caught my breath. "I can't. I can't drive." It felt ridiculous, even all these years after my mother's accident. I hated admitting it out loud. Hated even more showing him how weak I was. I felt so stupid. Who couldn't even drive a self-driving car?

Ash tilted his head and raised his eyebrows. "But I read in

your bio you grew up in suburban Connecticut, not the city, right? Isn't learning to drive a requirement in the suburbs?"

I didn't say anything for a moment, and we just stared at each other.

"I did learn," I finally said, my voice cracking. I was trying to hold back more tears. Unsuccessfully. I wiped at them furiously now as they started to fall down my cheeks. "I just... I haven't driven since college. My mom died in a pretty bad car accident and then...well, I haven't been able to drive ever since."

"Oh, shit." Ash put his hands to my cheeks and brushed away the remaining tears with his thumbs. "I didn't know."

"It's stupid," I said softly. "It's been a long time. I just..."

I managed to stop crying, but his hands stayed on my face, and he leaned in even closer. "It's not stupid," he whispered, and I could feel each word trace my skin. "Grief stays with you."

I remembered again what Mrs. Daniels had said: *When people leave us, they don't just disappear. They haunt us.*

My mother. Emilia. Angelica. It was true for all of them. For me and Ash.

And then it occurred to me that in the span of the last hour, Ash and I had both shared something very real and vulnerable with each other. There was something bigger between us now, more than a write-for-hire project, or money, or my career. More than the sexiest man alive. More than the failed writer. Standing here, holding on to one another, he was just Ash. And I was just Olivia. And maybe grief followed you forever, no matter who you were or how much money you had.

"Okay," Ash said softly, interrupting my thoughts. "Here's what we're gonna do. I'll drive us five minutes down the road to that winery with the pinot noir I told you about. Then I'll call Nate to come up and get us, and he'll drive us back to Malibu."

"But…your car?" I said meekly.

"Nate will figure it out." He said it in such a blasé man-
ner, the way only an extravagantly wealthy person with a
Tesla here and a Porsche there might. I couldn't help myself.
I started to laugh. Which Ash took as me agreeing to his plan.

I didn't want wine. But I was honestly ready to jump on
any plan that didn't involve me driving us back. Besides, arguing with Ash wasn't really an option. This much I already
understood, when Ash wanted something, Ash got it.

TWENTY-SIX

It was only a little past noon when we walked into the empty winery, and I wasn't at all excited about day drinking after my miserable headache last night, but I told Ash I'd try a few sips of the pinot noir he insisted was the absolute best. He ordered us a cheese plate too, and then we grabbed a small table by the window.

I sat down and looked out at the rolling vineyard and wide blue sky. Suddenly it felt like we were a million miles from anything or anyone else. Malibu, Boston, Ash's wealth and notoriety, my sad little writing career. Rose's accusations, and even my meltdown in the Tesla ten minutes earlier. "It's really beautiful out here." I sighed. "Peaceful."

"Pretty amazing place to live in a retirement home, right?"

"You mean *elder care suites*," I corrected him, teasing.

He smiled, and the lingering darkness had retreated from his eyes, stayed back somewhere five miles down the road, closer to Rose. "Are you making fun of me?" he asked. He was sunlight and sexiest-man-alive Ash again.

"Definitely not." I laughed. My headache had finally disappeared, and sitting here, I felt strangely calmer than I had all week. Maybe it was because I had just shown Ash something both real and terrible about myself, and here he was, sitting across from me, smiling.

The sommelier brought the bottle of pinot Ash had requested and uncorked it, offering Ash a taste. Ash swirled the wine around, sniffed it, and took a sip. "The best." He smiled. "As always." The sommelier smiled back, and I wondered if he knew who Ash was or not. If he did, it didn't seem to faze him. He filled Ash's glass up and started to pour one for me.

"Just a little." I held up my hand. But he either didn't hear or ignored me and poured a regular-sized glass before he walked away. Ash stared at me, expectantly, and I took the smallest sip. It was smooth, velvety, undoubtedly extremely expensive.

"You like it?" Ash asked.

"The wine is great." I picked up a piece of cheddar from the plate and nibbled on it. "I just finally feel normal again after last night. I don't want to have too much." I finished off the piece of cheese, leaned down, and pulled my notebook from my bag. "Okay, how about I'll eat cheese instead and ask you some more questions about Emilia while you enjoy your glass. We may as well work while we wait for Nate."

He reached across the table, gently pulled my notebook from my hand, and put it down next to me. "Or," he said softly, "we could forget about Emilia for the rest of the day after that trauma I just put you through, and we could...enjoy each other's company instead."

Enjoy each other's company?

I felt my cheeks turning hot, yet again. But the heat was weirdly less from embarrassment now than excitement. Did Ash just want to spend time with me? And what if maybe I wanted that too—would that be so wrong?

"You know," Ash continued, "we could just hang out for a

few hours. Talk. Drink some wine." He paused and took another sip of his wine as if to emphasize his point. "I feel like I'm finally getting to really know you, and now I want more, Olivia." He said it unapologetically, and though I wanted to ask him exactly what he meant by *wanting more*, I bit my lip.

It had been a long time since I'd done anything remotely close to dating, and in college, the few guys I'd dated before Jack had been getting together for cheap dinners, movies, and beer. I'd never been to a winery, in Ojai, with the sexiest man alive, telling me he wanted to hang out with me. Everything about Ash was outsized, extra. I had no idea how to manage my expectations. He wanted *more*. But what did *more* even mean for him?

I looked back up, and he was staring at my face, those intense blue eyes locked on *me*. The corners of his mouth upturned in a little grin, as if he could somehow see every last thought I'd just had, and it amused him. He reached across the table again, picked up my hand, held it in his own. His thumb very slowly traced the length of my palm, as if he were a fortune teller searching for my love line, and the slow, heated pressure of it made me breathless.

"You like spending time with me too, don't you, Olivia?" His voice was soft, but forceful.

I nodded, afraid to speak. More afraid to misspeak. Or maybe worse, misunderstand. Of course I liked being with him. I liked the way I felt when I was this close to him. I was charmed by him. A little in awe of him. He'd been so kind to me when I was sick last night and back in the car during my freak-out. How could I not be attracted to the *sexiest man alive*?

But the reality also was, I was a stumbling novelist at the low point of her career. An admittedly average-looking, curly haired Jewish girl from suburban Connecticut. My size eight jeans and frizzy curls didn't exactly scream his type, judging by that glamorous painting of the gorgeous Angelica in his guest room.

He liked spending time with me because I was helping him with this project. Because we were working together, and because he was lonely. Because we both had been stricken by a lingering grief in strange and accidental ways. Maybe what he meant by *wanting more* was that even he could use a friend to talk to, a friend to spend the afternoon with. He definitely was not talking about anything aside from that.

And thank god, because I needed this job to work out. I really did. My writing was the most important thing, the only thing. I could not lose sight of that.

TWENTY-SEVEN

I ended up drinking the whole glass of wine, and then I felt drowsy on the ride back to Malibu two hours later.

We'd spent the time at the winery talking, and I'd lost track of myself, sipping the delicious pinot as we chatted and waited for Nate, not really noticing its effect on me until we got into the back seat of yet another car—a black Escalade— and then I could barely keep my eyes open.

At the winery, Ash had insisted he'd wanted to know more about my life, and suddenly I heard myself telling him about my father, who I'd barely spoken to since he married Shawna. I turned down his yearly invitations to family Thanksgivings and Christmukkahs. Still, my dad very diligently sent a $100 check for my birthday each year in May, and I deposited it guiltily, then texted him thanks. Our one remaining inter- action, I told Ash.

"Well, you've met Rose," Ash said, empathizing. Then he'd added softly, "Ange was my only real family. Until she wasn't."

In the back of the Escalade, I ruminated over that in my head. At the winery, I'd thought Ash meant it was because she died. But Rose had said something about what Ash had done to her. Was there a betrayal? His or hers? And if there was, had it contributed to her death?

At that thought, I felt my head inexplicably drifting onto Ash's shoulder, and I couldn't stop it. The wine, the afternoon sun streaming in through the backseat car window, Nate's steady driving—I closed my eyes and drifted off, dreaming of the water, of a woman trying to keep her head above the white crests of the waves, my mother, or maybe it was Angelica. Or maybe it wasn't a woman at all, but the arched tails of the migrating gray whales.

"Olivia." Ash's voice came from somewhere in the distance, his hand gently nudging my thigh.

"Mmm," I murmured. "Just a few more minutes." My body was so heavy, and maybe I hadn't fully recovered from whatever had made me sick last night.

The next thing I knew, Ash's arms were under me. He was lifting me out of the back seat of the car and *carrying me* from his garage into his house. My body felt suspended in midair, and that completely woke me up. "What are you doing?" I protested, lightly swatting at his shoulder. "Put me down. I can walk."

"Can you?" He chuckled a little.

"Ash," I protested again. "Put me down."

"You sure? You really conked out in the car. You were snoring."

"I do not snore!" Oh my god, could I embarrass myself any more?

He laughed, and put me down gently, steadying me with a hand on the small of my back. But even once I was on my feet, he didn't let go of me. He kept his hand lightly on my back as we walked inside, toward the guest suite. "You're tired," he said as we stopped at the door to my room. "Take a nap, and I'll wake you up for dinner."

But he didn't move, and neither did I. We stared at each other, not speaking for a moment. Maybe I was still half-asleep and feeling impulsive, or maybe I just couldn't stand the thought of him walking away from me. Maybe it was his closeness that made me reckless, his smell, and his smile, and his intense blue eyes.

"I'm not tired anymore," I said softly. And even as I said the words, I understood they were an opening. An invitation. If he wanted them to be. But harmless enough if he didn't. He could still let go. He could still walk away.

But he didn't.

His hand still rested on the small of my back, and he used it now to pull me closer to him, so suddenly my body was pressed up against his. I could feel the heat of his skin even through both our shirts. "Are you sure?" he whispered.

I nodded, though I wasn't sure of anything, except that I didn't want him to let go of me.

He reached around me with his other hand to open the guest room door, then walked us both inside, shut the door with his foot, and spun me around so my back was pressed against it. He put his elbows against the door, on both sides of my shoulders, his face so dangerously close to mine that his breath traced my lips as he spoke again. "You want me to kiss you." He enunciated each word slowly. Not a question. A statement. He knew I did. He knew I shouldn't.

I nodded slowly.

"Say it," he said.

"I... I..." I could not bring myself to say it. Every sentence that came into my head started with, *We shouldn't do this... I can't do this...* And I didn't want to say those words either. Would it be so bad, to kiss him? Just this once. Just one time. How many single, straight women, free to do whatever they pleased—this close to the sexiest man alive—would be able stop themselves from kissing him?

Fifty thousand dollars. Your writing career!

"Tell me what you want, Olivia." He whispered the words directly against my ear, and as his breath hit my skin, I couldn't stop myself.

"I want you," I blurted, the words tumbling out of me much louder than I'd meant them to. I had the sudden mortifying image of Clara somehow hearing them all the way in the kitchen, suddenly stopping in her tracks as she scrubbed the counter.

An easy smile spread across Ash's face, and he leaned in those last few inches and touched his lips to mine. Softly, for just a few seconds, tentatively, like he wasn't sure how to kiss me yet. And the thought of me making him nervous, hesitant, made me smile a little. Made me feel brave. I reached my hand up to his face, traced the line of his jaw with my fingers, the way I'd wanted to ever since I first stepped foot in this house. Then I touched the coarse curls of his hair, and gently grabbed them in my fist, standing up on my toes to arch into him, to kiss him harder.

And then our kisses had a rhythm, a hunger. His tongue against my tongue, so I could still taste the blackberries of the wine from Ojai. He grabbed my hand and put it under his shirt. His muscular torso was so firm, his skin so hot. I ran my fingers up, along the length of his chest. He tucked his hand into the waistband of my jeans, and I could barely breathe. But I couldn't stop either. To stop would mean to think about what I was doing, and I didn't want to think. I wanted to feel every second of this.

But then all of a sudden, he stopped kissing me. He pushed me away and took a step back, straightening his disheveled shirt. He reached his hand to his lips, which were noticeably red and a little puffy. I touched my own, feeling the same. He stared at me, breathing hard, and I couldn't tell if he was annoyed now or crazy with desire. Or maybe annoyed because he was crazy with desire?

"I'm sorry," I said.

"Why are you sorry?"

I shook my head. There were probably a hundred things I should be sorry for. Did this ruin our project? It was obviously completely unprofessional. But the truth was, I didn't actually feel sorry for any of that. Not yet. The words came out more as a reflex than anything else.

He ran his hand through his hair, took another step back, glanced up and seemed to be staring off into space. I turned around to follow his eyes—no, not space. *Angelica*. His eyes must've caught on the painting of her above the fireplace. Is that why he pushed me away? Or was he just noticing her here now, watching us, in the aftermath, like I was?

"I should probably..." he said softly, nodding toward the door.

"Yeah, you probably should," I agreed.

Don't go. Please don't go. I stared at him, willing him with my eyes to intuit the words I was thinking even though I couldn't bring myself to say them out loud.

What do you want, Olivia?

I want you to stay.

"Yeah, so I'll just, let you..." His voice trailed off. He glanced at Angelica one more time, then quickly opened the door, walked out, and shut it behind him.

I flopped on the bed and sighed deeply, hugging a pillow to my chest. I put my fingers to my lips again, thinking about the way they'd just felt a few minutes earlier. My recent kisses with Jack had been boring kisses: quick kisses, routine kisses, verging on chaste kisses—but even when we'd first gotten together, back in college, Jack had never kissed me with the intensity Ash did. No one ever had. In the cold, quiet guest room, that thought terrified me, and a chill settled over me.

Ash was fire, and now that he'd left, now that I was alone here, I was suddenly cold.

I had gone from that heated moment back to this chilly, lonely one so quickly, I felt like I had emotional whiplash. I groaned and hugged the pillow tighter to my chest. How was I supposed to look Ash in the eyes later at dinner, much less *work* with him, without replaying every single second of that kiss? It would be impossible. I was going to have to leave in the morning, go back to Boston, and quit working on this project. Dammit. Charley was going to kill me.

A soft knock on the door startled me, and I jumped, dropped the pillow, and stood up. But before I could say anything, the door swung open, and Ash stood on the other side. His hair was still messy, and his shirt was still half-untucked. And for a moment he just stood there and stared at me, not saying anything at all.

Then he strode into the room, grabbed my hand, glanced quickly at Angelica, then looked away, back at me. "There are a lot of rooms in this house," he said, his voice coming out husky.

And as soon as he touched me, the chill evaporated; my skin was hot again, and I knew I was going to follow him. Forget reason, embarrassment, this job. My writing career.

I was going to follow him anywhere.

TWENTY-EIGHT

The room Ash led me to was in another wing of his house, one I hadn't been to yet.

He held on to my hand as we walked quickly, crossing back through the living room, past the kitchen. I kept my eyes focused on the back of Ash's head, his tousled curls, not wanting to see if Clara was standing in the kitchen, staring (surely, frowning) at me holding on to him. If she was, though, she didn't make a sound.

We were soon past the kitchen and down another hall with several closed doors, leading to what I assumed were more bedrooms. Ash stopped at the first one. Was this his bedroom? Had he shared this room with Angelica once? Or was this yet another guest room? I couldn't bring myself to ask; I didn't want to ruin whatever was happening by speaking.

"I moved in here a few months ago," he said softly, answering my unasked question. "I couldn't stay in the same…" His voice trailed off; he was unable to finish his thought. But surely, he meant the *same bedroom* he'd shared with his wife or the *same bed* he'd slept in with her, night after night.

Oh god, what am I doing?

I gently extricated my hand from his, but he shook his head a little and picked my hand right back up again. He opened the door to the room and led me inside.

It was minimalist and masculine in here, much like most of the rest of his house: pale gray walls, a king-sized bed in the center of the room with a dark gray comforter. There were double French doors that led to what I assumed was a balcony looking out over the ocean, but the heavy gray curtains were mostly drawn, letting in only the smallest slant of pale gray light, making the room feel strangely overcast. If a room could have an inherent sadness, this one did.

"Ash." I said his name softly. "Maybe we shouldn't—"

"Say what you said before," he cut me off.

What did I say before? Everything felt jumbled in my head, and all I could think about was the way his tongue had felt in my mouth, the way his hair had felt against my fingers. The warmth of his skin. I wanted to touch him, to feel that warmth again. But we shouldn't. *I shouldn't.* Ash would be fine tomorrow, no matter what was about to happen between the two of us. But would I?

"You said that you want me," he said. "Say it again."

Had I really said that to him, out loud? *I had.* And I'd meant it too. I bit my lip. And then I said instead, "I really need this job."

He nodded. "We can separate business and pleasure."

Could we?

He put his hand to my chin, gently turned my face so our lips were almost touching again, but not quite. "Say. It. Again." He breathed each word slowly, and I could feel them against my mouth more than I could hear or even comprehend them.

"I want you," I finally whispered. I almost hated that the words were true more than I hated that I'd said them. Twice.

He smiled a little, and then his lips were on mine. And I was underwater. I couldn't hear or see or think. I was drowning but I didn't want to come up for air; I couldn't even remember how to swim.

But then suddenly everything seemed to happen so quickly, like he'd pressed the fast-forward button on a remote I couldn't quite reach: my shirt was off, he unhooked my bra, he pulled my jeans down, pushed me back onto his bed. Then I was lying there on top of his comforter naked, and it was only when he pulled away from me to pull a condom from his nightstand drawer that my skin turned cold, and I could suddenly think again.

What the hell am I doing?

I barely knew anything about Ash except that he was, as Noah would probably say, both *gorgeous* and *self-centered.* Everything leading up to this moment had happened so fast. Too fast. We'd barely known each other a week. Wanting him was one thing. Kissing him was one thing. Getting naked five minutes later felt like another altogether.

I sat up quickly, scanned the floor for my jeans and my shirt, walked over, and scooped them up. I stepped hastily into my jeans, tripping over the legs a little. "I'm sorry," I heard myself stammering. "I think I should... I don't think we should..."

Ash shut the nightstand drawer and turned and looked at me for a second. His eyes were dark, but I couldn't tell if that was desire or disappointment, and whatever it was flickered away as he pulled his pants back up, buckled his belt, and walked towards me. He put his hands on my shoulders. "I moved too fast, didn't I?"

I shook my head, though that's exactly what had spooked me. The speed at which we'd gone from kissing by the door to about to have sex. I felt dizzy.

"It's been...a really long time since..." he said softly.

I bit my lip and nodded. And maybe that was my problem too. I hadn't even gone on a date since Jack had moved out, much less had sex. I fumbled with the button on my jeans and then pulled my sweater over my head, feeling static run up my hair.

Ash put his hand up gently to my head, smoothing my staticky hair back into place, tucking it behind my ears. Then he put his hand on my cheek, and it suddenly softened things again, warmed me. I was hot and cold, excited and unsatisfied all at once. "You don't have to go," he said. "I'll order us some dinner, and we can eat it here in bed and watch a movie."

My body suddenly felt heavy with exhaustion again, and I realized how much strength it had taken to stop things, to get off the bed, get dressed. If I sat back down, started kissing him again, I might not be able to get up the next time. "What would Clara think?" I said softly, taking a step back so it forced him to drop his hand from my face.

He chuckled a little. "I don't care."

I didn't exactly care either, except for the fact that it would just make me look embarrassingly unprofessional to spend the night in here. "I should go back to my room," I said, annoyed that my voice trembled with what sounded like uncertainty as I spoke.

"Is that what you really want?" Ash asked.

I nodded, afraid if I said anything else my voice would betray me further.

Ash reached his hand up to my cheek and stroked it softly with his thumb. "To be continued, then?" he said.

Back in the guest room, I found all the clothes from my suitcase washed and folded, piled up on the bed.

I tried not to think about Clara walking in here while I was down the hall, what she heard or what she saw while sorting my laundry. My face burned with private humiliation as I slipped into my XL Boston tee and my plaid pajama bottoms and stacked everything else in the closet. It was just past seven now, but I was exhausted.

I sat down on the bed and sighed. Tomorrow Emilia's journals would finally come back from FedEx, we'd go through them, and we could focus solely on work. Ash had said *to be continued*, but things always looked different in the light of day. The problem was, I now couldn't even imagine acting like nothing had happened in the bright glimmer of morning.

Maybe buying my return ticket to Boston for Saturday would ease my mind, set a hard deadline at least, so I grabbed my laptop to look up flights. But then I saw I had an unread text.

Noah: You up for a drink tonight? A cup of soup?

It came in ten minutes ago. Had I missed hearing it ding on my phone? Wait, where was my phone? I glanced around but didn't see it nearby.

I searched the bed, tossing up the comforter. Then crawled along the floor of the bedroom, and even checked the bathroom, before I finally remembered. The last time I'd had my phone for sure was when I'd shoved it in the back pocket of my jeans just before I'd followed Ash to the other wing of his house. I picked my jeans up off the floor where I'd just left them, but now the back pocket was empty. *Shit.* It must've fallen out in Ash's bedroom when he'd pulled my jeans off. Well, there was no way I was going back there now to get it.

Can't tonight, I texted Noah from my laptop. Maybe another night this week?

I shut the lid and put my laptop back on the nightstand, then burrowed under the covers and closed my eyes. I had a giant headache again, probably from the red wine I shouldn't have drunk, and all I wanted to do was close my eyes, sleep, and forget everything that had happened in the last few hours.

I would figure out how to get my phone back in the morning, along with everything else.

TWENTY-NINE

Sleep didn't make me forget, though. It just put my mortification off for a few hours.

I woke up around eight, and it all immediately rushed back to me. Kissing Ash in here, then in his bedroom. Those quick, awkward few moments I was naked on his bed. That feeling of crushing desire mixed with the emptiness that followed.

My head was too blurry to work through it all, and I knew I needed caffeine so I could make a real plan for today. I pulled a thin sweater over my pajamas and tiptoed out of my room, hoping I could make a quick cup of coffee in the kitchen without anyone noticing me.

But no luck. The second I stepped foot in the kitchen, Clara popped around the corner. "Rough night?" She stared at me icily.

Does she know?

Then she pointed to my hair, and I realized I hadn't even looked in the mirror. My curls must be sticking up—they always were. I reached my hand up to attempt smooth them. "I just wanted to make myself a cup of coffee before I got ready for the day." I forced a small laugh. "I was hoping not to see anyone looking like this." Though I was relieved that she, not Ash, was the one in the kitchen in my pre-coffee disarray. I definitely didn't have it in me to face him yet, but I turned around to look for him, half expecting him to suddenly waltz in from behind me. Because that would be just my luck.

Clara followed my gaze. "He had to run to the office for a bit. Said to tell you he'd be back this afternoon. I suppose you'll have to survive without him for a little while," she added, her voice exuding sarcasm. Or was it annoyance?

"Of course," I murmured. Had she actually witnessed me and Ash last night? Was she mad about it? I thought about that morning I saw her out on the balcony, in the flowing white dress (or nightgown?). I'd imagined from my spot on the beach the gown was sheer, but was it really? Ash had said last night he hadn't been with anyone since Angelica's death. Now I wondered if that was true.

Clara moved toward the counter with the espresso machine and pulled a small coffeemaker out of an appliance garage just next to it. "I can make you some coffee," she said.

"Oh, no, I don't want to trouble you. I can make it."

"No trouble at all," she said easily.

But if Clara actually had been with Ash, or *wanted* to be with Ash, was it really so crazy to think she might've put something in my coffee the other day? Certainly, she would want me gone, out of the house, away from him, if that were the case.

She opened the drawer and frowned. "Shoot, looks like we're all out of beans. I'll run to the store and buy some real quick."

"You really don't have—"

"I'll be back in thirty minutes," she cut me off, grabbed her purse from where it was hanging across the back of one of the chairs at the island, and before I could say another word, she walked out the back door.

I put my hands on the island to steady myself and closed my eyes for a second.

Yes, it really was crazy to think Clara had put something in my coffee the other day. Clara was Ash's housekeeper, and maybe she was a little icy, but she was going out of her way to help me. She just ran to the store to buy fresh beans. (Or more drugs to put in the coffee.)

No. Stop. Think, Olivia. Breathe. My brain was so fuzzy, I really needed caffeine. And my phone. If I had my phone, I could get a Lyft to the coffee shop I went to with Noah the other day.

The house felt eerily quiet now that Clara had left and Ash was at work. But even though I knew I was here alone, I still tiptoed down the hallway back toward Ash's bedroom, glancing over my shoulder like I was doing something wrong. *I wasn't.* I was just going to get my phone. Still, I put my hand on the doorknob and held it there for a moment before I finally got up the courage to open the door.

The heavy gray curtains were pushed aside this morning, casting a pale blue morning sea light in through the wide French doors, brightness streaming across the dark hardwood floors. Ash's bed was made, tight perfect corners, as if he'd never slept here, had never been here at all.

I closed my eyes for a second, remembering the heat I'd felt against my skin as he'd pulled me into this room last night, kissed me. The way my lips had felt every word that came from his mouth: *Say you want me.* Then, the chill I'd felt walking out of here only ten minutes later.

Focus, Olivia.

Right. I needed to find my phone.

I swept the floor with my eyes, but like the rest of the room, it looked completely spotless. There was nothing askew, nothing out of place. Maybe Ash had found my phone last night and picked it up off the floor. But every surface in the room was completely bare—the chest of drawers, the nightstands, the bed—all empty.

I thought about what he'd said last night, that he'd moved into this bedroom after Angelica had died, that he couldn't stand staying there without her. A morbid curiosity about her suddenly bubbled up inside of me, as if knowing more about her, understanding her, would help me understand more about Ash too. *Ange*, he'd told me yesterday at the winery, *was his family. Until she wasn't.*

I walked back into the hallway and stared at the closed door farther down the hall. I walked to it, held my hand on the knob for a second, before turning it, guilt washing over me. *I'm not doing anything wrong. I'm looking for my phone.* That was a lie; I knew it, even as I thought it, even as I turned the knob. I was invading something private, or something sacred. I was going into this room because I was in the house all alone, because I could, because something deep inside of me screamed that everything was wrong, but every time Ash was around, that scream was drowned out by something else. Something electric that made me stupid, that made me lose control of all reason.

I opened the door and walked inside.

In contrast to everything else in the house, this bedroom was strangely messy. The king-sized bed was unmade. A tufted red velour comforter sat in a ball by the bottom, making the bed look either recently slept in or perhaps untouched and left this way for months. Was this Angelica and Ash's former room, or was it Clara's? I wiped my finger along the edge of the nightstand, and my fingertip was quickly covered in dust. The surface hadn't been cleaned—or touched—for months. This definitely wasn't Clara's room—it was more like a museum, or a mausoleum.

Stacks of books still sat piled on the dusty nightstand. Were these the books Angelica was reading before she died, interrupted books, books Angelica never got to finish? When you died in an accident, the way she had, so abruptly, so tragically, you didn't get to know the endings of all the stories you'd started. That thought suddenly made me sad.

I shouldn't be in here.

But I made no move to leave. The books called to me, and instead, I turned them so I could see their spines. I'd long believed that a person's books can tell you everything there is to know about them. Jack didn't read books, except for comic books, and of course, that probably should've told me something too. My eye scanned from the top of the pile to the bottom: classics. *Jane Eyre*, *Rebecca*, *Wuthering Heights*, and sandwiched in between, I spotted the bright blue of a familiar cover. My cover. *Becky*.

I remembered again, seeing it in the guest room, just like this. Opening it, seeing that word scrolled across the title page: *Thief*. I'd convinced myself I'd imagined it. How did that word get there? It had felt even more imagined after Ash had me sign his clean copy of *Becky* in his living room. So what was this, sitting here? The copy he'd had me sign the other night, or the strange defaced copy I found in the guest room?

It felt more like a reflex than a thought, reaching for my book, picking it up, pulling back the cover, flipping to the title page. And though deep down I expected it, seeing it there again still shocked me: that bright, bold Sharpied word: **THIEF**.

So, I hadn't imagined it after all. But what did it even mean? And why was this copy sitting in here, on what I guessed was once Angelica's nightstand? Was it hers? But even if it was, who had moved it so I would see it? Angelica herself, if that Reddit thread had any merit. *No, that's ridiculous.* So, had Clara moved it? Or Ash?

"Olivia?" Ash's voice startled me, and I spun around quickly, holding the book behind my back, taking a small step backward to place it gently back on top of the other books on the nightstand and hoping he didn't notice. *Thief.* But I was not a thief. I was curious—what writer wasn't? "What are you doing?" His tone had a sharpness to it I hadn't heard from him before.

"I was...um...looking for my..."

"For this?" He pulled my phone from his back pocket, held it out toward me, but didn't take a step to come closer and actually hand it to me. I nodded, trying not to look as sheepish as I felt. "In here?" He raised his eyebrows and still looked pissed. "I found your phone on the floor in my room after you...well, I came to give it back to you last night, but you were already asleep."

I nodded again. "I thought I dropped it in your room. I just...got confused this morning," I lied. "And... I um, opened the wrong door and ended up in here." I wasn't a thief, but I was a liar. Most fiction writers were.

"You *got confused*?" It was clear from the way annoyance laced his tone that he didn't believe me.

"There are a lot of doors," I added softly. "Your house is really big..."

He just stared at me, his frown creasing deeper, and I stopped talking, realizing the more I tried to lie my way out, the further I was digging myself into a hole. He was standing just a few steps away from me, but it felt like an ocean between us. Yesterday, we'd been floating on the same life raft, and right now, it felt like he was about ready to drown me.

"I'm really sorry," I finally said. "I didn't mean to upset you."

His face softened a little, and I walked up to him to reach for my phone. But he didn't immediately let go of it. Instead, he gently grabbed my wrist with his other hand, pulled me closer to him, so our bodies were almost touching, but not quite. Up this close, he looked more amused than angry. He leaned in. "You wanted to see it, didn't you?" He whispered in my hair.

The book? My heart ricocheted in my rib cage, and I felt certain that standing this close to me, Ash could feel it too.

He tightened his grip on my arm, pulling me up against him. He'd gotten dressed up for work in a crisp white button-down shirt. But even through it, I could somehow feel the heat of his skin, and it was hard to breathe again. "You wanted to see where I fucked her, didn't you?" he whispered.

The realization hit me quickly, and I let out a little gasp. He wasn't thinking about my book on the nightstand. He was talking about this room, *this bed*, about Angelica. About whatever had almost happened between us last night.

As suddenly as he'd grabbed me, he let me go, and I stumbled a little, my body feeling weightless, almost ethereal. He gently put my phone in my hand, then took another step away from me.

When I looked up again, he was at a normal distance and appeared to be easygoing Ash. Calm Ash. Professional Ash. "I came back to the house because I forgot my wallet," he said coolly. "But I have to head back to the office this morning. Something urgent came up."

I nodded and crossed my arms in front of my chest. "Of course," I murmured. "I'll see you later."

"Oh, and Olivia," he called after me, as I walked into the hallway. I stopped and turned, glanced at him again. Now he had a little smirk on his face. "Maybe you should stay in your wing of the house while I'm gone?"

THIRTY

My phone was dead, since it was going on almost two days of not being charged. I plugged it in back in my room, and then went into the closet to get dressed.

Tension rattled my body, and I was shaking as I clasped my bra, mortified I hadn't thought to put one on before leaving in search of coffee earlier. Had Ash noticed I'd been braless as he'd pulled me up against him? *You wanted to see where I fucked her, didn't you?* It was such a disturbing thing to say, and yet even thinking about it made my heart pound all over again.

I took a deep, cleansing breath and threw on the outfit I'd worn hiking last week, minus the boots—jeans, my red tee, and my red flats, and by then my phone had enough charge to at least turn back on. I clicked on my messages, and my finger hovered over Noah's name. What had he said over Coronas just a few days ago at the hotel bar? *There are some rich creeps in Malibu.* But that seemed to reduce Ash to something simplistic, something that could be explained away with money, with privilege. It did not explain all the strange pieces of Ash's family history, the attraction I'd been feeling for him since I got here, whatever had happened between us yesterday and last night, and then, the weird way he had reacted this morning. Most of all, it did not explain why the word *thief* was written inside a copy of my book someone was moving around Ash's home.

It suddenly all felt like too much to handle on my own, and I knew I needed to get out of this house, get some air, clear my head. And I needed Noah too. Someone outside all of this that I could trust. But I wasn't totally sure he'd be willing to be there for me the way he once was.

Can you meet for coffee this morning? I texted him. My treat. When a minute went by and he didn't answer, I typed, Please??? Not even caring that this made me look desperate.

A minute later, my phone rang in my hand, and the abrupt sound of it made me jump. I sighed with relief seeing the name flash up: *Noah*.

"Hey, sorry, I'm driving," he said when I picked up, forgoing hellos. "Are you all right? Where are you? I'll come get you." His voice was thick with worry, and it made me feel a rush of emotion for him. For how protective he still was of me.

"I'm okay," I lied. "And I'll meet you—just tell me where." I wanted to see Noah, talk to Noah, get Noah's help. But I was not exactly ready to tell him where I was staying. "I'll get a Lyft."

"You're still in Malibu somewhere?"

I nodded, forgetting he couldn't see me. Then added a vague, "Yeah, Malibu."

"How about the coffee place we went to last week. I can be there in about forty-five minutes."

Clara was back from the store and in the kitchen when I walked out of my room again. I felt strangely nervous to tell her the truth about where I was going. Not that I was doing anything wrong or that any of it was any of her business. But

I suspected whatever I told her she would be repeated verbatim to Ash. So instead, I lied and I told her I was taking a walk. I *would* walk. Down Ash's long driveway to the PCH, and then I'd order a car to pick me up at one of the shops somewhere down there.

"Don't you want your coffee?" Clara frowned, and I felt a little guilty thinking about her going to the store, just to make me a cup of coffee I was afraid to drink.

"Could I take it to go?" I asked.

She obliged and when the coffee was ready, poured it into disposable cup. I asked her to tell Ash that I was out exploring Malibu, if he made it back before me. And then I walked out his front door and exhaled, feeling a sudden heady rush of freedom.

I walked quickly down the long driveway, waiting until I reached the very end by the main road, then looked behind me. You could barely even see the house from down here, but still I squinted, trying to make out if her face was on the other side of the tinted glass of the front windows. It was impossible to tell, and I held on to her coffee, hesitating for a moment before I poured it out into the bougainvillea that lined the end of the drive.

"Are you all right, Livvy?" Noah asked a half hour later as he slid onto the bench across the outdoor table from me. I nodded and forced a small smile. I'd gotten here first and had already sipped my way through half an Americano. The caffeine had cleared my head a little, and as I'd stared out at the Pacific, I'd made a mental list of everything that was bothering me.

1. *Thief*

2. Still not having seen Emilia's journals

3. The lack of Rebecca (and Emilia?) in the historical record

4. What Rose Asherwood said about Emilia's mental health and how she died

5. Angelica?

6. Ash this morning (and last night)

It felt like a lot of moving parts, not all of them connected. Or were they somehow? Ash had specifically brought *me* here to tell Emilia's story, he said because of *Becky*. But how had he even found my little failed novel, and why was there an elusive copy that someone had defaced with the word *thief*? And Ash could bring *any* woman to his house, his bedroom. Why me?

"You sure you're okay?" Noah said, reaching across the table and putting the back of his hand on my forehead. "You still look a little pale."

Noah's hand was warm, familiar, against my skin. When he touched my forehead, it felt like a hug, and I was instantly more at ease. I smiled, a genuine smile this time. I reached up and grabbed his hand, holding on to it on the table. "I'm fine, Noah. Really." I squeezed his hand as if to emphasize my point. "And thank you for meeting me."

He nodded, took a sip of his coffee, and let out a little sigh. "It was weird, Livvy. I've just had this really bad, sinking feeling all week, ever since we had beers the other night. And then when Jack called and said he couldn't get ahold of you, I kind of freaked out a little bit."

"You have a bad case of writer brain," I said, and he laughed a little, so I knew he understood exactly what I meant. "Probably felt weird to worry about me after not thinking about me at all for so long, huh?" I added softly.

He shook his head. "That's not true, Livvy. I always thought about you, even when we didn't talk. I still thought about you, a lot."

"Me too," I said. And it was the truth. There'd been so many times when I'd had the urge to text him but had stopped myself, thinking he wouldn't want to hear from me anymore, not after my book launch. I'd told myself that he'd moved on, moved past our college friendship. That he had an entirely different life in LA without me.

But here we were, sitting across from each other, and it occurred to me that even if nothing else came of this trip, even if this writing project failed completely, and I didn't get the career boost or the money I wanted, well, maybe at least this time in Malibu had given me my best friend back.

Noah cleared his throat a little, and I realized I was still holding his hand. I let go, and he entwined his fingers in front of him, cracking his knuckles, the way he used to back in college when he got nervous. Was I making him nervous now? I hoped not, and I really needed his help, so I had to get to the point.

"Okay," I said. "So can I pick your brain about this write-for-hire project I'm working on, and you'll never tell anyone I told you this stuff?"

He raised his eyebrows, as if to say, *do you really need to ask me that*? Ten years ago, I wouldn't have. "Livvy, of course. I'm dying of curiosity. Who are you working for?"

"You know who Henry Asherwood III is, right?"

"The Asherwood stores guy?" Noah asked.

At the same time, I said, "*People*'s Sexiest Man Alive."

Noah laughed. "Damn, you're still a devout reader of entertainment magazines?"

"Of course!" I laughed too. He used to make fun of me in college, when the only current events I knew about were the nuggets of celeb gossip I read in *People* and *US Weekly*.

"Okay, well, I can't exactly picture what he looks like, but I know he runs the whole Asherwood conglomerate. And his wife died, right? An accident in Malibu a year or two ago?"

"Wait. You really can't picture what he looks like?" It was funny to think of the way Ash was reduced to just *a faceless Asherwood stores guy* in Noah's eyes. Granted, that was totally on brand for college Noah, who'd nerded out over *National Geographic*.

Noah shrugged, and I started laughing again. "Okay, well, his looks are beside the point," I said. *But are they, really?* I shook that thought away. "He hired me to write a novel about his grandmother, who he believes was the true author of *Rebecca*. He found her journals, where she's written out the whole thing in her native French. He thinks she based the story on her own life, and he thinks Daphne du Maurier plagiarized her."

"Wait, what?" Noah frowned deeply, like he couldn't process anything I was telling him.

And saying it out loud now, to him, I realized how ridiculous it all sounded myself. Ash was so intoxicating that it was hard not to believe everything he said when I was with him. Away from him, when I'd expressed my doubts to Charley, she'd pushed them all away. But her interest was in selling the story, and incredulous or not, she probably could make us all a lot of money.

Noah was just Noah, and seeing the look on his face now, I suddenly started to sweat. *What the hell have I gotten myself into?*

"It kind of gets even weirder," I admitted to Noah. And then I told him about all the things that were bothering me: the journals I hadn't yet seen, the articles on Emilia stolen from the Malibu library (and just the lack of any information on her in general), Ash's mention of a first wife, Rebecca, and the fact that she didn't even seem to exist. I told him about the fact that Emilia had gone to the same finishing school as Daphne in France (but that connection between them felt tenuous at best), about the Malibu Lake house burning down, and finally, about how I couldn't even find historical evidence of that fire when I searched Newspapers.com.

Noah held up his hand to interrupt me for a second. "Okay, so this Asherwood stores guy hired you to write this totally bananas story about his grandmother. And there's no real historical record of it at all?"

"Well…kind of, yeah," I said. It was a pretty spot-on assessment. "I mean, Charley says we can call it a novel." He frowned again. "If I could find more information on Emilia on my own, I might at least have something to go on."

Noah glanced at his watch. "What are you doing the rest of this morning?"

I checked the time on my phone. It was just after ten, and at the prospect of going back to Ash's house, a large nauseating pit began to form in my stomach. "Nothing," I said. "What are you thinking?"

"I could take you to the UCLA library to see what we can find in the digital archives. I can't imagine they were 'stolen.'" He made air quotes with his fingers, his incredulity reaffirming my own. And I felt so silly for not having come to Noah sooner.

"That's a great idea. Are you sure you have time, and you don't mind?"

Noah stood and held out his hand to help me up. "Come on," he said. "If traffic isn't too bad, we can be there in a half hour."

THIRTY-ONE

It had been so many years since I'd stepped foot on a college campus, and being with Noah at UCLA, I suddenly felt like I'd stepped into another time. Another life. Twenty-one-year-old Olivia Finkemeier, whose mother hadn't died yet, whose writing career still shone before her with possibility. All she wanted in life was for someone to pay her to do what she loved: to write, to create stories, to weave characters and plots in a deliciously tangled web of words. All she wanted then was to graduate, to publish a novel, and certainly everything else would fall into place, and she would be happy.

But what happened to that girl? I'd left her somewhere so long ago, it was almost hard to remember she existed. That she was me.

I tried to imagine what college Olivia would think of this predicament I was in now. *Why would you want to be a ghostwriter, when you could be a real writer?* I imagined her saying to me with all the naivete and stupidity of a twenty-one-year-old English major.

But I pushed that thought away as I walked with Noah

through the gorgeous and sprawling UCLA campus, across the tree-lined mall, to the Romanesque redbrick library. "I've been doing a lot of novel research in here lately," Noah said as I followed him inside and we wound our way toward the digital archives room.

"Yeah?" I remembered how he told me last week that he had a new agent, a new story, and I realized I hadn't even asked him what his novel was about. That I had made our meetings this past week entirely about me. So, I had not only become a cynical and jaded writer in the years since college, but also a pretty awful friend. "What are you working on?" I asked him now. Then I quickly added, "Sorry, I should've asked you that before."

"No, it's fine. You obviously have a lot going on." He paused for a second, and I wondered if he didn't want to tell me. But then he said, "I found this true unsolved murder case from the '30s that I've become obsessed with. It's kind of a genre mystery/noir with a hard-boiled detective, not at all literary." He sounded apologetic.

Did he think that I, of all people, was about to judge him for what kind of book he was writing? "That's terrific," I said, and I meant it. "Publish genre fiction and sell a million copies, please."

He laughed and shook his head. "Well, who knows if it'll even get published. We'll see. Anyway, I think we can use the same newspaper archives I've been digging through for you to research these Asherwood women. The university has a special collection of local papers, even ones that are out of print now, so you may be able to find here what you couldn't online."

I nodded and followed him to the row of computers. I really wanted to ask him more about his true crime novel, and also, I really wanted to read it. In college, Noah and I always used to read each other's stories before class, before workshopping them. Noah was my first and best reader, and I was his. And the sensation of missing that, missing him, hit me so hard I blinked back tears.

Noah didn't notice—he leaned across me to swipe his ID to log in, and then he sat down next to me. "There you go," he said. "The world is your oyster. Or, the UCLA system is, anyway."

I shot him a grateful smile and then typed Emilia Asherwood's name into the search bar. Instantly, I understood that Noah was right. Nothing had been scrubbed, or stolen, or lost from here, as a list of articles about Emilia popped up from local California publications. There was her marriage announcement and society page articles about her going to charity events. I scrolled down until I found an article about the fire at Malibu Lake—Emilia was mentioned only insofar as it said she *perished in the fire*—but the article also said the cause of the fire was being investigated. I continued reading down to the next article, which said that a month later the fire had been deemed to be an accident, caused by a faulty gas stove. "Hmm," I said. "I guess Rose was wrong." But then again, she was, as Ash had told me, ninety-three, with a faltering memory.

"Who's Rose?" Noah asked.

"The third Mrs. Asherwood," I said, and he squinted at me, confused. "Emilia's younger cousin who ended up marrying Henry Asherwood after Emilia died."

"That's not creepy at all," Noah said.

"Right?"

But then I remembered I still hadn't found a thing on Rebecca, the alleged first Mrs. Asherwood, and I wasn't all that certain she'd ever really existed. "Actually," I corrected myself, "I'm not sure if Rose is the third Mrs. Asherwood or the second. Ash told me his grandfather had a first wife named Rebecca, but I haven't been able to find a single thing about her."

"Why would he lie about her?" Noah asked.

I shrugged—it was a good question. Why would he lie? I typed *Rebecca Asherwood* into the search bar. But nothing relevant came up.

"Try this." Noah leaned across me, and I was suddenly keenly aware of how close he was to me. How he smelled like gingerbread. And how much I'd missed him these last five years. I watched his fingers move across the keys as he changed the search to keyword rather than person and typed *Rebecca* and *Asherwood* in the keyword boxes.

One result.

But it was a recent article, from only five years ago, about Ash and Angelica's wedding: *Mr. Asherwood Takes a Wife*, the headline read.

I laughed out loud, and Noah glanced at me, his eyebrows raised. "This is about the dude who hired you? Who actively lives in this century, right?" I nodded and had to stifle another laugh at Noah calling Ash *the dude* who'd hired me. "What an awful antiquated headline," Noah said. "I mean, maybe *she took a husband*, for fuck's sake."

I felt this wave of grief for Angelica, and I wondered how any woman my age could not despise everything about a story and a headline and a *marriage* being framed like this. Ash had called her his only family, but Rose had mentioned something Ash had done to hurt her. What had it really been like for Angelica being married to Ash, living in that big glass cliffside house? Had she been isolated, lonely, before her death? I suddenly felt sad to think that just a few years after this chauvinistic article was written, she'd be dead.

I looked back to the article to see where the words *Rebecca* and *Asherwood* were highlighted, and finally saw them near the end, in a caption under a picture of Angelica in her wedding dress surrounded by her two bridesmaids, standing on what looked like the beach in front of Ash's house.

From left to right: bridesmaid: Ms. Rebecca Farmington, bride: Mrs. Angelica Asherwood, bridesmaid: Ms. Clara Landry.

I let out a little gasp as I read Clara's name and then looked back at the picture. It was definitely her, the same Clara who worked as Ash's live-in housekeeper and I was pretty sure actively hated me. "That's really weird," I said.

"What?" Noah moved closer to my screen, stared at the picture. "Oh. The bride looks familiar, doesn't she?" He pointed to Angelica. But I shook my head. She looked very much as she did in that large portrait that had loomed over me the last few nights. But Noah wouldn't have seen that.

"No, this woman. Her bridesmaid, Clara." I pointed to her in the picture and told Noah how she was working as Ash's housekeeper and how something about her had felt off in the few interactions I'd had with her. I stopped short of accusing her of poisoning my coffee—that still sounded too paranoid to possibly be true. "It's weird that she was Angelica's bridesmaid and now is Ash's housekeeper, isn't it?"

"Maybe," Noah said. "But not necessarily. What do you think it means?"

I shrugged. This probably explained why Clara disliked me, if she had noticed what was likely my obvious attraction to Ash. But aside from understanding that, this little tidbit got me nowhere. Rebecca Asherwood still didn't seem to exist. Emilia had died in a fire, deemed accidental. But none of that brought me closer to any real clarity with the story I was supposed to be writing.

My phone suddenly dinged with a text, and the sound made both me and Noah jump. I glanced down. Ash.

Where are you? Journals are here.

There'd been so many delays with the journals, so many weird questions swirling around in my head, that I wasn't sure I'd quite believed Ash when he'd said they would be arriving today. But if I could see them and get a translation, then maybe nothing else mattered. Maybe that was all I needed to write this story and collect my fifty thousand dollars.

"I have to go," I said as I stood and pushed in my chair.

"What? Now?" Noah stood quickly too.

I showed Noah my phone. And he frowned. "Are you going to his house? Is that where you've been staying?" I bit my lip, not answering him, but clearly, my silence was an answer. "Don't do that."

"I have to," I said. I quickly picked up my bag and my phone and started to walk back down the long hallway toward the door.

Noah ran after me and grabbed my arm. "Olivia, wait."

He never called me *Olivia*, and that alone made me stop and turn back to look at him. Noah's face always reminded me of a teddy bear—perfect round cheeks, brown waves of hair that fell across his forehead, and warm hazel eyes that couldn't hide emotion even if he tried. I used to tease him back in college that you could see everything he was feeling stretched across his face at the very moment he was feeling it. It was so clear now, he was worried about me. "I don't think you should go back there. Just quit this ghostwriting job," he said.

He made it sound so easy. But Noah's last five years had gone a lot differently than mine. How could he possibly understand what I was going through right now?

"Noah, look. I appreciate so much that you brought me here today. I really do. But our search turned up nothing damning. And now Ash says he has the journals back. I have to go see what's in them and salvage this project if I can."

"But why?" He didn't let go, of my arm or my eyes. "Is this what you really want to be writing?"

"It doesn't matter what I want to be writing!" My voice rose with frustration, and I tried to shake him off. "I have bills to pay. And this is a job."

He finally let go of my arm, but we stared at each other for another moment.

Then Noah did something so completely unexpected: he pulled me toward him in a hug, and when my face hit his chest, I suddenly felt like I was about to cry. I knew that if I started, here, like this, with Noah holding on to me, I might never be able to stop crying, or let go of him either. "The Olivia I used to know wrote because she loved it," Noah whispered into my hair.

I pushed myself back, away from Noah, turning the tears that threatened to fall into anger instead, righteous indignation. "Noah, the Olivia you're remembering was a stupid kid," I spat back at him. I was breathing hard enough that I could barely choke the words out. "You don't know anything about me now."

He stared back at me. I couldn't tell if he was stunned or upset or confused—maybe all three—his face wasn't transparent anymore. Maybe I knew nothing about him either.

I turned around and walked away. And this time he didn't go after me.

Excerpt from *The Wife*

It happens sometimes. Two writers get the same idea, but then, one publishes it first. And what becomes of the other novel?

Nothing. A book isn't a book until it's published, is it? And no one is going to want to publish a story that has already been told.

My friend in New York gives me one piece of advice: Let it go. You're talented. Write something new.

She tells me to call her when I do.

But I don't want to write something new. This story is my story. My fiction and my truth. I've poured every last piece of myself into my book—how can I just accept that someone else has written it first? And move on? What do I have if I can't burn my whole life to the ground, on the page? I'm not brave enough to do it for real. I can quickly light a match with my pen, but not with my trembling fingers. I have no money of my own, no career. I'd signed an ironclad prenuptial agreement. The one person I'd trusted entirely, my cousin, has already betrayed me. What am I supposed to do? What will I become?

First, I become an insomniac.

I lie awake each night next to my husband, so many thoughts running through my head. I watch him sleep, angered by the soft sound of his snore, and all I can think about is how I want him to suffer. I want to ruin him. My cousin too. I want to ruin both of them.

Can I really work up the courage to light that match? Can I really stand in the water and watch the flames engulfing this house, incinerating him and her and everything in this wretched life of mine?

Once, in the middle of the night, I sit on the edge of our bed. I pull a match from the matchbook in my nightstand, and I light it quickly, using the flame to illuminate his face. He's sleeping so easily, so peacefully. But what would happen if I were just to drop the match on his pillow and run?

All of a sudden, he sits up. The flame grows and glows against my forefinger, too close. Too hot.

"What are you doing?" he asks as he quickly pulls the match from my hand and shakes it out. "You'll burn yourself."

The first time we ever met was at a party, and he rescued me. I'd tripped, and in a split second, there he was, holding on to me just before I hit the ground. And here he is, thinking he needs to rescue me still.

He doesn't understand yet that I want to destroy him. That I don't want him to save me anymore. He should be thinking about how to save himself.

The book that is my book—but not mine at all—was actually published a month before my friend called from New York to let me know about it.

After that night with the match, I decide to go look for it at the small bookstore in town. It's mostly to torture myself, because what good will it do to hold it in my hands? To see and imagine what might have been mine had I written my story faster, sooner? I'd let the idea fester for years after I'd started it back in school, but what if I hadn't? What if I'd finished it then like I'd planned, before I'd ever met my husband?

I find it on the fiction shelf—just one lonely copy in the whole entire store—buried in an alphabetical row. Not even on display or face out. No one would find it here unless they were looking for it, like I am.

I flip through the pages, feeling their coarse texture between my fingers, my eyes scanning over such familiar names and familiar thoughts, my chest vibrating with disappointment or some intangible loss, or jealousy. There is Rebecca, and there is fire. And Maxim de Winter, who may as well be my husband.

I flip all the way through, and tears of frustration, of this heady intangible loss, well in my eyes, making the words and the pages blur. So, when I reach the end, the biography and photo of the author, everything looks fuzzy for a few seconds.

But then I blink my tears away, and the author's face comes into focus. Something about it feels familiar. At first, I think I must be imagining it. But then I read her biography, and I understand, I'm not imagining it at all.

I know her.

THIRTY-TWO

It took me over an hour to get back to Ash's house, and I felt a little carsick from the Lyft ride in such horrendous stop-and-start traffic all up the Pacific Coast Highway. I was relieved to finally be out of the car, and I inhaled deeply as I rang Ash's doorbell, trying to center myself and quell my rising nausea. The cool salty air soothed me, and the car sickness began to pass. But then I thought about Noah, just standing there staring sadly at me in the library, and my stomach somersaulted again.

Clara finally opened the door, took one look at me, and frowned. "What happened to you?" she asked, holding the door open for me to walk inside.

I smoothed my hair with my hands, tucking my curls behind my ears, and took one more deep breath. "Nothing *happened*," I said. "I ended up meeting a friend from college for coffee." Not even a lie, and yet I thought about that photo of Clara I'd just seen in the digital archives at UCLA, and my voice trembled a little as I spoke. I cleared my throat, stepped into the foyer, and glanced around. "Where's Ash?"

"He got tired of waiting for you and went for a hike." Clara huffed out the words, as if she were annoyed at me on his behalf. I pulled my phone out of my back pocket and went to text him. But she put her hand out and gently lowered my phone. "He doesn't like to be bothered while he's hiking. Come on, have you eaten yet? I'll make you some lunch."

"I'm not hungry," I said. "I'm actually feeling a little carsick." But then my stomach betrayed me by growling at the mere mention of food. And I realized I hadn't eaten all day.

Clara raised her eyebrows. "Well, I'll tell you what. I'm going to eat, and I'll put out a plate for you. You can do what you want with it."

I followed her into the kitchen and sat down at the island while she opened the large Sub-Zero fridge. "Turkey sandwich okay?" she asked. "Mustard, mayo, lettuce, tomato…?"

I nodded. "Whatever you're making for yourself, make one for me too. Don't go to any trouble."

"No trouble," she muttered, and I watched her assemble the bread, deli turkey, lettuce, and tomato on two plates and then carry them over. She put a plate down in front of me, then sat across from me. I knew I was being ridiculous, but I waited for her to take a bite of her sandwich first before I deemed mine safe to eat too.

"Can I ask you something?" I said after polishing off half the sandwich. I realized I was actually very hungry, because this tasted like the best turkey sandwich I'd ever eaten in my life. Clara didn't answer me, just took another bite of her own sandwich. But she didn't say no either, so I kept talking. "You were…friends with Angelica?" I asked.

She stopped chewing for a second mid-bite, and her breath caught in her chest audibly. The expression on her face reminded me of a stunned bird that had just accidentally flown into a window. And she didn't move or say anything for a few long seconds. "Why would you ask me that?" she finally asked.

"I was doing some research on Emilia, Ash's grandmother, and just the Asherwood family in general, and I came across a photo from Ash and Angelica's wedding. You were in it. You were a bridesmaid along with someone named Rebecca?"

She put her sandwich down, wiped her hands on a napkin, and then twisted them in her lap. "Angelica wasn't my friend," she said. "She hated me."

"Hated you? But you were in her wedding?"

She hesitated for another moment, then added, "She was my cousin."

Her cousin?

I thought again of that morning I'd seen Clara on the veranda in a white dress, her hair blowing in the wind. How I'd thought about the Reddit post about Angelica still being alive, and I'd wondered for the briefest moment if that was her. Maybe there was, I realized now, the slightest family resemblance between Clara and Angelica. Their facial features were different, but their hair fell in the same pretty auburn waves against their shoulders. "Is that why you're here now?" I asked her. "Because of Angelica?"

"No. Not for her," Clara said pointedly.

For whom then? *For Ash?*

Before I could ask her anything else, the back door swung open, and a sweaty post-hike Ash jogged inside. His eyes caught on me, and he smiled that gorgeous sexiest-man-alive smile. No trace of whatever irritation he'd felt toward me earlier this morning. "Oh good, you're back." He spoke with such an easy nonchalant kindness in his voice that I almost wondered if I'd been wrong reading into everything that had happened between us in the past twelve hours. The worst thing about this write-for-hire project was how much it made me doubt myself, question everything.

No, Livvy. I could hear Noah's voice in my head now. *You haven't imagined any of it. Get the hell out of there.*

"She was out meeting a friend," I heard Clara saying to Ash, and it brought me back to the kitchen. I looked up, and Clara was putting her dirty plate in the sink. Then she walked out without another word.

"A friend?" Ash strolled over to the island, easily leaning his weight on his elbows, just across from me. He stared at me, his face almost uncomfortably close, and I was pretty sure he looked annoyed. It felt like Clara had tried to get me in trouble, though I had done nothing wrong.

"Yeah," I said, trying to keep my voice just as breezy as his. "A friend from college who teaches at UCLA now. He actually let me use the library there, and I was caught up doing some research on Emilia when you texted me. It took a while to get back up here. Traffic in LA sucks." I stopped talking, realizing I was babbling now as nervousness pushed its way up in my chest.

Ash raised his eyebrows. "He let you use the library to research Emilia?" I couldn't tell if he wanted to know more about Noah, or if he was...jealous? I thought again about the moment on his bed last night, me half-naked and vacillating between desire and regret all within the span of five minutes. Then him earlier this morning asking me if I wanted to see the place where he'd *fucked* Angelica. "You signed an NDA, Olivia," Ash was saying now.

"Oh," I stammered, flustered at the way I'd misunderstood his question. "Well, Noah just let me borrow his ID to access their computers and the digital archives. That's all." Ash frowned, like he was certain I was lying, and I almost felt a little guilty. But if I never admitted that I'd told Noah anything, Ash would never know the difference. "Seriously," I added. "You don't have to worry about it."

His frown creased deeper. "You didn't have to go all the

way to UCLA. I told you to ask me whatever you wanted to know." Now he sounded a little hurt.

"I'm used to doing my own research." I said it apologetically, though I didn't feel sorry for anything I'd done this morning. And as much as Ash kept telling me to ask him, whenever I did, he was never forthcoming. "Anyway." I tried to bring the subject back to the reason I was here. "The journals. You got them back finally? Can I see them?"

Once we went through them, once I got Emilia's story straight from the source itself, I could get out of here. And suddenly I wanted to be far away from him and Clara and Malibu more than anything.

He stared at me for another moment, not saying anything. But then he relented: "Give me a half hour to shower and change, and I'll meet you in the living room."

I plopped down on the cool white leather sofa while I waited for Ash and scrolled on my phone.

I'd gotten a text from Noah while I'd been eating lunch with Clara, which simply said: I'm here. If you need me...

My finger hovered over it for a second, but I wasn't sure exactly how or what to respond, so instead I googled *Angelica Asherwood's cousin*. Nothing relevant came up.

Then I searched for *Clara Landry* and found her LinkedIn. It looked like she graduated college, UC Santa Cruz, two years after I did, which would make her around twenty-nine or thirty, and her latest job, as of three years ago, was working for a tech company in the Bay Area as a marketing assistant. That seemed like a far cry from *housekeeper*. So, what was she doing here now? If not for her dead cousin, who she claimed *hated* her, then for what? Or for whom?

"All right!" Ash's voice boomed, startling me. I looked up and he was walking in from the hallway, carrying a box. His curls hung damp against his forehead, and he was dressed more casually than he was for work earlier, in jeans and a white linen shirt. He came and sat down next to me, close enough that I caught a whiff of that intoxicating cedarwood aftershave. I closed my eyes for a second to center myself. When I opened them again, Ash had put the box down on the coffee table in front of us. He leaned forward and pulled out what appeared to be a typed manuscript.

It didn't look like a journal, and certainly not an almost ninety-year-old one. "What exactly is this?" I asked him.

"She translated everything from the journals for you and typed it up. It's all right here in English for you to read."

I nodded but felt weirdly disappointed. This wasn't what I'd been expecting at all when he'd said the *journals were back.* "What about her actual journals, the ones written in French?" I asked. "Can I see those too?" I wanted to feel the pages between my fingers, examine her handwriting, breathe in the words she'd written even if I couldn't exactly understand them all with my rudimentary French. I felt like I needed to see her journals so I could imagine how she had once written these words, and hopefully, in doing so, envision an Emilia I could actually write a novel about too.

Ash shook his head. "Those aren't back yet."

I sighed, feeling a little like he'd lied to me. Or at the very least, misled me. His text had specifically said the journals were back. "And what about the authenticator?" I asked him. "Did she send a report I can read?"

"Not yet." An easy smile washed over his face, and something struck me as strange about his too-breezy reply. But I didn't want to argue with him, because I wanted to see what he did have. I picked the manuscript up off the coffee table and swallowed back the rest of my questions.

I could still feel Ash's eyes on my face as I flipped open to the first page. It began just as Ash's handwritten translation had: *Last night I dreamt I went to Malibu again.*

I looked back up, and he was still staring at me. Did I have turkey on my face? I reached up to brush my cheek with my hand, and Ash reached up too, caught my hand with his own.

"Your eyes, in this light," he said softly, like he was looking at me now, *truly looking* at me, for the first time. "They're two different colors."

I nodded. "Heterochromia. Just a weird genetic thing. I used to think it was the most interesting thing about me." I realized I was rambling again, so I stopped talking. He smiled a little and was still staring at me. I definitely could not focus enough to read this manuscript under these conditions. "Do you mind if I take this to the guest room to read it?" I asked him.

He shook his head then leaned in, just a little too close. He reached up, tucked a misplaced curl behind my ear, and then put his thumb gently on my cheek, just below my eye. I remembered what he'd said last night: *to be continued.* "I could come with you," he said now. "I've been thinking about you today."

Was that before or after he yelled at me this morning?

"Last night was…" He didn't finish his sentence, and I wasn't totally sure whether he was about to say something good or bad.

For some reason, I thought about Noah hugging me back at UCLA, about his text: I'm here. If you need me. And I had the urge to push Ash away, to pick up my phone and call Noah, ask him to drive up here, to pick me up, and to take me immediately to the airport so I could go back to Boston and forget I'd ever met Ash.

But Ash had finally, finally handed me *something* concrete. (At least, I thought he had.) Noah wasn't wrong, that I used to write because I loved it. But if I wanted to get back to that place, I had to claw my way out of this terrible publishing hole I'd managed to fall down the last few years. This was my way out. I couldn't run away, not now.

I stood up. "I'm going to go read this," I said firmly. "And then we can…talk more later."

Ash frowned a little, but he didn't protest any further, and I walked back to the guest room with the manuscript, alone.

The manuscript told me everything, and it told me nothing.

Ash was right, that it was *Rebecca* or… *Rebecca* was it. Every piece and every line and every word felt so familiar, I knew I'd read it all before, many times. But in this version, the husband's name was Henry Asherwood, his first wife still Rebecca, and the narrator had a name, Emilia. They lived in Malibu Lake, not in England, and Henry Asherwood owned a department store.

As I turned the pages, I felt my pulse quicken in my fingertips. Because the more I read, the more I understood that every detail and every sentence and every emotion was exactly how I remembered Daphne du Maurier's novel unfolding.

It felt like reading *Rebecca* but in a funhouse mirror. A book I knew by heart, but as I read this, it made everything look slightly different.

When Ash had said that his grandmother had written *Rebecca*, I hadn't expected that even the words themselves would feel so familiar. This wasn't a retelling. Instead, it felt as if one woman had the other's manuscript in front of her and had copied it down exactly. Not just the idea, or, the story, or the gothic feeling of it, but the cadence of the sentences and the phrasing too. All that was different were the names and places.

What am I supposed to do with this?

I heard a knock at the door, and I looked up and realized it was almost dark out. I was squinting to read the words now in the gray light of dusk, but I'd been so caught up that I hadn't even thought to turn on the light.

"Olivia." The soft sound of Ash's voice came through the door. "I made dinner if you want to take a break and eat."

I pictured dinner, and inevitably wine, with Ash out on his veranda, the soft roar of the ocean in the distance, the chill in the air. Ash looking at me, sitting too close, so I could barely remember how to breathe, much less think. That felt like the last thing I needed. But I wasn't sure what else I was getting out of this manuscript either. I groaned a little because this writing project felt further out of my grasp than ever, and if I went to the veranda now, I was probably going to have to address his *to be continued* from last night.

"Olivia?" he called again through the door. He wasn't going to take no for answer, and I supposed I had to eat.

"I'll be there in five minutes," I finally said.

THIRTY-THREE

"They must've known each other at finishing school," I said to Ash, cutting into the steak that he'd already mentioned twice he'd grilled himself. I'd joined him for dinner promising myself I would keep the conversation strictly about our project and the manuscript he gave me earlier. "The text reads so similarly to *Rebecca*, almost exactly. Like Emilia transcribed it directly from Daphne du Maurier's book. Or vice versa," I added quickly, as my knife made its way through the filet. It was bloodred in the center, and I wasn't a big red meat eater to begin with, even when it appeared before me fully cooked. I sliced a small piece of the edge and chewed it carefully.

Ash poured me a glass of red wine without asking if I wanted any, then put the goblet down in front of me. I acknowledged it with a nod but did not move to take a sip either. I definitely didn't need wine. I didn't need anything else confusing me, obscuring things, blurring any already fuzzy lines between *business and pleasure*. "So, they met in school, and then they stayed in touch?" Ash asked, taking a sip of his own wine.

I nibbled on the edge of my steak and thought about it for a minute. "Was there any correspondence with your grandmother's things? Letters?"

"Correspondence," Ash mused, with a weird sort of careful certainty and a half smile. Maybe it was the wine, but his voice drawled out lazily, more relaxed than this morning. "I don't think so."

"And what about the authentication of when the journals were written?" I pressed him. "We need to get that back and verified to even begin to broach the idea that Emilia could've written this first. Before Daphne." The truth was, I didn't believe that myself. My working theory was that Emilia had been copying Daphne du Maurier, not the other way around as Ash believed. Maybe Emilia didn't actually set the fire, but maybe Rose was also right, that Emilia had been struggling with her mental health just before she died. Had she come across an old classmate's novel and then written her own version of it in her journals?

"But she did write it first," Ash said, frowning, as if he knew exactly what I was thinking.

"I don't mean to upset you," I said quickly, before I lost my nerve. "But honestly, what you gave me today reads like fan fiction. Like your grandmother read *Rebecca*, then rewrote it with a few changes."

"But she lived it. It had to be hers *first*." Ash finished off his glass of wine, and then looked up to stare at me. His expression was so intense, even in the darkness and tiny glow of the twinkle lights, I could feel it from across the table as a heat rising on my skin. "The story belonged to her," he added. I bit my lip and didn't say what I was really thinking—could a story really *belong* to any writer?

"I don't know," I finally said. "Carolina Nabuco and Edwina McDonald thought that Daphne du Maurier took their idea too."

"Who?" Ash asked. *Exactly.* All these years later, no one even knew their names.

I explained to him about the multiple claims of plagiarism that existed after *Rebecca* first came out. How nothing had ever been proven, but much had been contemplated and written about the similarities to Nabuco's *A Sucessora,* which was published in Brazil years before *Rebecca.* Some scholars speculated that Daphne du Maurier may have read *A Sucessora* before she wrote *Rebecca,* as Carolina Nabuco had been sending the book out, trying to sell the English translation rights to Daphne du Maurier's eventual publisher. And then, how separately, an American author, Edwina McDonald, claimed Daphne had stolen her novel, *Blind Windows.* Her son had even taken Daphne to court after his mother's death, a plagiarism trial had ensued in New York City in the late 1940s, but ultimately Daphne du Maurier had won the case, I told him.

"Well, none of that negates our story," Ash said with a frown.

"True. But it doesn't prove anything either."

His frown creased deeper, and he grabbed the bottle of wine to pour himself another glass.

I remembered what Charley had said when I first told her about my idea for *Becky. There are no new stories,* she'd said. And besides—who really owns any story? *A Sucessora* was *Rebecca* was *Jane Eyre.* What made a story, any story, unique was how a writer told it. Her voice. And maybe that's what was bugging me most of all about the manuscript Ash had handed me this afternoon. The fact that Emilia's voice sounded *exactly* like Daphne du Maurier's.

My phone buzzed on the table next to me. I glanced at it—a text, from Noah: Call me. I put it on Do Not Disturb and stuffed it in the pocket of my sweater.

"So maybe we don't have proof," Ash was saying now. "But you just said someone sued Daphne du Maurier for plagiarism." Ash swirled the new wine in his glass before taking a sip. "I would bet anything that she was a thief."

Thief.

The word hung there in the cool evening air, haunting me even now. A breeze blew off the water, and I rubbed my arms.

"Sued her and *lost*," I emphasized.

"But still," Ash pushed back. "Maybe she didn't meet the legal definition of plagiarism. But that doesn't mean she didn't steal something."

"People have been retelling stories for as long as stories have been told." I could hear my voice elevating as I suddenly felt like I was defending myself, though it made no sense why I would have to. *Becky* barely sold any copies. It was the smallest of blips in the *Rebecca* canon. This wasn't about me. This was about Ash, his grandmother, and some impossible—and I was beginning to believe, unprovable—story he wanted me to write about her. "And I still have so many questions about that manuscript you gave me. Who translated the journals and how close of a translation is—"

"Olivia." Ash cut me off, leaned across the table, and grabbed my forearm. His eyes were wide, and I wondered how much longer we could keep going round and round in exhausting circles like this. All night?

I sighed, steeling myself to argue with him some more, but to what end? When did I just decide to take Noah's advice, walk away, give up on this hopeless project instead? I inhaled deeply, and suddenly my lungs felt like they were burning. I coughed.

"I think the house is on fire," Ash said.

I turned around, and smoke billowed up from the first floor, making white wisps across the new night sky behind me. That's why my lungs were burning—smoke.

I jumped up quickly, accidentally knocking over my still-full glass of wine. I grabbed at napkins to wipe it, but Ash

quickly pulled me away from the table, to the other end of the
veranda, where there were wooden steps leading down to the
beach.

I ran down them, still holding on to him, forgetting about
our weird conversation and our weird night last night, and
that weird manuscript back in the guest room. Smoke swirled
above our heads, and we were both breathing hard as we hit
the sand.

I almost ran straight into someone. She yelped a little as I
stepped on her foot, and Ash turned on his phone's flashlight.
Clara. Her hair was messy, her face streaked with black. "Are
you okay?" I asked her.

She ignored me and turned to Ash, her face illuminating in
his flashlight, clear enough so I could tell she appeared honestly spooked. "The grill." She choked out the words.

"Oh my god, Clara, did you call 911?" Ash asked.

She shook her head. "I put it out... The fire extinguisher..."
She gasped out the words, then collapsed into a sitting position down in the sand, as if her legs couldn't hold her weight
anymore.

Ash sank down next to her, whispered something I couldn't
hear. Then he lifted her up in one quick sweep of his arms,
like she was a child, or a rag doll, not a full-grown grumpy
woman.

"What are you doing?" She tried to protest as he lifted her
higher, but her voice came out weakly, and Ash didn't even
flinch.

"I'm taking you to the ER, to get checked out," Ash said.

"I'm fine," Clara protested again, but her voice sputtered
on a cough as she spoke.

Ash ignored her and turned to me for a second. "Olivia,
Nate's up in the garage. Can you have him check the fire?
Maybe call the fire department too, just in case, to make sure
it's completely out." I nodded. "God, this is all my fault." Ash's

voice broke, and it reminded me of the way he'd sounded when we'd walked out of Rose's room, genuinely upset.

"You couldn't have known," I said, though I had no idea if that was true or not, if the grill caught fire because there was something wrong with it or because Ash did something stupid, like forgot to turn it off.

But before I could say anything else, Ash was already striding back up the steps, carrying Clara. Rescuing her, the same way he'd pulled me out of his Tesla yesterday during my panic attack.

As I watched them walk away, I wondered if this was the real Ash. The man who picked you up and carried you to safety when things fell apart. Kind, protective, gentle. Sweet. But if it was, how was I supposed reconcile that with the version of him who had confronted me in Angelica's old bedroom this morning?

I did find Nate in the garage as Ash said I would. But I took the long way there, by the barbecue grill, which was out by the pool on the side of the house opposite of the beach—wanting to see for myself that the fire was truly out before I did anything else. It did appear to be, though there was an ashy, foamy mess on the red bricks and a discarded fire extinguisher. What looked like the sweater Clara had been wearing earlier when she made me lunch was now on the ground and torn, covered with fire extinguisher foam and black ashy streaks.

I picked up her sweater and hung it over a patio chair, then wandered around to the garage. Nate was already on the phone with who I assumed to be the fire department, and I supposed Ash had asked him to call as he'd left to drive Clara to the ER. My presence here felt irrelevant.

"Wild night," Nate said to me when he hung up his phone. "But then, there's never a dull moment around here." He laughed a little.

"Really? It's felt pretty quiet here this week otherwise," I said.

"Well, you know, working for a guy like Ash, he always keeps me on my toes." I remembered Ash calling Nate to drive to Ojai suddenly to pick us up and realized maybe this week hadn't felt *quiet* to him at all. "But I guess that's nothing compared to when Angelica was here. The two of them together." He whistled a little under his breath. "I used to feel like I was just trying to stay alive in the middle of a hurricane."

It appreciated the metaphor, though it surprised me coming from a guy whose primary job was to operate a car. I hadn't made much more than small talk with Nate this entire time, but his commentary on Ash and Angelica now intrigued me. "It's really tragic what happened to Angelica," I said, wanting him to tell me more.

Nate hesitated for a moment, and then simply nodded.

"She was the hurricane?" I prodded.

He shook his head. "The two of them together. In the back seat of the car. The way they would fight…and then make up…then fight all over again."

I thought about what Ash had said this morning when he'd found me his bedroom. And I closed my eyes for a second, not wanting to imagine the two of them together. Not fucking, and not fighting either. But then I thought about the article I'd found earlier at UCLA, the way I'd felt this morning in her untouched room. I was eager to know more about Angelica. How she lived, and how she died.

"What was she like?" I asked Nate. "Aside from being married to Ash, I mean. What was she like as a person?"

Nate didn't say anything for a moment. "She was different than Ash," he said. "She didn't come from money the way he did, you know?" I nodded my head. I really did know. "But after a few years of marriage, she was an Asherwood through and through."

"What does that mean?" I asked him.

He shrugged. "Glamorous...yet extremely unhappy." That actually seemed to be a pretty fair assessment of everything in Ash's orbit. I nodded. "They fought a lot at the end," he added. "I would've put money on a splashy and extremely expensive divorce. But then she suddenly died."

She suddenly died.

I considered what Charley had told me, that Angelica had been rumored to be shopping a tell-all book. The *real* Ash seemed kind and protective, but also overly so when it came to his family. What if Angelica had found some of the Asherwood family skeletons Rose had mentioned? I couldn't imagine Ash just letting that go, letting her sell a book about it after they got divorced.

But before I could ask Nate any more questions, a fire truck sped up the long driveway, lights and sirens blaring, as if Nate had forgotten to tell them that the fire was already out.

THIRTY-FOUR

Ash and Clara weren't back from the hospital by the time the firefighters declared the house safe a few hours later, and by then, I was exhausted. I wandered through the long, dark hallways back to the guest room, not daring to veer off path in the empty house as I had earlier this morning.

The manuscript pages were still spread across my bed where I'd left them before dinner. I'd read almost the whole thing this afternoon, and I felt pretty skeptical that the ending would give me any more clues about this project. But I would worry about that tomorrow morning. I yawned and gathered the pages back into a pile—I was too tired to think about Emilia or Ash or Angelica or *Rebecca* any more tonight.

I grabbed my phone to scroll lying in bed, and realized I'd forgotten all about Noah's earlier text. Now I saw three missed calls from Noah and three more texts from him too. I hesitated for only a second before pressing the icon to call him back.

"Livvy," he said, breathless, like he was out jogging, though I was sure he wasn't. College Noah had hated running as much as I had. "Thank god. I was ready to send search and rescue."

"Sorry," I said. "We were having dinner, and there was a small fire. And some chaos ensued."

"Shit, are you all right?"

"I'm fine." Though I didn't say it out loud, the fire wasn't even close to the strangest part of this day. "It was minor," I added. "But I had my phone on silent and just got back to my room and saw all your texts and calls. What's going on?"

Noah didn't say anything for a few seconds, and I heard him still breathing heavily on the other end of the line. "I figured out why she looked familiar," he finally said.

"Clara? I told you, she works here."

"No," Noah said. "Angelica Asherwood."

I thought about what Nate had said, about a hurricane, about her becoming an unhappy and glamorous Asherwood. Noah had known her too? I sat up. "Really, why?"

"After you left, I did a deep dive on her, and I found her maiden name in another article: Peters, and it mentioned she graduated from Brown." Noah paused like he was letting that sink in, but I didn't exactly understand what he was trying to say.

"Yeah…so…?"

"So…we graduated from Brown."

"As did like a million other people." But even as I said it, I remembered noticing Angelica had been around my age. "I didn't know her at Brown," I added.

"Yeah, you did," Noah said. "We both did." I heard his words, but I still didn't quite understand or believe them. "She wasn't *Angelica Asherwood* back then, obviously. After I saw she went to Brown and her maiden name was Peters, I got out my college yearbook."

His college yearbook? Granted, I'd been in a haze of grief during my senior year, but I didn't even remember us having a college yearbook. And I still couldn't process what Noah was trying to say now. "I don't understand," I told him.

"I went back through the yearbook until I found her. We didn't know Angelica Asherwood or even Angelica Peters, but we knew a girl named Angela Peters. Remember her?"

I rolled the name around in my head, and it was vaguely familiar. Maybe? "I'm not sure," I said.

"Spring semester of senior year. The semester your..." His voice trailed off. *The semester my mother died.* The semester I put one foot in front of another in a fog, with Noah gently pulling me through classes and assignments. I had barely any memory of that whole semester, except for Noah being there with me, quite literally holding me up. Noah walking into my apartment that morning I was lying on the cool tile bathroom floor, in a daze of pain meds. Making me promise I'd never try anything like that again. I went to classes. I did some of my work that semester. I must have—because I didn't fail out of school, and I graduated in May. I met Jack. But I couldn't conjure one other single concrete memory of that period of time other than Noah, my mother's funeral, and playing tennis with Jack. "She was in our writing seminar that last semester," Noah said.

I rubbed my temples, trying to remember that specific class and who was in it. But I'd taken a lot of writing seminars in college, and they all blended together in my head now ten years later. "I don't know," I finally said. "If you say so."

"Livvy." Noah's voice was quiet, serious. His tone was suddenly scaring me. "She's the one who wrote the *Rebecca* story."

Excerpt from *The Wife*

I know her.

I don't recognize her name. And even in her author photo, she's unremarkable in almost every way, unmemorable. Except one. Two-color eyes. One green, one blue. She'd written a story about it in the one writing class I'd taken in college. Heterochromia. *I don't remember what the story was about, but I remember that was the title of it, and of her mismatched eyes. She was definitely in that class with me.*

That was the class where I first wrote and workshopped my story: "Mrs. de Winter Goes to the Ball." It was a short story reimagining a scene from my favorite novel, Rebecca, *only told from the point of view of Rebecca's ghost. I rewrote the ball scene—Rebecca's ghost watching as the second Mrs. de Winter tries to imitate everything about her, down to her dress. At the end of the story, my Rebecca swirled the air in the room just so, causing her former husband to trip.*

The class had hated my story and hated me too. They all knew each other from having taken English classes together for four years. I was a history major who took the senior writing seminar as an elective. The workshop comments said things like "farcical," "ridiculous," "old-fashioned," and years later I can still remember the worst one word-for-word, from the professor himself, a middle-aged man who hadn't published anything in over ten years, but who had the gall to tell me that my story was "amateurish" and "would appeal to no serious reader."

The written workshop comments had felt like bee stings, so hurt-ful they were visceral, throbbing, and I took the comments back to my apartment and set them on fire in my sink. I lit the match and watched them burn into ashes.

But the thing is, I couldn't burn them from my memory so easily. I'd put my story in a box and couldn't bring myself to look at it or even think about it again for years. That box traveled with me across the country from Providence to LA, sat in the tiny closet of my studio apartment in the West Valley. Then later, in my large closet in my Malibu bedroom. I stumbled across it again a few years into my marriage, and suddenly then, I knew Rebecca. I am Rebecca. Screw everyone in that stupid workshop—I would do what I had set out to do all along and write a Rebecca retelling from the point of view of Rebecca's ghost.

And not just the ball scene, but the entire novel. And instead of England, I set it in Malibu. It was a retelling, but a tell-all too. My husband and Maxim blending together in my mind, on the page.

But then the girl from the workshop years ago had taken my idea. The girl with the two-color eyes stole my premise. She'd gone and written and published my novel first.

I buy the lone copy of her novel from the bookstore, and I'm so angry as I walk back out to my car, I can barely see straight. My hands shake as I throw the book on the passenger seat and start the engine.

I know I'm torturing myself. This book is published; this book is already real. What can be done about it now? Her words are out there, mine aren't. It's already too late for my story. There's no use in reading her book, engaging with it. Hating it. And yet I know I will. I know I will read and obsess over every last word of it.

I drive out of the parking lot, filled with this incandescent, blind-

ing rage, taking the steep curves too fast, speeding the whole way back to my house.

I still haven't calmed down by the time I pull up my long driveway and park the car. And even when I pick up the book again, take it inside, and sit with it in my writing room, at my desk, my hands are still shaking with rage.

I flip back to the slightly familiar photograph of the mostly unfamiliar author. I can't stand to look at her, and I take a Post-it note and cover over her face.

Then I pick up a pen and write across it: You are a thief. I am the first Mrs. de Winter. And I will fucking haunt you.

THIRTY-FIVE

"You really don't remember her story?" Noah asked, still breathing hard into the phone. I couldn't tell whether he was extremely upset or extremely excited by what he'd figured out.

I shook my head, forgetting he couldn't see me. "Noah, I don't even remember what *I* wrote for that class, much less what anyone else wrote." After college, I threw away all my workshopped stories and workshop comments, and even my undergraduate story-collection thesis. I felt like a different person after my mother died, a different writer, and *All the Little Lights* sprung from that Olivia, not the college girl who'd workshopped what I'd later feel were empty and ultimately meaningless stories.

"Well, I remember her story was terrible," Noah said. "She got eviscerated in the workshop."

"Didn't we all?" I laughed bitterly. I was never totally sure how Noah went on to endure two more years of those soul-crushing writing workshops for his MFA and kept his sanity intact. Sometimes I would wonder if half the reason I chose to move to Boston with Jack was because it gave me an out for graduate school. I loved writing, more than anything. (Or, I used to.) But sitting in a circle of twenty other writers, all with different opinions and critiques and worldviews they were bringing to my very personal work, had been a confusing sort of torture that had paralyzed me, made me lose all sense of why I loved telling stories in the first place. Somewhere deep down, I knew I would've given up writing altogether if I'd had to endure two more years of workshops. I don't think I ever could've written *All the Little Lights* under those conditions.

"Angela—or, uh, Angelica—wasn't in any of our other writing classes," Noah was saying now. "I think she took our seminar senior year as an elective. And like I said, her writing wasn't very good. Or memorable, for that matter." He said it bluntly, not mean, but just matter-of-fact. "But the thing is, I did actually think about the fact someone in college had written a *Rebecca* story when your book came out a few years ago. I assumed it inspired you, to be honest."

His words took a second to sink in, and I pushed myself to remember this girl he talked about and her story. *Angela Peters*. Bad writer, crashing our workshop as an elective, senior year, *Rebecca* story.

I looked up and stared at Angelica's portrait on the wall in front of me, wanting it to elicit a memory of some younger, less glamorous college-aged girl with her face.

But I couldn't picture any of it. My mind felt entirely blank. I could not even bring myself to conjure one single real image or memory from our writing class that entire semester. "Noah, I really don't remember any of this. Honestly."

He was quiet for a minute. "Well, that was a rough semester for you." That was putting it mildly. "But subconsciously, maybe it all stayed with you."

"Wait, you think I subconsciously took some story idea

from a girl in college I don't even remember? I was doing bare minimum work that semester. I hardly read any of the workshop stories, much less paid attention or showed up for the critiques. I really don't remember this Angela person or her story." I couldn't stop my voice from rising, anger, defensiveness spreading hot up my chest to my throat.

"I'm just trying to piece together what's going on." Noah sounded defensive now. "I'm not saying you did something wrong, Livvy."

"Aren't you?" I snapped at him, though even as I said the words, I knew this wasn't his fault. Whatever anger I was feeling right now wasn't because of him. But I couldn't control it either.

"Well, let's look at the facts," Noah said calmly. "Ideas aren't copyrighted. And she never actually published anything." But for some reason I thought about what Ash had said at dinner, that just because a court didn't find someone guilty of the legal definition of plagiarism, it didn't mean they weren't guilty of something. Was I guilty of something I didn't even mean to do or realized I'd done?

And then it all suddenly hit me. "This is why Ash brought me here to Malibu, isn't it?"

Noah sighed, like he was relieved I finally got the urgency of what he'd been trying to tell me. "That's what worries me. Not what *you* did. What he might do." He paused for second. "You have to get out of his house, Livvy."

But I could barely process what Noah was saying because everything that had happened the last week with Ash was rerunning through my mind. Was anything real? Emilia? Her journals? Fifty thousand dollars? Was this all just some sort of twisted revenge plot against me for a writing sin Ash believed I committed against his dead wife by writing *Becky*? I thought again about the word *thief* inscribed inside my book. Who wrote that? Ash? Angelica? The perfect storm of the two of them together? Oh God, I'd almost had sex with him last night. I felt like I was going to throw up.

I put my phone down and switched it to speaker because my hands shook too much to hold it up to my ear.

"I'll come pick you up right now." Noah was still talking, his voice coming out of the phone sounding distantly urgent and strangely disembodied. "Text me the address. I'm walking out the door to come get you."

"No," I said, and my voice was shaking with rage now. "I'm not going anywhere."

"Livvy," Noah pleaded with me. "This Asherwood guy might be unstable. You can't stay there."

"If he wants to play this game," I sputtered angrily, "I can play too." But even as I said the words, I wasn't sure whether they were true or not. Ash was still an Asherwood, and I was still me.

What I loved most about the character of Rebecca was how she always somehow one-upped Maxim, even after she was dead. And that was what drew me to telling her story to begin with. Not anyone or anything else. Not some seed planted in my subconscious. It was my own pure love and curiosity for the original character that led me to write *Becky*.

"Livvy." Noah said my name softly into the phone, pleading with me. "Please?"

But nothing Noah could say was going to change my mind. Now that I knew what was really going on, there was no way in hell I was leaving Malibu without beating Ash at his own game.

THIRTY-SIX

I slept fitfully all night, tangled up in half dreams of Angelica. She was a painting, then a doll, then an unfamiliar girl whose auburn hair obscured her face as she sat across from me in a classroom. In my dream, I was suddenly back at Brown with Noah, but somehow Ash was there too, waiting for me outside University Hall, reaching his hand out to hold mine. I took it, but then he held on too tight, yanked my arm, and pulled me down the steps. I woke up early the next morning, sweating, still feeling like I was tumbling.

I checked my phone. It was just after 7:00 a.m., but I already had a text from Noah. If I don't hear from you at least once before 5 PM I'm sending the police.

Does this count? I texted back, adding an upside down face emoji, attempting to make light of his worry. But I swallowed hard as I hit Send.

Check in at noon, he texted back quickly.

Yes, sir.

Three dots appeared, then disappeared, then reappeared. And let me come pick you up later.

I stared at it for a second, not sure if it was an invitation to hang out or a demand to pack my stuff and leave. Probably the latter. I knew he was worried about me. But I'd spent the last few years dealing with my life just fine without Noah's help. Okay, maybe not *just fine*. But I was here. I'd survived it. I didn't need Noah to take care of me the way I had back in college. I could handle Ash all on my own.

I'll text you later, I finally wrote. Promise.

I silenced my phone and got dressed, remembering a bra this morning. I needed all my armor to face Ash and to figure out what to do next.

I wandered into the kitchen, and Clara was sitting at the island, already drinking a cup of coffee. "You're up early, after last night," I said.

She grimaced into her cup and took another sip. "I'm always up with the sun, no matter what time I go to bed," she said. "You want some coffee?"

I hesitated. Maybe it hadn't been crazy to think she'd slipped something in my coffee. If Ash thought I stole something from Angelica, what did her cousin, Clara, think about me? Had he and Clara been in on this whole plot or whatever it was together all along? Or maybe Clara knew nothing and Clara's coffee had never been a problem. Maybe it was all Ash. Ash's cardamom scone? I remembered the way he'd kissed me the other night, and my stomach twisted in disbelief.

"Coffee?" Clara repeated, interrupting my thoughts.

"No thanks," I said. "I'll just grab a glass of water instead."

Clara shrugged, unconcerned, as if to say *suit yourself*. I took a glass from the cabinet and poured myself water from the tap.

"There's sparkling in the fridge," Clara said. "And limes and lemons."

"This is good," I said, and brought my water to sit across

from her at the island. First things first. I needed to figure out where Clara really stood and how she was involved in all of this. "So tell me," I asked sweetly, "how are you feeling this morning? That fire was pretty scary last night."

Her face softened a little. "Honestly, I'm totally fine. Ash overreacted. It was a small outdoor fire. I put it out. I wasn't going to die of smoke inhalation."

"He cares about you," I said. She laughed a little into her coffee. "Are the two of you...together?" I realized, even as I said it, how inappropriate my question was, given what had almost happened with me and Ash the other night. But Clara didn't know about that. At least, I wasn't sure if she did or not.

"God no," she said. "My cousin would literally come back to life just to murder me if anything happened between me and him. Not that I would want it to anyway," she added quickly. So quickly that it sounded like an overt lie. I thought about the way Ash had picked her up last night, carried her up the stairs, looked after her so gently. Of course Clara wanted him. How could she not? Ash was Ash.

But I smiled at her and played along. "Can I ask you a question?" I said. "Why are you here? Housekeeping doesn't seem like it's your passion." I didn't think it would help to mention that I'd googled her, and her LinkedIn agreed with me.

She shrugged. "Ash needed some help. I was in between jobs." She cast her eyes down quickly into her coffee cup, avoiding looking right at me. She definitely was lying, but the question was, *why*? "And remind me again," she said, looking back up and meeting my eyes, "why are *you* here?"

"I'm writing a book about Emilia," I said, my gaze un-flinching, my voice verging on defiant. Though even as I said the words, I understood they probably weren't exactly true anymore.

We held on to each other's eyes for a moment, as if who-ever blinked first would have to admit they were the biggest liar. Finally, she looked away and took another sip of her coffee. And I took that as my opening to keep asking questions. "Did your cousin ever mention me?" I asked her.

"Angie?" She raised her eyebrows. "Mention you?" I nodded. "Why would she? Were you the one Ash was screwing around with before she died?"

"What? I just met Ash last week!"

She rolled her eyes, and I couldn't tell if she didn't believe me, or if she just didn't care. Or maybe it was that Ash had screwed around so many times it would be impossible to keep track.

I guessed it shouldn't surprise me that a man like Ash would cheat on his wife. But it felt oddly disappointing too. What he'd said to me in his bedroom the other night—that it had been so long since he'd been with anyone—made it seem like, if nothing else, he'd been a devoted husband to Angelica up until the very end. But now, even that much felt like a lie. "If Ash was cheating on your cousin," I said, "then I really don't understand why you're here helping him out now."

Clara bit her lip and didn't say anything for a moment, as if trying to decide whether or not to tell me more. "I didn't talk to my cousin all that much," she finally said softly. "But every once in a while, she'd get drunk and call me. And she did, the night before she died. She'd had too much champagne, and she'd called me in the middle of the night. The last thing she ever said to me was that Ash betrayed her, and that she was going to destroy him."

Destroy him. The thought chilled me. If that's what Angelica had been intending, did Ash know? I couldn't imagine that he would let anyone destroy him. Not even his wife. Especially not his wife.

"Anyway," Clara continued, "the next day, Angie had her accident. She was dead, and Bex has been missing ever since."

I shook my head, confused at that last part. "Bex?"

"Our other cousin, Bex. We're all only children, and our moms were three sisters. So Angie, Bex, and I grew up together, kind of like sisters ourselves. Bex worked for Angie as her personal assistant the few years before her death."

Bex? As in, Rebecca? I wondered if she was referring to the other bridesmaid from the article I'd found in the digital archives— the girl on the end, Rebecca Farmington. Her name being Rebecca was whole reason I'd stumbled onto that article in the first place. Angelica had been planning to *destroy* Ash. Now she was dead. Clara was here. Bex was...missing? "What do you mean... Bex is missing?" I asked Clara. Could a grown woman just disappear, without a trace? Could a man as rich as Ash just make it so? I swallowed hard at that thought.

"No one has heard from her since the night Angie died," Clara said. "Ash told us she was so overcome by grief that she fled to Europe. But that was over a year ago, and we still haven't heard a word from her."

"It doesn't sound like you believe him," I said.

"I don't know what to believe yet." She paused. "But that's why I'm here. She's why I'm here." She spoke so calmly but firmly now, I actually believed her. "I promised my aunt I'd figure out what really happened that night Angie died."

So, it wasn't just people on Reddit who had questions about the night Angelica died. It was her own family too. The realization rippled through me, chilled me. "And have you? Figured anything out?" I whispered, trying to find my voice again.

I suddenly heard Ash's footsteps coming down the hallway, and Clara put a finger to her lips. I nodded to show her I understood.

"Good morning," Ash's voice bellowed into the kitchen. "How's everyone feeling today?"

So many questions swirled through my head, about Angelica, about Bex, about why Ash had truly brought me here,

I could barely think, much less form a reasonable answer. I managed a half smile, and Ash turned his attention to Clara, offering her what appeared to be a genuinely concerned look. My heart softened again. *No. I am not going to let myself be sucked back in.*

"I'm fine, really." Clara finished off her coffee and stood. She smiled sweetly at Ash, and I marveled at the way she was masking everything she'd just told me, working here in this house, for him. "Do you need anything?" Ash shook his head, and she started to walk out of the kitchen. "I'll be in the laundry room if you change your mind," she called out behind her.

For a moment the air in the kitchen was hollow and still, until Ash turned to me and smiled. He reached across the island and put his hand on mine. I tried not to flinch as he touched me, but everything Clara just told me and what Noah said last night raced through my head. My reaction to Ash's touch now was immediate, visceral. I jumped a little and pulled my hand back.

"Hey," Ash said softly. "What's wrong?" He sounded so kind, so concerned. Not at all like a man who had brought me all the way to Malibu just to get some sort of twisted revenge. Could Angelica's story that Noah remembered from ten years ago have been a giant coincidence? *(No, writers don't believe in coincidence.)* Was it possible Noah was mistaken? Even if he wasn't, there was still the smallest chance Ash didn't know anything about it.

But there had been so many strange occurrences since I'd come to Malibu that I could no longer just explain away. The missing journals, the lack of anything concrete pertaining to Emilia's story or the illusory first wife. The similarity between this supposed translation of her journals and the original *Rebecca*. It read like someone had simply rewritten the original with the Asherwood family's names and places. Had they?

Was Ash truly diabolical enough to have paid someone to do just that? And then there was the larger question now swirling around in my mind—if Ash had gone to such lengths to lie to me, what exactly had he been capable of doing to Angelica?

"Why did you read *Becky*?" I blurted out.

"What?" Ash frowned.

"I mean, how did you even find out about it to read it? It barely sold any copies. It didn't get any publicity."

He didn't say anything for a moment, and then he said softly: "Ange."

My heart started pounding so fast when he said her name, the sound of it echoed in my ears. I remembered Noah's worry, that Ash might be *mentally unstable*, and I inwardly chided myself for saying anything, alone with him now. Even if I screamed, it would echo off all the glass or be swallowed up in the rush of the Pacific. And anyway, no one would hear me but Clara, who I wasn't sure would come to my rescue from the laundry room. I felt my hands start to tremble, and I clasped them tightly in front of me.

"Olivia?" I jumped a little at the sound of his voice. "You look like you've seen a ghost."

"Angelica," I said softly. She was here, but she wasn't here at all. She drove everything Ash did, even a year after her death. She had brought me here too, hadn't she? Noah had said it last night. Now Ash was confirming it.

"Ange was reading *Becky* just before she died," Ash said. "She loved everything Daphne du Maurier. *Everything*. She was actually the one that first suspected Emilia and Daphne might have gone to the same school." He paused for a moment. "Anyway, I found *Becky* on her nightstand just after her accident, and so I picked it up to read myself."

It all sounded logical, understandable. But then, I thought about the copy on her nightstand yesterday, the one with the word **THIEF** Sharpied in it. Had that been there when he read it? Or had Ash himself written it in there? I looked up, and Ash was smiling at me now, looking calm, his demeanor easy.

"Shortly after I read *Becky*, I discovered Emilia's journals. And then it all felt meant to be. You, Angelica, Emilia. All of it."

Me. *Angelica. Emilia.* The two of them were both writers who had died tragically young. That thought chilled me, and I folded my arms across my chest to try and keep from visibly shivering. The last thing I wanted right now was for Ash to touch me, to warm me, to confuse me any more.

But he didn't seem to notice. He glanced down at his watch. "Shoot, I have to go into work for a few hours. Will you be all right here today? I'll be back for dinner."

I nodded, and Noah's invitation to pick me up later hung in the back of my mind. But maybe Noah was wrong. What if Angelica's love for Daphne had driven her to find Ash and his family to begin with, driven her to read *Becky* too? And what if Ash was telling the truth? What if he didn't even know about her college story or the fact that we were at Brown together?

THIEF. That one little Sharpied word rattled around in my brain, making me feel unsettled.

"No, wait!" Ash exclaimed, oblivious to all the worries running through my head. "It's Friday. LA LIT is tonight. You promised you'd come with me, remember?"

I had promised that, and it was hard to recall now how excited I'd felt about it just a few days ago. LA LIT! But it would still be exciting to go, wouldn't it?

I could practically hear Noah's voice in my head shouting at me to say I'd changed my mind. To run away from here, and to never talk to Ash again. But I forced myself to smile even wider, and then I heard myself say, "Yeah, of course. I wouldn't miss it."

THIRTY-SEVEN

Ash left for work, and the house felt exceedingly quiet. I couldn't stop thinking about Angelica as I walked back to the guest room, sat down on the bed, and stared up at the portrait of her. How was it possible we'd started in the same place years ago, in a writing workshop at Brown? We both loved *Rebecca* and had somehow both ended up right here in this very room, in this very opulent Malibu house. Only I was alive, and she was dead.

"What really happened to you?" I whispered.

Had she died in an accident? Was she murdered? Had she been reading *Becky* before she died because of her love for Daphne du Maurier or because of some hatred for me? Did she think I was a *thief* or a former classmate whose work she admired? Had Ash brought me here to soothe his own grief or out of some twisted sort of revenge?

But of course, a portrait of a dead woman gave me no answers.

I flopped back on the bed and sighed. My eye caught on the manuscript Ash had given me last night, still piled up on the nightstand. I picked it up, thumbing through the rest of the pages. There was a Malibu Lake party scene—where Emilia found herself accidentally tricked into wearing the first Mrs. Asherwood's dress by their housekeeper. Just as in the original, the narrator in *Rebecca* had been tricked into wearing a copy of Rebecca's gown for the costume ball by Mrs. Danvers, shocking and angering Maxim. Henry Asherwood too, is angry, and Emilia ends up crying in her bedroom.

Even in the furthest stretches of my imagination, I no longer believed this could be a translation of Emilia's journals. So what exactly was it, and why had Ash given it to me?

A knock on my door startled me. "Olivia, are you in there?" Clara's voice.

"Yeah," I called back, sitting up and shuffling the manuscript pages back into a pile. "Come on in."

"What's all that?" Clara asked as she walked in, pointing to the pages on the bed.

I stared at her for a moment, still unsure whether or how much to trust her. She said she'd barely talked to Angelica, but what if Angelica had called her drunk once, claiming I'd stolen her story? Was Clara the one who'd written *thief*? Or did she truly just want to uncover her cousin's whereabouts and she couldn't care less about me?

"Well, Ash wants me to write his grandmother's story," I finally said. "This is a translation of her journals." Then, to try and feel her out a little more, I added, "Allegedly."

"What?" she said through a sliver of smile. "You don't trust him?" I didn't trust him, but I didn't trust her either, so I didn't answer.

She tilted her head to the side and then jumped back a little, seeming to catch a glimpse of the portrait of Angelica on the wall. "That terrifies me every time," she said softly, shaking her head.

"Really? Terrifies you. Why?"

"Her eyes. They were *exactly* like that in real life." She paused for a second. "It almost feels like they're still judging me in this painting."

I wondered what they would've been judging her for. Maybe Clara's attraction to Ash had been as obvious to Angelica as it was to me.

Clara reached her finger up to touch the canvas, and then ran it carefully along the edge of the pearlescent dress that hung across Angelica's shoulders. "I actually know where this dress is," Clara said. "You know what you should do, if you really wanted to mess with Ash? Wear this dress to LA LIT tonight."

I tried not to laugh, wondering if Clara too, was familiar with *Rebecca*. But I bit my lip. Dress aside, if Clara knew about LA LIT, she must've been eavesdropping when she said she was in the laundry room earlier. Or had Ash told her he'd invited me? Oh, who was I kidding? She had probably been eavesdropping on me this whole week.

"Ash despised this dress," Clara was saying now. "Angelica was friends with the designer. Good friends, and Ash was jealous. It's why she wore it for her portrait, I'm sure. Just to fuck with him." I considered everything she was saying for a moment. But even from the little I knew of Ash, the idea of his jealousy in that kind of situation felt spot-on. "She loved everything he despised," Clara added. *A hurricane*, Nate had said. But Nate had probably driven them countless places. Clara said she hadn't been in touch with Angelica all that much.

"You really know a lot about her, considering you hated each other and didn't talk much," I said.

Clara frowned. "I never said *I* hated her. She hated me." She paused for a moment and lowered her hand. "She was still my cousin. We grew up together like sisters."

I thought about my own sister. I hadn't spoken to Suzy in months, and aside from a quick text exchange every few weeks, which usually involved Suzy sending a cute picture of my niece, Lily, and me texting back a heart, I knew nothing real about her life now. I didn't hate Suzy. And I didn't think she hated me? There was just this wide gulf between us that had felt weirdly insurmountable since our dad had remarried Shawna and Suzy hadn't been angry like I was. But suddenly, I missed her, and I promised myself I'd call her as soon as I got back to Boston.

"Anyway—" I realized Clara was still talking, and I shook thoughts of Suzy away for now and looked back up. "We got interrupted earlier in the kitchen. You said yesterday you came across an article with me and Bex in the picture. I was wondering if you found anything else about Bex in your research?"

I shook my head. Though, of course, I hadn't been looking. I could tell her with a fair degree of certainty that Rebecca Asherwood had never existed. But Rebecca "Bex" Farmington—I had no idea. I'd barely found anything about Angelica, other than the newspaper article, the Reddit landscaper who was convinced she was alive, and Rose's comment about her that had struck me as odd. *What you're doing to Angelica.* I wondered again what Rose thought *he was doing* exactly. Did she mean how he'd been cheating on her, or was it something else?

"What about Rose?" I said to Clara. "Have you been to visit her?"

She shook her head. "Rose?"

"Ash's grandmother," I clarified. "I mean, step-grandmother."

"Oh, that Rose. Right. I met her briefly at their wedding." She shot me a skeptical look.

"When I met her the other day, she said something weird about Angelica that seemed to spook Ash a little bit." I paused for a second. "Maybe she knows something about what really happened that night of Angelica's accident, about Bex going missing too?" I thought about it for another minute. I certainly wasn't getting any answers from Angelica's portrait, or this stack of pages Ash had given me. Maybe another visit to see Rose today, without Ash, could help me understand what had really happened to Angelica, and why Ash had really brought me out here. "Do you drive?" I asked Clara.

"Umm, yeah. Why wouldn't I?" Her eyebrows shot up as if I'd asked her the most ridiculous question in the world. But I let it pass. I didn't have to like Clara to help her or to use her to help myself.

"How would you feel about driving us up to Ojai?"

THIRTY-EIGHT

The ride to Ojai felt extremely long, and the quiet that sat between me and Clara only seemed to make the trip drag on.

As we got closer, Clara finally broke the silence to ask me where exactly she was driving to in Ojai, and I realized I had no idea how to get there. I put *Green Oaks Care Suites* into my phone, and then at least we had Siri's voice to cut the silence.

I thought about how annoyed Rose was last time with Ash for not calling first, but I had a feeling that even if I could get her number from Green Oaks, she would hang up on me. I asked Clara if we could hit the McDonald's drive-through on the way, hoping we could soften our surprise visit with a bribe.

"Seriously?" Clara raised her eyebrows, but did not move her eyes off the road. "You couldn't have eaten before we left?"

"Not for me," I clarified. "For Rose. Just trust me."

She sighed; she definitely did not trust me. But as I amended the directions in my phone, she followed Siri to the closest McDonald's.

I still felt nervous ten minutes later as we walked into Green

Oaks together. I had the weird sense that I was entirely out-side of my body, watching myself do this thing I shouldn't be doing. Ash had never told me not to visit Rose again. Still, I intuitively knew Ash would see this as a betrayal. *And what did he do to Angelica when he thought she betrayed him?* My heart-beat quickened at that thought, and I clutched the greasy bag and Diet Coke tighter in my hands.

"Do you remember which room?" Clara asked as we turned down a long hallway. I shook my head, but then pointed out that each door had the person's name engraved next to it on a fancy gold plate. *Of course it did.* "Oh, right over there!" Clara pointed to the gold *Rose Asherwood* plate, and it was the first time I'd ever heard her sound genuinely excited about anything. I hoped I hadn't gotten her hopes up for nothing.

"I have to warn you, she wasn't in a very good mood the last time I was here." I tried to temper her expectations a bit. "And Ash said her memory isn't always the greatest."

Clara nodded, but pulled the paper bag from me with one hand and knocked on Rose's door with the other. "Yes, dear, come in!" Rose shouted from the other side, and Clara opened the door before I could warn her that Rose most certainly would not have sounded that friendly if she'd had any idea it was us.

Rose was sitting on her couch today, her wheelchair tucked off to the side, and she was dressed in a floral dress with a thick strand of pink pearls around her neck and a wide-brimmed white hat perched sideways on her head, like she half expected to get up off the couch and walk straight into the Kentucky Derby. She glanced at Clara, then at me, and frowned. "Who the hell are you?"

"Hi, Rose," I said, brightly, forcing a confidence I didn't feel at all. "I came with Ash a few days ago to visit, remem-ber? I'm Olivia, the writer. And this is Clara..." I paused for a second, unsure if I should introduce her as Angelica's cousin or Ash's housekeeper. I glanced at Clara, hoping she'd introduce herself.

But instead, she said: "We brought you a burger." She held out the brown bag. "Olivia said it's your favorite."

"And a Diet Coke," I added hopefully, holding out the soda in my hand.

"What are you trying to do, kill me?" She frowned, and Clara shot me a look that said *what the hell*. But then Rose beckoned with her hand for Clara to come closer. "Just take it out of the wrapper and hand it to me," she ordered Clara. "I suppose it would be rude of me not to have a bite. And put the Diet Coke down right here." She pointed to a coaster on the coffee table in front of her.

Clara and I obliged, and then we sat down on the love seat across from her. Rose took one bite of the burger, then two. Then devoured the whole thing and ordered Clara to walk back into her kitchen for a napkin as she daintily lifted the straw to her lips to sip her Coke. Clara returned with a napkin, and Rose dabbed at her face. "So, tell me why you're here," Rose said brusquely. "What's so important that you're trying to bribe me with fast food on a Thursday morning?"

It was definitely a Friday morning, but I bit my lip, not about to correct her on that fine point. "I had a few more questions for you," I said. "If you don't mind."

"I already told you. I don't want to talk to you about Emilia," she said curtly.

I nodded. I knew she didn't. But Emilia, the write-for-hire project, was not the reason I'd come back here. "What about Angelica?" I asked her now.

She raised her eyebrows. "What about Angelica?"

All the lies I could tell her ran through my head. On the tip of my tongue was that Ash had given up on Emilia and now wanted me to write a book about his dead wife instead.

But Clara jumped in and spoke first. "Angie was my cousin. I think you and I actually met at the wedding?"

Rose frowned, but then she said, "Yes, and in Malibu once too? Thanksgiving, was it?"

Clara shook her head. "That was probably our other cousin, Bex. She was Angie's assistant."

Rose nodded, like this made sense to her. "Ah, yes. Her assistant. The little tramp."

Clara's face turned bright red, and I felt embarrassed for Rose's brashness. "Do you know what she did for Angie? She gave up everything for her!" Clara's voice broke on the end of the sentence, and anger flamed on her cheeks.

Rose put her Diet Coke down and stared at her fingers. She wore a giant pink ring today, pearls in the shape of a rose. Of course. It was probably custom-made and worth millions of dollars. She ran her fingers slowly across the pearls as if deciding what else to say to Clara, if anything. "I love Ashy, like he's my own," she finally said. "I always have since he came to live with us as a little boy. And Angelica is a doll." She paused and ran her forefinger back around the pearls another time. "What am I supposed to call that girl who works for Angelica and seduced him?"

Seduced *him*? I thought about Ash's eyes on me, his hands on me, his lips on me. I could barely suppress an eye roll at Rose's narrative that seemed to leave him blameless.

Then I glanced at Clara, trying to get a read on her face, at the revelation that maybe it was her cousin Bex whom Ash had been *screwing around with*, as she'd put it earlier. Clara's expression was blank, though, and I wasn't sure what to think.

"The Asherwood men." Rose shook her head and continued. "They're all weak, you know. I never expected my husband to be faithful. It might be hard for you young ladies to understand, but a man like Ash, like his father and his grandfather, well, they can never be satisfied with just a simple woman, like me. Like Angelica." Rose seemed the furthest thing from simple, as did Angelica. And what Rose was saying sounded an awful lot like Ash cheated on Angelica, and Rose was now excusing it away with some awful rich-boys-would-be-rich-boys logic.

But I swallowed back my criticism, not wanting to say anything that would make Rose stop talking to us altogether. "Last time I was here," I said instead, "you mentioned something about *what Ash was doing to Angelica.* Is that what you meant? That Ash was cheating on her with her cousin?"

She was silent for another moment, and I didn't think she was going to answer me. But then she said, "Ash pushed her too far. And now she wants to destroy him. Destroy our family. He will never let that happen." Her words hung in the air for a moment, and it was eerie the way she was still talking about Angelica in the present tense. Like her memory failed her when it came to Angelica's death, over and over again.

But was it her memory failing her, or was there something else she knew? *No. Angelica is dead.* That Reddit poster had probably spied Clara walking on Carbon Beach. But goose bumps suddenly pricked my forearms.

"What are you saying?" Clara asked. "Did Ash do something?"

"What am I saying?" She stared at Clara, moving in closer to her face. "What was I saying?" Her eyes were suddenly stones, cold and dark and distant, and maybe what Ash had said about her not being entirely lucid all the time was actually true. "I don't know what he was thinking. You're not even half as pretty as Angelica is."

It appeared Rose was confusing Clara and Bex right now. Or, Clara had been lying to me about what her relationship was with Ash. I glanced at Clara again, and now she had turned pale, her eyes glassy, looking a little like she might throw up.

I took a deep breath and cleared my throat before I let what

I really wanted to ask finally tumble out of me in a rush: "You told me last time I was here that Emilia's death wasn't an accident. You said there was a *long history* of that in this family. Do you believe Angelica's death wasn't an accident either?"

Rose tilted her head and stared at me. Her eyes were sharp and bright again, like diamonds now. "People will see what they want to see and believe what they want to believe."

I frowned. That was no kind of answer.

"You think Ash is some kind of magician who will change your life? Well, magicians saw beautiful women in half or make them disappear." She snapped her fingers, and I thought about Bex. About Angelica. Is that what Ash had done to one or both of them? "Leave Ash alone. Go home. You're out of your depth, young lady."

Excerpt from *The Wife*

There are all the stages of grief in letting go of my story. I reach peak anger when I buy that other woman's book—and then, I can never bring myself to read it all the way through. I'm too livid to focus on the words. Instead, I tuck it in a drawer in my writing desk with a copy of my college story and my own manuscript. Tuck it all away, for good.

That makes my anger fade into depression. If I don't have my book to write or to publish, then what do I have? I have a husband and a cousin who I have to interact with each day, pretending to love, pretending to be oblivious to what's going on. It's exhausting.

I start drinking again, and then my depression numbs its way into acceptance.

My husband reaches for me in bed at night, and I don't even have the will to pull away. Sex is a weapon and a drug with him. It has kept us together all these years and torn us apart. But now, I let him undress me, put his hands on my bare skin, and I yield to him. My body responds the way it always has to his touch, and it's animalistic, whatever remains between us now. Desire and love, my body and my brain, are strangely disconnected. And sometimes, I feel it even then:

I am already hovering above, already watching my life from somewhere else. Already a ghost.

THIRTY-NINE

Our return trip to Malibu was far less silent.

Rose's personal acupuncturist had shown up right after Rose had yelled at me about being out my depth, and then Rose had thrown us out of her suite.

"I really don't like that woman," Clara spat out as soon as we'd both fled to the parking lot and had gotten safely back into the car.

I nodded, realizing that our shared dislike of Rose gave me and Clara something to talk about. "I'm not sure she was all there today, though," I said. "She seemed to maybe be confusing you and Bex." I put it out there tentatively, wanting to judge Clara's reaction.

"You think?" Clara huffed, and I could practically feel the anger rippling off her skin, a truth of its own. "Angie loved Rose, and god, I have no idea why."

"It's disconcerting that she still talks about Angelica in the present tense, isn't it?" I mused.

Clara nodded as she pulled back out onto the main road. "It is. But like you said, she wasn't all there." She paused for a few moments as she merged into traffic. Then she added, "And it's hard to accept when someone you love dies just like that."

That much, I could understand for sure. And yet, my writer brain turned and twisted, and I couldn't stop myself from saying more. "I actually saw some post on Reddit speculating that Angelica is still alive, that she faked her death."

Clara stopped at a red light, then turned to me and frowned. "You can't possibly believe that."

I shook my head, but I wasn't sure what I believed anymore. What was true and what was lie. What was real and what was fiction. "I just kept thinking about it the whole time Rose was talking about Angelica in the present tense."

Clara sighed. "What got me was that thing she said about Angie wanting to ruin Ash. And how he would *never let that happen*. Then all that weird stuff she said about Ash sawing you in half and making you disappear, when you asked her about Angie's death being an accident."

"Do you think Angelica's death was an accident?" I said softly.

Clara cast me a quick sideways glance before turning her attention back to the road. "Yes…no…maybe?"

"I mean, Ash is a lot of things, but he's not a murderer, right?" I added.

Clara bit her lip, as if trying to decide how to answer. Finally, she said, "You're the fiction writer. You tell me. If this were a novel, would Ash have cut the brakes in her car?"

"Too melodramatic." I laughed, but the sound caught in my throat, coming out more like a tiny cry. "But I guess people always say the truth is stranger than fiction."

"Well, definitely the Asherwoods' truth is stranger than fiction." Clara said it lightly, like she was trying to make a joke now, but the frown on her face said otherwise. Whatever had happened to Angelica, and Bex, it truly wasn't funny. I was pretty sure we both agreed on that. "I guess if I'm really being honest," Clara added softly, "I'm not sure what Ash might be capable of."

I nodded, and it occurred to me, if this were actually a *Rebecca* retelling, then, God, Ash would definitely be a murderer.

But it wasn't. It was real life, and Ash truly seemed so damaged and broken over Angelica's death, I still couldn't fully bring myself to believe that he was responsible for it.

Just then, my phone rang, and Noah's name popped up. I'd totally forgotten to check in with him at noon like I'd promised. "Shoot," I said to Clara. "I have to take this real quick."

She nodded and kept her eyes trained steadily on the road.

"Hey, Noah. Sorry, I'm fine. I just went on a little road trip with Clara."

"Wait, what?" Noah asked. "I thought we didn't like her?" I was certain his voice was loud enough for her to hear it through the phone, as she chuckled a little to herself, and I mouthed *sorry* at her.

"Anyway, we'll be back in Malibu soon, but I didn't realize what day it was when we were texting earlier. I'm actually going to the LA LIT Gala with Ash tonight, so you can't come pick me up."

Noah was silent on the other end of the line, and I couldn't tell if he was worried or annoyed or upset with me. LA LIT was the kind of thing we would've dreamed of going to when we talked about our writing careers back in college. "I don't understand you, Livvy," he said after a minute. "What are you still doing there, all mixed up with this guy and this stupid writing job?"

I didn't say anything, because I couldn't think of a way to explain it to Noah that could possibly sound close to reasonable: Ash had brought me here, enchanted me, terrified me, excited me. Rose had said I was out of my depth, but maybe it was more accurate that I was in too deep now to just walk away.

"Seriously," Noah said, taking my silence as an argument.

"I don't get it. You did this with Jack in college, and now you're doing it with him."

"Doing what?" I shot back, annoyed he was bringing Jack into this.

"It's like you want to sabotage yourself," Noah was saying now. "You can't face whatever's going on in your life, so you just cling to the worst and prettiest guy who will destroy you." He paused for a second, and then he added, "And you only come back to me when you need help picking up the pieces."

His words were daggers, meant to wound. And I remembered how mean Noah could be sometimes. I thought about the huge fight we got into just before graduation when I told him I was moving to Boston with Jack, not going to UCLA with him, and Noah had told me then I was my *own worst enemy*. It wasn't my book party that started the chasm between us—it was that night, those words he'd said to me then. The book party just finished things off.

"I'm sorry I asked for your help yesterday," I finally shot back. "Just forget all about this whole thing. In fact, don't even give me another thought."

I heard him breathing through the phone, and for a second, I thought he was going to apologize, but I was too angry to listen even if he did, and so I quickly ended the call.

I wasn't sure how much Clara had heard or understood of my call with Noah, but to her credit, she didn't ask me about it. Instead, she changed the subject entirely, asked me about Emilia, and exactly what kind of book Ash had hired me to write.

"I don't know." I leaned back against my seat and sighed. I felt a pressure ache forming just above my eyes: Noah's angry words. Rose's strange warning. Clara reminding me how bizarre the Asherwoods' *truth* really was. "I'm not even sure the book is actually going to happen," I finally said.

Clara raised her eyebrows. "But you're still here." Was she pointing out the obvious or asking a question?

"Well, I promised Ash I'd go to LA LIT tonight and…" My voice trailed off because I wasn't sure what else to say. And, what? Why *was* I still here? That nagging voice inside of me that always wanted answers, that same voice that drove me to write fiction—that's why. Now it was telling me there was more to know about Angelica's death, and I just couldn't let it go. But what I finally said to Clara was, "No writer could pass up LA LIT."

She nodded. "I was serious about that dress from the portrait. I know where it is if you want to wear it tonight. You could really get in his head." She sounded a little gleeful at the prospect.

I considered it. Ash had been in control all week—why shouldn't I *get in his head*? Walking into the gala in Angelica's dress that Ash despised would be such a *Rebecca* moment. In *Rebecca*, Mrs. Danvers convinces our unwitting narrator to wear a replica of a dress Rebecca once wore to a ball. Charley called my situation in Malibu *meta*, but at this point I kind of felt like the universe was trying to trap me in a *Rebecca* retelling of my own, if only to punish me for thinking I could ever be good enough to write one. Like the *Kirkus* review hadn't been bad enough.

"You want me to go grab it for you?" Clara asked as she pulled back into Ash's garage and turned off the car.

I thought about it for another minute, but then I shook my head. "No, I'm good. I'll wear something else."

The truth was, I was getting pretty tired of retellings. Of writing them, of living them. Of being trapped by their constraints. Whatever I was going to do next, I wanted it to belong completely and only to me. I wanted to write the rest of my story my own way.

FORTY

Everyone thought that the center of the publishing universe was in New York, but the LA LIT Gala seemed to exist if only to prove that school of thought wrong. A mix of big-name authors (think Stephen King) and Hollywood names (think Steven Spielberg) got dressed up and came together once every March for a silent auction to raise money for literacy charities across California. If someone had told me at this time last year that I'd be attending, and with *Henry Asherwood III*, I might've passed out from shock. Now I just kind of wanted to pass out, skip the whole night, run back to Boston, and hide in my apartment.

I wore my own dress. It was a simple black A-line that I'd thrown into my suitcase last minute just in case. Just in case *what*, I hadn't known, and for sure I never would've imagined this. But I was thankful to have the dress now. Ash had sent a red one up from the warehouse that I'd found on my bed when I got back from Ojai, but I tossed it aside, just as I had done with Clara's offer of Angelica's old dress. Tonight, I wanted to be me. In my own clothes.

Nate drove me downtown—Ash had texted he was coming straight from work and would meet me there. And Nate was back to making small talk in the car. The air quality had turned bad late this afternoon, and a fine brown pillow of dust hung across the ocean at dusk. Nate chatted about this as we got stuck in traffic on the freeway on-ramp, and I murmured in response as if I were listening.

But I wasn't really. I was thinking about what Rose had said earlier, that Ash could make a woman *disappear*. That I was *out of my depth*. Had Angelica been out of her depth too? She had been at Brown with me. And Nate had told me the other night that she wasn't like Ash, at first. Until she was. *Glamorous but unhappy.* Ash had drawn her in and then, had she gotten caught, tangled, unable to get out?

I felt the car move forward, and we were finally on the freeway. Nate stopped talking. I glanced at him—his jaw was clenched, and his eyes were focused steadily on the road. He didn't say anything else until we got off the exit, and he pulled into the line of cars all waiting, I assumed, to let out their passengers at the red carpet in front of the LA Public Library.

"Why don't you text Ash?" Nate said. "Let him know we're in the line in the Tesla."

I pulled my phone from my purse and saw I had a text from Noah. I'm really sorry. Can we talk?

Dammit, Noah. Why couldn't he just leave me alone?

I swiped away from it and texted Ash instead.

"First time at LA LIT?" Nate asked, back to making small talk. I nodded. "Should be fun," he said.

Fun wasn't exactly what I was feeling. A nervous energy coursed through me as so many questions ran through my head. I thought about what Clara had said earlier, that she really wasn't sure what Ash was capable of. Was he a broken man or was he a murderer? Was the truth stranger than fiction or was the truth just simple and boring? Had Ash reached out to me because Angelica was reading *Becky* before she died or because he truly thought I was a *thief*?

"Angelica loved LA LIT. It was her favorite night of the year," Nate added.

I thought about what Charley had said, that Angelica had been rumored to have been shopping a book. And what Noah said, about her story in college. Angelica had been a writer, or at least, had wanted to be one. She had been here, once, just like me. With Ash. And now, she was gone.

"What did you think about Angelica's death?" I asked Nate, nervously pulling on the skin around my thumb.

Nate shook his head, like I'd confused him. "What did I think about it?"

"Did you think it was suspicious? The car accident, I mean. You're a professional driver. You must know a lot about cars. About the Asherwoods' cars."

Nate sighed and ran his thumb along the edge of the thick leather steering wheel. "The police investigated, declared it an accident," he said.

I nodded. "But what do *you* think?"

He didn't say anything for a moment, just kept running his thumb across the leather, back and forth, around and around. "She complained to me about her car a few days before it happened. She thought the steering felt off, and I told her I'd take it in to the dealer to get looked at."

I thought about what Clara had said earlier, half joking, about Ash cutting the brakes. Had she been hovering somewhere close to the truth? "The steering felt off?" I repeated.

He nodded. "I should've taken the car in as soon as she told me." He paused for a moment, and his thumb caught on the letter *T* of *Tesla* in the center of the wheel. "But Angelica complained about a lot of things."

My car door suddenly opened, and I jumped. I looked up, and there was Ash, dressed in a white tux. It felt impossible, but somehow he was even more gorgeous than usual, though I noticed there was a darkness in his eyes too. My whole body tensed up as he reached for my arm to pull me out of the car.

I hit the sidewalk and straightened my dress, trying to take a deep a breath as Ash tugged on my arm, then grabbed my hand, pulling me toward the red carpet that lined the street in front of the library. My heart pounded so hard, I was positive he could feel it beating down my arm, through my fingertips, as we hit the edge of the red carpet. It should have been pounding from excitement, from the idea of walking a red carpet, walking into LA LIT with him. But instead, all I could think of was what Nate had said in the car. *The steering felt off.*

"Smile, Olivia," Ash breathed into my hair. He stopped to pose, put his arm around me, pulled me tightly against his side. "At least act like you're enjoying this."

All around us, there were suddenly a million flash bulbs, the sounds of screams, laughter. I should have been scanning the crowd for celebrities, but instead, I felt numb, blinded by the flashes of light.

All the Little Lights.

The title of my first novel rattled around in my brain. It had come from a scene where my main character is driving high at night, careening the wrong way down a highway, and all she can process, all she can understand in that moment, are *all the little lights* coming toward her, blinding her. As the lights grow closer and closer, in the moment before she causes an accident, she has a sort of clarity, where it comes to her: this is all her fault.

But I had no clarity at all as Ash took my hand again and ushered me through the large double doors into the gala, and orbs of wayward light still floated across my retinas. I blinked a few times, but the lights lingered, and it took a few minutes before I could see clearly again.

The inside of LA LIT was packed, and there were so many

people, we didn't make it very far past the door until we got swept into a crowd.

Ash leaned down and tried to whisper something in my ear, but it was too loud. I couldn't hear him. All I could feel was his breath against my hair, my skin, and a chill came over me. I pulled back to rub my arms.

He mimed drinking, and I supposed he was asking if I wanted one. I nodded, and he mouthed that he would be right back.

I stood in the swirl of people and looked around. It felt more Hollywood here than publishing, and I struggled to find a familiar face in the crowd. Everyone was dressed up, achingly beautiful. Glamorous. What was it Nate had said about the Asherwoods? They were *glamorous but unhappy.* Diamonds sparkled everywhere, and I reached up self-consciously to touch my own tiny opal earrings that had once belonged to my mother. My black dress felt suddenly both too plain and too banal. I probably should've put on the red one Ash had sent up from the warehouse or taken Clara up on her offer to take Angelica's dress. *Angelica. Angelica loved LA LIT.*

Ash suddenly reappeared in front of me, holding out a glass of champagne. He had only one for me, nothing for himself. "Go ahead," he shouted to be heard above the crowd. "I'm driving."

I frowned. It felt unlike him not to drink. And besides, he always had Nate for situations like these. So what if his car was here too? Nate could come back for it later the way he had in Ojai. I thought again about that day I'd gotten so sick. I'd drunk Clara's coffee, but I'd also eaten his cardamom scone.

I pushed the champagne back toward him. "You should drink it," I shouted. "I'll call Nate later when we're ready to leave."

"Nate's busy," he shouted back, pushing the champagne back towards me.

I stared at him, stared at the drink. It bubbled and fizzed on top the way a good champagne should. But I thought about the number one rule from college: don't ever drink a beverage that was out of your sight for any period of time. And writer brain be damned. Even Clara said she wasn't sure what he was capable of. Maybe he *had* slipped something in my scone the other day.

"Did you drug me?" I asked Ash. The background noise flooded my ears, and the way Ash's face turned in confusion, I wasn't sure at first whether he'd heard me.

But then he frowned, grabbed the champagne flute from me, put it to his lips, and chugged the whole thing. "Satisfied?" he shouted back.

I just stared at him, but no, I wasn't feeling satisfied at all.

He set the empty glass down on a nearby table and then grabbed my arm. "We need to talk," he said. "Outside. It's too loud in here."

He pulled me back out through the crowd, the double doors, past the red carpet, and I breathed in damp, polluted air, more relieved to be out of the party than I'd ever been excited to be in it. Ash finally stopped walking in front of his Porsche, and he opened the passenger door and gestured for me to get in. I didn't move. A car was much scarier to me than the glamorously packed LA LIT, than the inside of Ash's empty glass house too. "We could talk out here," I said, crossing my arms in front of my chest.

Ash glanced around the street and shook his head. Laughter echoed nearby—I looked around too, and there were a lot of people out, still wandering toward the red carpet. Ash wanted to talk in his car for privacy, not to hurt me. At least, I was fairly certain that was the case. I hesitated for another moment, but then I got in.

Ash ran around to the driver's side, got in himself, but he thankfully didn't start the engine. He turned to face me instead. "What's going on? I thought we were getting along really well. Why would I want to drug you?" His words tumbled out in a rush, and he sounded hurt.

Maybe it had been a crazy thing to think. Maybe I'd just had a virus. "I'm sorry," I said, retreating to my natural propensity to apologize in times of stress.

"And why did you go talk to Rose?" His tone shifted. He sounded angrier now.

"I just…had some more questions for her," I said vaguely, squirming a little in my seat.

"Questions about Angelica?" he snapped.

I swallowed hard. "I don't know," I finally said, trying to sound noncommittal.

"What the fuck do you think you're doing, Olivia?" He let out a little noise of disgust and pounded the side of the steering wheel with his palm.

I jumped at the sound it made, remembering Noah musing about him being *unstable*. His hand hovered by the start button, and I had this sudden overwhelming sensation of being trapped. I was out of my depth; I should've insisted on talking in the street. Ash had just chugged a glass of champagne, and he could drive off now, speed away too fast, eventually veering off the edge of a cliff in Malibu, killing me in a car accident. The way Angelica died. The way my mother died. He was in the driver's seat, and I closed my eyes for a moment and forced myself to breathe slow, deep breaths.

"Why did you really bring me to Malibu, Ash?" I finally said. My heart rattled in my chest as I spoke, but I had to know the truth.

"You know why," he said.

"Angelica?" I said softly. He nodded. "Did she tell you I was a thief?" My voice caught on the word *thief*, and I had to gulp back a little sob as I said it. I was not going to cry. Not like this. In front of him.

"Aren't you a thief?" he said calmly.

And then the only thing I could think to say to him was the truth: "No. I'm not a thief." He raised his eyebrows. "*Rebecca* didn't belong to her, Ash," I continued. "*Becky* was mine. It was all mine. I wrote it because I loved *Rebecca* as a teenager. Because it was one of the only books that brought me comfort after my mother died. Because after my father remarried, I couldn't stop wondering how Rebecca would've seen the second Mrs. de Winter. It was *my* story. It was deeply personal. And it failed. And that failure is mine too." I was breathing so hard, and tears stung my eyes, but I blinked them back.

Becky was a failure. I was a failure. Whatever game Ash had been playing with me only compounded that, because the truth was, if *Becky* had been a runaway bestseller, or even a moderately decent seller, I never would've considered taking a write-for-hire job in the first place.

"Ange started writing again a few years ago," Ash said quietly. He moved his hand away from the start button, ran it through his hair, and sighed. "For a period of time, she was always writing, and I hated it. Because then some pretend world was on her mind and she didn't have the time or energy to focus on me, you know?" I fought the temptation to roll my eyes. He and Jack could've had quite the pity party together, as I remembered Jack saying almost those exact same words to me just before he left.

"Ash," I said softly. "None of that has anything to do with me."

He nodded. "After she died, I did find *Becky* on her nightstand like I told you." He paused for a moment. "But then, also, one of the last searches on her phone was you."

I felt chilled at the thought of Angelica researching me the way I'd tried to research her. Was it really because she thought I stole her story or because she wanted to know what became of an old classmate? Or because, as Ash had told me once, Angelica was obsessed with all things *Rebecca*? Like I was.

"Then I found the novel she'd been working on in her desk," Ash continued, and I thought about what Charley told me. Angelica had been shopping a book proposal before she died. Maybe it wasn't a celebrity memoir at all, but a novel? "I read them both," Ash was saying now. "Your book and hers. And they're essentially the same story." He paused. "Two writers have the same idea, and one steals it from the other, publishes it first. Whose story is it?" I swallowed hard, remembering how he'd said something very similar at dinner the other night, as he was arguing with me about Daphne and Emilia. But now it was clear that what he'd really been arguing about was Angelica and me. "She left a Post-it on your book that made it abundantly clear you'd stolen it. It was her story, her life. Our life. And you even have a line about me in your book."

"What?" I had no idea what he was talking about.

"The very first line: 'Becky stood staring at the house of ash, where her life had once existed.' House of *Ash*. That's me."

It was so weird to hear my words, my familiar first line, in his voice. To hear them rattle with sarcasm and annoyance in a way that made them feel completely surreal. I shook my head. "No, that's not you. *Ash* because the house burns down in *Rebecca*." My voice shook with anger as I spoke now. "What does fire leave behind? *Ash*."

"So, I'm a metaphor?" Ash frowned.

I shook my head again. He wasn't a metaphor. My book, that line, had nothing to do with him. Or Angelica. And I still didn't understand why Ash brought me here, why he lied, and what he thought he could possibly accomplish. "But even if you did think that line was about you, and even if you thought I was a thief, why not just sue me? Why go to all this trouble to bring me to Malibu under false pretenses?"

"Lawyers make things too complicated." Right, like he would've needed proof that any of what he just said was true. "It unnerved me to know you'd stolen something from Ange, something personal that belonged to her. To us. To know that it was the last thing she'd been thinking about before she died."

"But I didn't steal Angelica's story from college," I emphasized again. "I don't even remember ever reading it."

He ignored me and kept talking. "And that line about Ash. I couldn't let that go. You already knew me, but I knew nothing about you. I had to meet you and see what you were like. See if I had anything to worry about going forward."

"Worry about?" What could a man like Ash possibly have to worry about from a person like me?

"Angelica died. Just like Becky did in your novel. And you made the husband a murderer."

"But Maxim *is* a murderer in *Rebecca*."

"Debatable," Ash said. "Is it really murder if someone wants you to kill them?" His words were so cold, they crept across my skin. And suddenly all I wanted to do was to get out of the car. I reached for the door handle, but Ash was faster, and he hit the lock button first. "We're not done talking," he said calmly.

Rose's and Noah's words both echoed in head. I was out of my depth. And Ash might just be unstable enough to drive off and crash this car just to teach me some crazy lesson.

"Anyway, none of that matters now," Ash continued, his voice still calm.

It mattered to me, but I couldn't interject that before he kept talking.

"As soon as I met you, everything changed. You're smart and pretty and funny, and you weren't going to do anything to hurt me. No, just the opposite. You needed me to rescue you. Just the way Ange did when I first met her."

I shook my head. Rescuing me and rescuing my career weren't one and the same. I didn't need any man to rescue me, and definitely not one who was lying to me to do it.

He reached across the seat and grabbed my hand. I tried

to yank out of his grasp, but he wouldn't let me go. "Then I started to see everything differently. It almost felt like you were a part of Ange that was still here. And when I was with you, she felt alive again."

His words were ice, and goose bumps pricked my bare arms.

"So Emilia's story," I finally managed to say. "Her journals? *Rebecca?* It was all a lie."

He shook his head. "No, she and Rose did go to school with Daphne. Angelica figured that out, like I told you. And then I really did get her journals after my grandfather died. They were in a box in my attic for years. When you asked to see them after you arrived, I went to the attic to bring them down, but the box was missing."

"I don't believe you," I said. "If you'd actually shown me the journals, you would've exposed your own lie. Her story had nothing to do with *Rebecca.*"

"Didn't it?" he asked. "Young woman married to a rich older man…"

"That's not what *Rebecca* is about. You're missing the whole point." But my voice faltered a little. I wondered what would've happened if he'd just shown me the journals. Would I have bought into all of it? Seen what he told me was there instead of what was really there? Would I have tricked myself into believing they were *Rebecca,* just because he was as intoxicating as hell, and he said they were?

"Anyway, I swear on Rose's life this much is true. I went to the attic to get them for you after you asked, but the box really was gone. I haven't been able to figure out what happened to them." He reached for my arm again, but I was quicker at pulling away this time. "Olivia." He said my name softly. "If you think about it, I didn't really even lie."

But even that was a lie. He'd lied so much! All that stuff about Emilia being the true author of *Rebecca?* And Rebecca Asherwood—his grandfather's supposed first wife—who didn't exist. And were the journals in French or had he just said that to stall for time? Ash's face looked so sincere now, it was like he couldn't even remember or care about half the lies he'd told me.

"Wait—what about that manuscript you gave me yesterday that you said was a translation of her journals? If what you're saying now is true, that makes no sense."

He gave a sort of sheepish shrug. "I paid someone to write that quickly when you wouldn't stop asking so many questions about her journals." He paused for a minute. "But it's what her journals *could've* said, if I had found them."

"Ash, can you not see how that's a lie?" He stared at me, but didn't say anything. "The truth is, you brought me all the way out here just to mess with me. But I'm not a fucking toy. I'm a person. I'm a fiction writer—"

"I didn't expect to like you so much." He cut me off. As if that made everything better.

"Let go of me, and unlock the door," I said as calmly as I could.

But instead of letting go, Ash squeezed my hand. "Olivia, don't go yet," he pleaded. "I'll pay you double what I offered before. And you can write whatever you want." He paused for a moment and tilted his head, his deep blue eyes as intense as always, locked now on my face, like it was the only thing he could see. "Just stay with me for a little longer, while you write. It's been so nice to have you in the house. You can't leave now. Please, just say you'll stay?"

It would be so easy to do what Ash was asking, to stay in the car. To stay at his house. To walk back into LA LIT on his arm. To take the time to write a new novel without money worries or all the pressure that it would have to be a bestseller. It would be easy to hand my life and my body and my whole self and my writing career over to him. And then, money and success would follow, just like Charley said they would. It would all be so easy.

But it wasn't what I wanted. I'd told Noah that I could play Ash's game too, but maybe the only way to win was not to play at all anymore. "No," I said.

"No?" Ash echoed me, like it was a word he couldn't even comprehend.

I finally yanked my hand away from his and tugged on the door handle. "Let me out of the car," I said.

"Olivia." Ash said my name so quietly, so calmly, that I already knew the sound of his voice would haunt me, even if I made it out of his car, away from Malibu. "I won't take no for answer."

What is he capable of? Would he ruin my career? Trash my life? That was already done and done on my own. Or would he actually try to hurt me? I heard Rose's voice in my head. *Magicians saw beautiful women in half or make them disappear.* But I didn't believe Ash was a magician. He was a liar. And he was a little boy who threw a tantrum when he didn't get what he wanted. And maybe, he was still a grieving husband too. Was a man who became so obsessed with what his dead wife left behind—on her phone, in her desk, on her nightstand—the same kind of man who was capable of murdering her? In this moment, I didn't think so.

"You have to let me go, Ash," I said firmly.

He stared at me for another moment, but then he finally hit a button on his door, and I heard the click of the lock popping open.

My hands were shaking, but I pulled on the handle again. The door opened, and I got out and ran into the street. I could still see all the little lights flashing by the red carpet up ahead, but now they were no longer blinding me.

And instead of walking toward them, back to LA LIT, I crossed the street and walked away from the lights altogether.

Excerpt from *The Wife*

I stumble across the journals by accident.

My husband commissions a portrait of me, and I'm looking for the dress I want to wear for the sitting. It had been made especially for me by my friend Benj, an up-and-coming designer, to wear to LA LIT the year before. My husband had commented that the bust looked like gloved hands across my breasts, and I'd spat back that Benj had been inspired by his own hands as he'd been dreaming up the design one morning in bed, beside me.

It was such a stupid lie, meant only to cut my husband—Benj has a longtime boyfriend—but my husband was so blinded by jealousy he'd stolen the dress out of my closet one night while I was sleeping and had hidden it somewhere. "When you find it, you can wear it again." He'd smirked at me over breakfast the following morning.

In response, I'd gone and thrown his car key in the ocean while he was on a conference call. Then, over dinner, I'd told him with a coy smile that I'd misplaced it. Cars meant nothing to my husband. Keys could be remade. He had another one by the end of the week.

Now I am determined to find that dress for my portrait, certain it's in the house. The Pacific is too much effort for my husband. He doesn't like the feel of sand between his toes.

I spend a full afternoon crawling through closets, but I am victorious at last, as I illuminate the dark and musty attic crawlspace with the flashlight on my phone. It shines on the beautiful white fabric of my dress! I pull a spider web off the gloved bodice and curse my husband. But as I lift the dress, my eye catches on the box underneath simply labeled: Emilia.

Emilia?

Her name is familiar, but foreign too. An old lover, a family member? I'd heard it before, but I can't place it at first.

I drag both my dress and the box down the steps, where I tell my cousin to take the dress to be cleaned before my sitting tomorrow, with not a single word about it to my husband.

"Are you sure you want to wear this one?" she questions me. The gall of her to question me. "You have so many others."

"Yes, I'm sure." I glare at her.

A little noise escapes from her chest that reminds me of the squawking sound a seagull makes as it dives headfirst into a wave. It is jealousy and it is exasperation. As if to say, he loves you, he wants you, and this is how you repay him?

"I mean it," I tell her. "Not a word."

She frowns but leaves with the dress, and I take the Emilia box to my writing room.

Inside is a pile of journals, dated from the 1930s, and as I begin to read, I remember exactly who Emilia was: my husband's biological grandmother. She'd died when his father was very young, and he'd never known her. But then, inside these brittle yellowing pages, her life unfolds before me.

A life of a woman married into this family. So much like me, but nothing like me at all. Emilia was young and naive and barely spoke any English when she moved to Malibu from France and married. Her husband was devoted to her, and after a few years, his devotion suffocated her, isolated her, as he stashed her away up at Malibu Lake. Eventually, she could only remember to breathe again when she escaped at night, and found solace in the arms of a groundskeeper named Teddy.

Teddy?

From there Emilia detailed her affair with Teddy and her subse-

quent pregnancy, a baby I assume must be my husband's father as I do the math with the dates. This delicious realization hits me as I'm sitting there on the floor.

My husband isn't the man he thinks he is or says he is. My husband isn't even truly a real part of this wealthy family, is he?

I start to laugh, and then I laugh so hard I can't stop.

"What are you doing?" my cousin asks as she walks back into my room. I look up, and outside it has grown mostly dark. But I've been too riveted to notice. "And why is it so dark in here?" She flips on the light. It floods my eyes, and it makes me laugh even harder. "What's so funny?" she asks.

"I never would've found this if he hadn't hidden my dress." That thought is so bone-shakingly hysterical that I keep laughing, and tears run down my face.

"Are you all right?" my cousin says, sitting down on the floor behind me, reaching for my arm to hold on to me, as if she believes I've become unmoored in her absence. "I'm worried about you." Concern edges her voice, and I hate that she still cares so much about me.

"This is the story I'm going to tell," I say, holding up Emilia's journal. "This is the story I was meant to write," I tell her.

This is the story that will destroy him.

FORTY-ONE

I had Noah's address in my phone from the return address on the last birthday card he'd sent me, probably about three years ago at this point, so as I put it into Lyft, I just hoped he still lived there. I was afraid if I called or texted him, I'd lose my nerve or he'd tell me not to come, and neither one of those felt like good options.

The driver let me off in front of a three-story apartment building in Westwood. It had no elevator, Noah lived in 304—on the third floor—and by the time I made it up there in my dress and heels, I was out of breath and sweating, and I was sure my hair was a frizzy mess. But there was no turning back now. Literally. The Lyft driver was long gone, all my stuff was trapped at Ash's, and my heart actually physically hurt when I thought about the awful phone conversation Noah and I had had earlier this afternoon. I couldn't lose him again, not now after just getting him back. If one good thing came out of the last week, it wasn't a revival of my writing career, but instead a revival of my relationship with Noah.

I reached up to knock, but suddenly the door swung open

before I could even hit it with my fist. Noah stood on the other side, dressed in a full black tux, his wavy hair gelled back, so I could see his entire face clearly, even the way his expression immediately softened when he processed that I was standing here, on his doorstep. "Livvy." He said my name so sweetly that I suddenly felt like I was going to cry again.

"Noah." I said his name back, and I put my hand on his arm, running my finger down the smooth sleeve of his tux jacket. "I'm interrupting something. I'm sorry. I should've called." I was embarrassed by this grand sweeping notion I'd had in my head, of this dramatic scene where I just showed up here, unannounced. Classic writer brain.

"No." He shook his head and picked up my hand gently, holding on to it, bringing me inside his apartment. It felt opposite in every way to how Ash had just grabbed me and dragged me down the street to his car. "Come, sit down." Noah led me to the beat-up couch that could've quite possibly been a relic from college, sat down next to me, but he still didn't let go of my hand.

"But you're all dressed up," I said. "You were just about to go out."

"Livvy," he said. "I was dressed up to go to LA LIT. To find you."

I started to laugh, and for a minute, I couldn't stop. It was a tangle of nerves and relief. And understanding that it was the right thing to walk away from Ash, to come here, to show up, just like this. "So let me get this straight," I said when I finally stopped laughing. "After all these years, we both could be at LA LIT right now, and yet we're sitting here on your couch instead?"

Noah started laughing too, and then he pulled me into a hug, and my head hit his chest, and every emotion I'd been trying not to feel for months, for years, hit me all at once: happiness, sadness, anxiety, anger, and relief too. But suddenly I wanted to feel them. I wanted to feel everything. I remembered that it was okay to feel with Noah.

"I'm so sorry," I said, finally forcing myself to let go of him after a few minutes of holding on too tight. "You were right. No more gorgeous, self-centered men. And I won't run to you for help anymore. I promise. I came here to say that. And to apologize in person. And I hope you'll forgive me."

"No," he said quickly.

"No? You won't accept my apology?"

"No, I want you to run to me for help." He paused, reached up, and tucked a wayward curl behind my ear. "I mean, I don't want you to get yourself in situations where you need help. But I want to be there for you if you do. All the time. I want to be the person you call when you need something. I've always wanted to be that person for you." His hand had moved from my hair to linger on my cheek, and I suddenly noticed how green his eyes looked in this light, and with his hair back this way. "I hated it when you were with Jack," he added. "And I hated it even more this last week when you were with that rich Asherwood asshole."

"I wasn't with Ash," I clarified. Well, maybe for one weird hour, but that barely even counted. "Not really," I added softly.

Maybe I had made a mistake by coming to Malibu, by letting myself get sucked in by Ash, and by thinking something like that, someone like him, was what I needed. But I hadn't let it define me for very long. I was feeling pretty good about myself for getting out of Ash's car, refusing his offer to stay in Malibu and write whatever I wanted. And then suddenly, I remembered Charley. Shit.

"Well, the good news is I am completely done with Ash," I said. I felt a little nauseous as I digested the bad news myself. And maybe once Noah fully understood and believed it, it would change everything he'd ever thought and felt about me too. We became friends as writers, were pulled apart as writers, and were brought back together again as writers. What if I wasn't a writer anymore? "The bad news is," I finally added, "my writing career is definitely over."

"No, Livvy. It's not over." His thumb trailed down my cheek, and then my arm, and then he picked up my hand gently again, holding it between his own.

"It really is, Noah. I'm serious. Charley is going to drop me."

"So?"

"So, do you know how hard it is to get an agent?"

"I do," Noah said. Okay, fair enough. He did. "But look, Livvy, you'll write another book. You're a writer. That's what we do. And then you'll get another agent if you need to." I frowned, unconvinced. "And you know what, fuck the Asherwood stores guy and his crazy story he made you sign an NDA for. No one wants to read that anyway."

I shook my head—obviously, many people would want to read that. Hence Charley's obsession with it. But I couldn't help but smile a little bit at his attempt to make me feel better. When Noah said I was a writer, I almost thought it was true again. "I wish I could believe all of this half as much as you do," I told him.

"Come on, Livvy. This one weird thing happened. You can't just give up on writing because of one thing."

"One weird thing, which followed the absolutely abysmal sales of my second novel and no publisher even wanting my third novel." I finally put it all out there, the whole truth. All my failures as a writer naked before him.

Noah shrugged, unfazed. "My first two novels didn't sell, and my first agent dumped me. You know that. This whole writing thing isn't for the faint of heart." I smiled again. Not because Noah had also faced failure, but because I forgot how nice it was to be with someone who just completely understood everything about me. "You know what you should do?" Noah was saying now. "You should use this. What did our writing professors always say in college? *Write what you know.*"

"And we knew nothing back then. So it was the dumbest advice ever."

"Yeah, but now here you are. You know some crazy shit. Use it for your next novel."

"What?" I laughed a little. "Ash? No way." I didn't want to think about Ash ever again, much less write a novel about him. I kind of wanted to pretend that this whole strange week had never happened.

"Forget about the Asherwood stores dude. But write about a ghostwriter who gets tangled up with a bizarre story she's hired to write." He paused and squeezed my hand.

For some reason I thought again about Angelica, about the way she was frozen in that terrifying portrait in Ash's guest room, and the way she had started off at Brown like me, but then, her glamorous and unhappy life had been cut so short. I was always drawn to writing about troubled women. Maybe Noah was onto something.

"And then promise me," Noah added, "that I'm the first one who gets to read your draft."

Excerpt from *The Wife*

Her story is my story, and my story is her story.

The men in this family, they trap, and then there is no escape, no way out. Except death.

Only my husband's grandfather's second wife got out alive, and only she understands me. But she hates it when I complain to her about my husband. She calls me weak, and she will neither confirm nor deny what was written in the journals.

"It was all so long ago," she says. "Who cares about any of that?" I give her a look. Well, my husband might care. Everything he is is wrapped up in his name. Being a part of this family. She grabs onto my sleeve: "Don't you dare ever tell him."

Or what? She's ninety-three years old and mostly confined to her wheelchair in a nursing home. I shake off her hand with a small laugh.

The journals, I realize after that, are my answer to everything. When I write the book about them, about what she wrote, about the fact that my husband is a fraud, it will utterly eviscerate him.

And then, you see. That's exactly why he kills me.

The day I die, I drive up to Malibu Lake with my cousin and take the journals with me to poke around a little. I ask the old woman housekeeper if she's ever heard of Teddy, the former groundskeeper, and she shakes her head, seeming genuinely confused. A part of me wonders if Teddy was real, or if Emilia was a writer too? What is a trapped woman to do but escape through her words on the page? They let her out, they let her go. Writing sets her free.

I'm not a wife when I'm a writer. I'm not a captive when I tell a story. This story is truth, but it's fiction too.

In Emilia's last journal entry, she wrote of fire. She dreamt of fire the way I have. She wanted it to heat, to destroy, to incinerate every piece of her miserable life.

I find myself walking around Malibu Lake, thinking of her. She is me and I am she. Did she set this whole place on fire, or was the fire truly an accident, a tragedy like the rest of her life?

I circle the path around the lake, thinking of her words, of my words, and then suddenly there my husband is, standing in front of me, blocking my way.

My heartbeat quickens as he grabs my wrists. I try to shake myself free, but he won't let me go. He holds too tight, and it hurts. "What are you doing here?" I demand.

"I could ask you the same question?" He frowns and grips me tighter.

He won't let go. He is never going to let go.

He stares at me so fiercely that I wonder if he's spoken to his step-grandmother in the nursing home, if he knows what I told her about Teddy. Or maybe he's always known?

But does he understand it now, the power I'll have if I write it down, if I tell the whole world? His face is so dark, it seems to cast a shadow over the entire lake, and then I know one thing for sure. He will destroy me if I don't destroy him first.

I yank my arm harder, finally pulling free. "I'm going back home," I say. "And don't try and follow me. You should spend the night up here, alone."

"Babe," he calls after me—and this will be the last thing he ever says to me. "Be careful driving."

FORTY-TWO

Noah really wanted me to stay out in LA with him, but I told him I had to go back to Boston. There was the matter of my apartment and all my things. And then there was my sister and my dad in Connecticut too. The crazy week I spent in Malibu made me miss and long for my down-to-earth family. And I knew I needed to do better with them. Try harder. Noah was right about so much, not the least of which was that I had been sabotaging myself and my relationships for years. I had been my own worst enemy. And I was done with that version of Olivia.

The day after LA LIT, I booked the red-eye back to Boston, and I texted Clara and asked her to let me know once Ash left for work so I could come get my things. She said he'd confined himself to his bedroom and was *refusing to come out*. I couldn't tell if that was meant to make me feel bad or relieved that I'd left him in his car at the gala, but then she offered to pack up my stuff and meet me for coffee so I didn't even have to go back to his house. I thanked her and took her up on it.

"I don't know what happened last night," Clara said as she

wheeled my roller bag onto the Starbucks patio by Noah's apartment and sat down across from me. "But whatever you did, it messed with him more than the dress would've." Her words crackled in the cool morning air, sounding almost diabolical. I still wasn't sure whether Clara hated Ash or loved him, and her tone now didn't exactly clarify that. Maybe it was a little bit of both.

"I didn't *do* anything," I said firmly. "I called him out on his bullshit and then left him at LA LIT."

"Well." Clara flipped her hair behind her shoulders. "Good for you. Not too many people do that." Whether she meant calling him out or walking away, I couldn't tell.

"I'm sorry I couldn't help you find your cousin," I told her. And I meant it. Maybe I'd come to Malibu for Emilia, but eventually I'd stayed for Angelica and Bex. It did bother me to be leaving now without closure, but I supposed that was where my fiction writing would come in. Writing stories always gave me answers and endings that didn't exist in real life.

"It's not your family," Clara said, sounding weirdly possessive. But it fit how Clara had treated me like an intruder all along. "I mean." Her voice softened. "You don't have anything to feel sorry for."

But I did truly feel sorry for her. Even spending a week caught up in the Asherwood world had started to make me feel like I was losing my mind. I couldn't imagine what years must've been like for Angelica, or for her cousin Bex, who'd been living there with her. Or God, poor Clara, working as Ash's housekeeper for the last year.

"Look," I told her. "I know you don't like me very much. But can I give you a piece of advice, for whatever it's worth?" Her face was blank, and it was hard to read her expression, whether her eyes were channeling hate or curiosity about what I was going to say. So I continued talking: "Your cousin isn't in that house. You're not going to find her working for Ash, as his housekeeper."

Last night, I'd decided that Ash had been too obsessed with Angelica to murder her. But now, face-to-face with Clara again, in the light of day, I wasn't feeling as sure. So I told Clara what Nate had told me, about Angelica complaining about the steering in her car before she died.

"The steering? You really think Ash did something to her car?" Clara asked, raising her eyebrows.

"I'm just saying, I don't want you to get hurt," I finally said. "I'd get the hell out of that house if I were you."

Clara offered me a tight-lipped smile in response, and then stood and lowered her sunglasses over her eyes, getting ready to leave. "You're sweet to worry about me," she said. "But don't. I know exactly what I'm doing; I have everything under control." Her voice was cool and steady.

It was funny, I remembered saying almost those exact words to Noah a few days ago in my hotel bar, and I had the urge to grab Clara, to tell her it was impossible to have everything under control with a man like Ash. But even if we weren't enemies, we weren't exactly friends either.

So I didn't. I just sat there and watched her go, her heels clicking confidently against the pavement, as she walked away.

Charley and I didn't exactly break up when I called her the next morning and told her that I'd come home empty-handed, given up on the Asherwood project altogether. But Charley did mention something about us *taking a break*, and maybe *touching base on another project down the line*. I understood that she would probably be letting all my calls go to voice-mail from now on pretty much no matter what.

"It's such a shame you couldn't make this work, Olivia."

"He was lying about everything," I emphasized to her.

"When you're a ghostwriter, it's all a lie." Charley sighed, and I knew even if I tried to explain it to her until I turned blue, she wouldn't ever truly understand it. I felt words in my soul; Charley saw them as dollar signs. I couldn't write what I couldn't understand or feel, what I couldn't love, and definitely what I couldn't trust. No matter how much someone would pay me.

I knew I had to believe in what Noah told me. There were other books for me to write and other agents to sell them. "Take care of yourself, Olivia," Charley finally said.

"Yeah," I said softly into the phone, and I realized saying goodbye to her felt harder than saying goodbye to Jack. "You too."

And somehow six months floated by.

Spring turned to summer turned to fall. My niece, Lily, turned five, and I went to her birthday party in May. I even joined my dad and Shawna and Suzy and Lily in Cape Cod for a weekend in July, and I didn't hate it.

I got a job working at a coffee shop down the street from my apartment, and it paid me enough to pay my rent and gave me the time to write. I'd taken Noah's advice and had started a novel about a write-for-hire job gone wrong when the writer gets tangled up in a murder mystery. It was a little bit inspired by Angelica, but also Clara and Ash. It was a modern-day gothic suspense novel, and it might even also turn out to be a love story. I hadn't totally decided yet. It was going slowly. But at least it was going, which was better than where I'd been last fall.

Noah and I spent hours on FaceTime, talking about writing and life and stupid stuff too. We binged Netflix together until 3:00 a.m. for me (midnight for him) since he had to get up and still teach classes on weekdays, and we texted each other every last thought and every last emoji. And then in August, Noah emailed me his manuscript for feedback, and I stayed up all night reading it. Even though I assured him it was literally the best mystery novel ever written, I then nitpicked the crap out of it, like I had with his stuff back in college.

After he incorporated my notes into his draft, his agent sold it, and the yet-to-be-written sequel, in a five-way auction for a seven-figure advance. And Noah claimed it was my feedback that got the novel to auction level.

"Okay," I said to him over FaceTime as we both drank champagne, toasting across the country to celebrate. "I'll take half your advance, then."

"Ha, yeah, right." He took a sip of his champagne and then moved in closer to his phone as if he were studying my face. Noah had a way of doing this—even over FaceTime, I could tell he was watching me, writing me in his head. Exactly what he was writing, though, I wasn't sure. He was harder to read than he used to be, and definitely harder to read over Face-Time. "I would like to buy you something, though," Noah said casually.

"You don't have to buy me anything. I was joking!"

Noah nodded. "Well, it's a present for me too." He paused for a few seconds and just stared at me. Then he said, "Let me buy you a plane ticket to come out here and visit me next week. I want to have a drink with you in person to celebrate. Somewhere really fancy."

I remembered that was Noah's description of Malibu: *fancy*. And suddenly I thought about the Pacific Ocean, the cliffs of Malibu, Ash and his house, and my stomach started to hurt. "I don't know," I said. "I have to work."

Noah frowned, and he looked so truly devastated at the thought that I might reject his offer that I looked away from my phone for a second. "Can't anyone cover your shifts?" he asked.

"Yeah…probably," I said slowly, still not able to look at his face.

"So, you'll come?" His voice warmed me with its hopefulness. It was the thought of being in the vicinity of Malibu again that made me hesitate. Not Noah. I wanted to see Noah, and not just through a screen anymore. But I had to put Malibu and Ash in the past; I couldn't let him dictate my future.

"Yeah," I finally said to Noah. "I'll come."

FORTY-THREE

I was so happy to see Noah waiting for me at baggage claim
that I forgot to be nervous about being back in LA. It was a
big city, and I tried to reason with myself that I wouldn't just
run into Ash. Nor did I plan to go anywhere near Malibu
when I was here. But I still wasn't able to calm myself down
on the flight—I'd spent the first two hours trying to read
the same paragraph, until I finally gave up, ordered a glass
of wine, and lulled myself into a troubled half sleep instead.

But then there Noah was, sitting on the edge of a baggage
carousel, his elbows resting easily on his knees as he scrolled
through his phone. I stopped walking and just stared at him
for a moment. I'd seen him probably a thousand times on
FaceTime these past six months, but it was so much better
seeing him just there, just across the room, knowing I was
about to hug him. I thought about his amazing book sale,
and it hit me that he was about to become a big fucking deal.
But here he was, still just my Noah from college. Looking
as calm and easygoing in his jeans and his UCLA sweatshirt
as he always had.

He suddenly looked up, saw me, and a giant smile spread across his face as he stood and waved, then came toward me in a few giant strides. "Livvy!" His arms were already around me as he said my name, and my cheek hit his chest. I gripped him tightly, never wanting to let go. "You're here," he said into my hair. He reached a hand up and tugged gently on the end of a curl. Then took a step back and looked at me. "You're really here."

"And you're extremely good with words," I teased him. "Like definitely good enough to write some words worth a million dollars."

He laughed and took the handle of my roller bag with one hand, my hand with his other. "Come on, I'm illegally parked."

I held on to him, running through baggage claim, toward the glass doors. "You should've just waited in the car and circled," I said.

"No, I wanted that moment."

"What moment?"

"That moment when I saw you coming down the escalator. And then our eyes would meet, and I'd get up and run to you."

I started laughing. "You were totally looking at your phone when I came down the escalator."

Noah shrugged sheepishly as we reached his car. He was parked at the curb, emergency flashers on, and it appeared he hadn't yet gotten a ticket. He quickly popped the trunk to throw my suitcase in, then opened the passenger door for me. As he pulled away from the curb, I heard him exhale a little. And I wasn't sure whether it was about not getting a ticket, or that I was here, sitting in the car next to him, with him, at last.

Two hours later, after I'd showered and changed at Noah's apartment, we were sitting across from each other at an outdoor table at what Noah said was one of his favorite spots in Santa Monica. The October air chilled, and a thick gray layer of fog dropped over the Pacific, reminding me too much of those nights out on Ash's veranda. But Santa Monica felt altogether different than Malibu, more real and more alive, and in the distance, the lights from the pier illuminated the gray sky.

We ordered a bottle of Nebbiolo—a ridiculously expensive bottle that Noah insisted we get to celebrate his book deal—and a plate of oysters to share.

"Are you warm enough?" Noah asked, offering me his jacket.

"I'm fine," I told him. "Really." I didn't mind the feel of the cool sea air on my skin, and then Noah reached across the table for my hand, warming me anyway.

"I need to tell you something," Noah said. "And I didn't want to say it over FaceTime, so I'm glad you're finally here, because I need to tell you face-to-face."

He suddenly sounded and looked too serious, very un-Noah. It worried me. "Are you okay?" I asked him.

"Yeah." He paused for a second, clasping my hand in between both of his, rubbing his thumbs gently across my knuckles. "But the thing is, I've been wanting to tell you something for a very long time. And every time I've gone to tell you, starting all the way back in college, something else has happened and I haven't been able to."

As if on cue, my phone started buzzing against the table. I glanced at it, and Charley's name lit up the screen. *Charley?* I hadn't spoken to her since the write-for-hire project fell through, and I'd been pretty sure we were never going to speak again. Why would she be calling me now?

"That's weird," I said. "It's Charley."

I looked up, and he was staring at me so intensely, and I remembered what he'd just been saying, that he'd been trying to tell me something but kept getting interrupted. "Sorry," I said. I tapped to reject the call. "I can let it go to voicemail. I can't imagine it's anything important."

Noah exhaled, as if he'd been holding his breath for days. Or years. "I'm in love with you, and I want to be with you." He said the words so quickly they tumbled out in a rush, nearly unintelligible.

"What?" I asked. Partly, I wasn't sure I'd heard him right. And partly I just wanted him to say it again. *I'm in love with you.*

"I've been trying to tell you how I've felt since college, and the universe never let me. Your mom died and then you found Jack, and then you published a book, and then..." His voice trailed off for a moment. I thought of all the stupid mistakes I'd made in those years, and I realized not being with Noah all that time was probably the biggest one. "And I kept think- ing," Noah was saying now, "that maybe that meant we just weren't meant to be together. Maybe the universe kept stop- ping me from telling you how I felt for a reason. But screw the universe! I don't want to be apart from you anymore. I had to tell you. So there it is. I love you. I'm in love with you, Livvy."

He had been trying to tell me how he felt, all this time? "Since college?" I repeated.

He nodded and gave me a kind of sheepish look, like when I said it so simply like that, he couldn't believe he'd kept it in for ten whole years.

"Noah." I squeezed his hand. "I wish you'd told me back then, but maybe it's better that you didn't."

His face fell, and he cast his eyes down. "Why? Because you don't feel the same way?"

I shook my head. "No, because I would've definitely fucked it all up back then. I was a mess senior year, remember? And I was arguably also a mess when *All the Little Lights* was pub- lished."

"And now?" He raised his eyebrows a little, and if we

weren't having this particular conversation, I was pretty sure he'd be teasing me about what a mess I'd been six months ago in Malibu too. And it occurred to me that maybe he loved me because of all that, not in spite of it. Maybe he just loved me for me. Mess and all.

"Now," I said, squeezing his hand again, "I want to be with you too."

If I were going to write the scene that happened next between me and Noah, to include in my loosely-based-on-real-life ghostwriting novel, it would be the hottest sex scene I'd ever written. But some things were too personal to even try and fictionalize them.

Noah knew me better than anyone had ever known me, and when his hands were tracing on my bare skin, it felt like they already understood every inch of me, every exact right way to touch me. He was perfectly attuned to every small move and every tiny noise I made, and he knew exactly where to touch and how to linger.

As I was just about to fall asleep, hours later, naked and still lying half on top of him, his hands running lazily through my curls, I drifted off with the thought that I had never felt more satisfied and more comfortable at the same time in my entire life.

Until, sometime just before dawn, I dreamt I went to Malibu again.

I was walking there on the beach below Ash's house. Flames and smoke leapt from the grill area, and Clara was screaming.

Just come back, Ash was yelling to her, or to me. *I'm not going to hurt you. I just want to help you.*

And I knew he was lying, he was a lying, lying, liar, but I walked toward him, toward the fire anyway. I felt the heat burning up my skin, but I couldn't stop myself.

I woke up sweating and shaking. But my limbs were still

entwined with Noah's, who was certainly dreaming of something much better, if the half smile on his face was any indication. And I told myself again, Malibu, Ash, all of it, were nothing to me now except a bad dream.

But then suddenly I remembered: Charley.

FORTY-FOUR

Voicemail from Charley Bingham, 5:45 p.m. October 2nd:

Olivia, call me as soon as you get this message. It's extremely urgent.

I was sitting on the edge of Noah's bed, and had replayed Charley's message three times, still unsure what to make of it, when Noah finally woke up.

"Hey." He reached for my bare shoulder, gently pulling me back down on the bed towards him. "It's early. Come back and lie with me."

It was just after seven in LA, which meant it was after ten in New York. I played the message for Noah, now hearing it myself for a fourth time, and then he asked me if I'd called her back. "Not yet," I said. "What could she possibly want? We're not really even working together anymore." God, I hoped it wasn't another work-for-hire opportunity. But why would it be? She'd clearly been upset with me over the way the last one had turned out.

"Just go call her," Noah said, sitting up, kissing my shoulder gently. "It's probably nothing."

I thought again about my dream, and it felt like a weird premonition, like I already knew that Charley had something to say about Ash, and that I wasn't going to like it, whatever it was.

"Olivia," Charley's voice sounded bright, normal, when she answered the phone on the second ring. "How have you been?"

"Pretty good," I said, and I realized as I said it that it was actually true. I was actually *very good*, if we were just talking about my last twelve hours and my current situation with Noah.

"Oh, great. Well, listen, I don't want to beat around the bush, but I heard some news yesterday, and I didn't want you to be blindsided by it."

I wasn't sure why it hadn't occurred to me before this very moment, but I suddenly felt certain she was about to tell me she'd brought in another one of her clients to work with Ash, and that writer, whoever she was, had written whatever Ash wanted her to, and they'd sold his book for a million dollars. I sighed, bracing myself. "I appreciate the heads-up," I said.

"Well, the thing is…" She stumbled for a second, which was completely unlike her. "Apparently there's a novel coming out in the spring called *The Wife* by a debut novelist, Bari Elizabeth Xavier. Pseudonym, of course, and they're keeping the identity of the real author hush-hush. But it supposedly tells the story of Henry Asherwood's wife and makes a lot of outrageous claims under the guise of fiction."

"Wait," I stopped her, confused, because this wasn't at all what I'd been expecting her to say. "His wife? You mean Angelica?"

"The one who died in the car accident? Or not..." Charley added.

I still hadn't forgotten that whole Reddit thread that swore Angelica was still alive, walking the beach in Malibu. *The truth was stranger than fiction.* "What do you mean *or not*?" I asked her.

"Well, like I said...the publisher won't say who actually wrote the book. But there's a lot of theories already swirling around the industry. The novel is told from the wife's point of view. Makes a lot batshit claims about the Asherwood guy I set you up to work with." Was that supposed to make me feel vindicated? Because it didn't. I felt like I was about to throw up. "But anyway, why I called is that it also mentions you."

"Me?"

"I mean, not by name. But she writes about *Becky*—also not by name. But apparently, it's very clearly you from the descriptions. They launched the book in-house yesterday, and my phone was ringing off the hook."

"But someone can't just write a novel and include real people in it," I said. "Isn't there like a legal team at the publisher or something?" I was certain Ash had a legal team, and that they might not be so happy about a novel that made *batshit claims* about him, as Charley so delicately put it. But what had Ash said to me in his car at LA LIT? Lawyers make things complicated.

"You can do whatever you want if you disguise it just enough and call it fiction." She sighed heavily. "That's what I was trying to tell you, Olivia."

My heart beat furiously in my chest at the thought of someone—Angelica—(or Ash and some other writer he hired?)—writing stuff about me and calling it fiction. Ash had said I was the last search on Angelica's phone. Had she really survived the accident, and then written about me the way I was sort of writing about her in my new novel? *Two writers get the same idea, and one publishes it first,* Ash had said.

An idea doesn't belong to any writer, I'd argued with him.

"Look, it's not that big of a deal." Charley was still talking. But her voice betrayed her. Clearly it was kind of a big deal, or she never would've called me.

"You've read it?" I asked her.

"Well, no...not yet," she stammered. "But I can have them overnight you a galley. The Boston address still the best one?" she asked.

"No, I'm actually out in LA right now. Can you send it here?"

"Los Angeles?" She stumbled a little again, like she couldn't believe I'd come back here.

But I didn't owe her any explanation; I didn't owe her anything. I gave her Noah's address, and then I hung up the phone.

Excerpt from *The Wife*

I walk away from Malibu Lake, his words echoing in my head. Be careful driving.

Why does he say that to me? Has his step-grandmother told him what I plan to do, and has he done something to my car? Is that why the steering has felt loose all week? Or is he just playing the role he has played so long? Concerned husband. Loving husband.

I shake the feeling off and walk down to the driveway. I'll be fine. It's a short drive back home, and my husband doesn't know enough about cars to do something anyway. He could've hired someone. But that would be too messy. He likes everything neat. Tidy. If he wanted to kill me, he'd poison me. Now, that would be easy enough. Drop something potent in a glass of red wine, and I'd be dead in an hour.

I shiver at that thought as I reach the driveway, and then I notice that my car is gone. I glance at my phone, and my cousin texted me a half hour ago. Went to the store to pick up some lunch. Be back soon.

She's always doing that. Taking my things without asking. My clothes. My car. My husband. She would probably secretly love it if my husband poisoned me. She might cry for me, but then, I would give her exactly two months before becoming the second wife. To forget all about me. To cling to him.

I am thinking these horrible things, anger brewing inside of me, paralyzing me, so I am still standing there by the driveway a few minutes later when I hear the housekeeper screaming from inside the house about an accident. I hear her and my husband running down the path from the lake, so I hide behind a tree and watch them hop into his car, his tires squealing as he drives off.

And somehow intuitively I know, they think it was me driving.

★ ★ ★

I'm alone up here again, and I walk along the lake. The world feels newly quiet, still. My husband isn't calling for me, wanting me, holding on to me. He's driving fast into the canyon, wondering if I'm gone.

That quiet voice inside of me was right after all: he really did something to my car, and he thinks he's gotten away with it. Why wouldn't he? He gets away with everything.

I stop walking and stare out at the quiet lake. The water is so still, until it ripples a little from the slightest breeze. A cold disturbance that gives me a chill too. I am still here, but I am not really here at all. And that's when it hits me: I can't go back to Malibu. I can never go back again.

But if he thinks I'm dead, if the whole world thinks I'm dead, then am I finally truly free?

Away from here, from him, can I be a woman and a writer? Daphne du Maurier or Charlotte Brontë, or maybe even, Sylvia Plath. What was it she wrote in "Lady Lazarus"?

"Dying is an art. I do it exceptionally well."

I can do it exceptionally well. I turn and walk away from the lake, toward my new uncertain future, as a ghost. Or a ghostwriter.

FORTY-FIVE

A year later

When I first read the galley of *The Wife* Charley sent me, it felt like the end of the world. If I'd thought my writing career was over when I'd dropped out of Ash's writing project, I was one hundred times more certain it was over when I realized that Bari Elizabeth Xavier called me out as a plagiarist in her debut novel. There was a line where the main character put a Post-it note over my author photo and said she would *fucking haunt me.* That completely decimated me, and I couldn't get out of bed for two whole days, until Noah dragged me out and insisted he wished someone would *fucking haunt him.*

"Seriously, Livvy, like how cool would it be to have your own personal ghost?"

I'd groaned and thrown a pillow at him, but then I'd taken his hand, and gotten up and gotten dressed again too. Because what other choice did I have? I couldn't afford to take legal action, which Charley said would be fruitless anyway.

I was a failed writer, until I was a failed ghostwriter, until I was reduced to a plagiarizing "fictional character."

"I don't want to be haunted," I told Noah. "I want to be left alone."

"Come on, Livvy." Noah tried to cheer me up. "You and I both know that most books that are published never find their audience. I bet no one even reads this one when it come out."

But Noah was wrong.

As soon as *The Wife* came out, it was an instant *New York Times* bestseller (of course it was).

People bought it for the deliciously "fictional" trashing of Ash and the Asherwood family, but then, their curiosity was piqued about me and *Becky*. Within a month of *The Wife's* publication, sales of *Becky* took off too. And by the summer it had gone into its fifth reprinting, spent six weeks on the *USA Today* bestseller list, and I was in early talks with Netflix for a limited series.

Charley actually started emailing me again, and she asked me a few times what I was working on next. I decided if Angelica and Ash wanted to haunt me, well, I would haunt them better. So I finally wrote her back, and told her that I was writing a novel inspired by my week in Malibu with Ash. I pitched it to her over email: *A writer gets caught up in an affair with a disturbingly handsome billionaire and discovers his darkest secret—his dead wife may actually be alive.*

My phone rang a minute later, and before I could even say hello, she started talking. "Olivia, don't you dare take that project to anyone else." Her voice came through wildly excited. "I will sell the shit out of it."

"Publishing is the weirdest," Noah said as we toasted my first royalty check for *Becky*, which arrived almost a year to the day since he'd told me how he felt about me. And just a few weeks before the launch of his own book in November.

"I hate everything about it," I said, but I smiled a little as I sipped my champagne and stared at my check sitting on the table in front of me. I'd spent so long thinking *Becky* was a failure that it was still hard to believe that now it wasn't. I'd thought Ash would resurrect my career, but definitely not like this.

"Sure, you hate it. But then you love it even more. And you couldn't be happy if you weren't writing," Noah said as he clinked his glass to mine.

"If we do this for the rest of our lives, we might lose our minds," I said, sipping more champagne.

"True story," Noah said, and then he added, "But at least we'll lose them together."

After *The Wife* was published, Ash came under a lot of fire. Everyone wanted to know if the details in it were true: Did he cheat on Angelica, murder Angelica? Was Angelica alive and the author of the novel? Was he really even an Asherwood to begin with?

He put out a statement reaffirming Angelica's death, saying it was backed up by dental records and the coroner's report, that the police had investigated and declared it an accident. He was the only living Asherwood heir, and there was no question about his ancestry. He might've made some mistakes in his marriage, but hadn't we all?

Then he dropped out of the limelight for a while and checked himself into rehab—for what, it wasn't entirely clear, but Noah said we should just assume it was for sex addiction. Because that was the trendy thing to be rehabbed for these days.

By the time I got my royalty check, Ash was already dating a young singer/actress everyone was calling "the next Taylor Swift," and the Asherwood brand acquired another major department store chain, sending its stock prices soaring. When Ash was named *People*'s Sexiest Man Alive for the third time a few months later, no one would even remember that he went to rehab, much less that he might've possibly tried to murder his wife. Or even if they did, I guess it only made him that much sexier.

I did a lot of interviews once *Becky* gained new popularity, and people always asked me what I thought the truth about Angelica and Ash was. I would shrug and say I didn't know, and just reiterate that *Becky* was completely my story. My writing, my imagination. My retelling of a classic. But the words were entirely mine.

Deep down, though, I had a theory.

Ash hired another writer after I left, and then she wrote *The Wife* for him. He actually craved the attention that came with its publication, negative or not, and calculated it all himself. I understood now, I was never special to him. He'd never wanted *me*. He wanted a woman, any woman, to want him. To write any lies he wanted to tell. And my guess was, he'd found someone else willing to do it.

Clara seemed to disagree. I caught her talking about *The Wife* one morning on *The View,* of all places.

Angie is alive, Clara said, crying into a twisted tissue. *In my heart, I can still feel her.* I rolled my eyes, because Clara was sobbing an awful lot over a woman who'd hated her. *After reading her words, I'll never believe she's truly gone.*

I thought about our conversation on the ride back from Ojai, when Clara got annoyed when I'd brought up the Reddit post. And then the last thing she'd said to me that morning at Starbucks, that she had *everything under control*. Did she still? Even down to this act or whatever it was on national television? Or had Ash's glamorous world finally broken Clara the way it had Angelica? And me. I puzzled over this a lot, and in the end, I decided I needed to give the character loosely inspired by Clara in my new novel her own point of view, so eventually, I could figure her all out on the page.

As for Bari Elizabeth Xavier (it was not lost on me that her initials spelled *Bex*), she would later go on to publish a second novel. But this one would be a quiet family drama about sisters, and it would get panned by the trades. Critics suddenly wondered if it wasn't her writing that was so great after all but the stunning topic of her debut. Then, I never heard much about it—or her—after that. And I almost felt sorry for her, because I'd been there before too.

Did I go back to Malibu, ever again?

Once.

Noah decided to leave his adjunct position at UCLA after his first book came out and was a huge success. With his advance money and my royalties from *Becky,* we bought a little house by the water, near Narragansett, not too far from Providence, thinking it would be good luck to return to the place where we first met and first wrote. And I wanted to be closer to my family, and his mom was still in New York, where he'd grown up.

I asked him to go with me, to walk the beach in Malibu one last time before we moved back east. Just to remember for myself everything that had happened there that had brought me back to him and back to writing and back to myself. To face it in real life, the way I struggled to in my recurring dreams about it.

And so we did. He parked at the hotel I'd stayed at, and then we walked up the beach, holding hands, strolling along the edge of the water.

"Is it that one?" Noah stopped and pointed. Maybe it was because he'd heard me talk about it too many times, or maybe it was because I'd finally let him read the manuscript of my next novel, where I described such a similar house with such a similar man, but he pointed to the right house.

"Yep," I said. "That's the one."

Ash's house was there, exactly as it once was, looming and impressively terrifying with its walls of one-way glass.

"It looks so cold," Noah said. "Too much glass. When we're rich, let's never live in a house like this, all right?" I laughed. And then looked up at the house for another moment. It felt weirdly less menacing here than it did in my dreams. And Noah was right. It was too cold. Hollow and empty, glamorous and unhappy, much like *the sexiest man alive* himself.

I stared at the glass and wondered if he was home. Could he see us out here? Was he watching us down on the beach? I half expected him to come running down the veranda steps, towards us in the sand, calling out to me, trying to hug me, or trying to push me into the sea, drowning me.

But everything was quiet and still. Ash and his house were watching us or they weren't. Angelica was still alive or she wasn't. Bex had been found or she was still missing. Clara was my ally or not. And I realized that it didn't matter to me. None of it did. I'd walked away from Ash and his stories when my life and career were in shambles. I could definitely walk away now that they weren't.

"Let's go," I said to Noah.

"You're ready?" Noah looked surprised. "We just got here."

"I'm more than ready," I said.

And I held on to his hand and walked down the beach, turning my back on Ash, on Malibu. I wasn't a ghost or a ghostwriter. I had my own story to tell.

EPILOGUE

Last night I dreamt I went to Malibu again.

And in my dream, I set his house on fire, and then I ran down the beach into the cold water of the Pacific to escape. The water pulled me under, filled my lungs, suffocated me. And all the while I was drowning, I was also hoping he would save me, that he would dive in after me, pull me out, tell me I was the one he loved, he really loved, all along.

Clara, Ash would say. *There was never anyone else but you. It was always you.*

He would forget all about Angie, about Olivia, about that trashy starlet he's been sleeping with, and he would only see me. Only want me.

But then I awoke with start, to the bright white light of morning, a few hundred miles up the coast from Malibu, in my bed in my apartment in Redwood City. I remembered again that Ash and Malibu were far away. I was above water. Malibu was just a dream. Ash was just a dream.

Sometimes, now, my biggest regret upon waking in the morning is that I hadn't really burned his house down. Once,

I almost did, but I'd chickened out and put the fire out before it could rage out of control.

The last thing Angie had said to me before her accident was that I was a coward. She'd yelled it at me on the edge of Malibu Lake, as she'd asked me about my feelings for Ash. I'd denied them, denied everything, of course, and that's what she spat back in my face. That one tiny, looming word: *coward*.

In my dreams, though, I wasn't a coward at all. I was brave. And maybe that's why, even now, they're still filled with flames, with smoke. And Ash coming through all that. Just for me.

But then in my waking hours, I had to remember that Ash lived on, somewhere down the coast, his life, his house, still perfectly intact. And that he'd long forgotten about me.

Even after all I'd done for him. Even after writing that book that put him back in the spotlight as the *Sexiest Man Alive*. He hadn't even called me. Not to thank me, or yell at me, or find out how I was. Or to say he wanted me again.

Hate and love are two sides of the same coin. Angie had shown me that. I'd spent all those wasted years with her, taking care of her, helping her, wanting to be her. Me, not Bex. If Olivia had bothered to do any research, she would've learned that everything I told her about Bex was a lie. Bex had moved to London years ago. We all knew where she was.

It had been me and Angie in Malibu for so many years. Me wanting her life, her husband. She had everything, and I had nothing.

Ash came to me once. One solitary quiet afternoon, but then after that, he pretended it had never happened. Angie was still sleeping in his bed every night in the months that followed. I could hear them sometimes, with my ear pressed to the door. He still wanted her, again and again.

So it wasn't fair when she wanted the one and only thing I had that was truly mine: writing. Angie had taken one writing class at Brown, and then all those years later she thought she could just write a novel. And there I was, the one who'd wanted to be a writer all along and had majored in English at UC Santa Cruz. It was why I'd gone to work for her in the first place—so I would have the time to write.

She couldn't be me, though—she discovered her one silly book idea had already been written, and then she threw her hands up in the air and gave up.

But even after she died, Ash pushed me away. I couldn't be her either.

Except, as it turned out, in fiction.

This morning I woke myself up from my recurring dream, pushed Malibu and Ash to the back of my mind, again. And then I checked my email, and I saw one from my literary agent:

Clara, just wanted to give you a heads-up. Olivia Fitzgerald is shopping a book loosely based on her experiences working as a ghost-writer in Malibu. Do we have anything to worry about?

Olivia Fitzgerald. That was another fire I should've ignited, if only I'd been brave enough to grind more Percocet into the coffee. But I stopped at two. I only wanted to mess with her, not murder her.

I wasn't a murderer, and I wasn't an arsonist. An opportunist? Maybe.

I read Angie's manuscript after she died, and I knew that her novel was crap, but the story that another writer might've written it, might've stolen it, that part was perfection. I didn't expect Ash to actually bring Olivia to Malibu, and to complicate everything by bringing Emilia into the picture too. I was already working on *The Wife*, and I knew it was going to be my big break. There wasn't room for another Asherwood novel, for another writer. I couldn't let Olivia take what was rightfully mine.

As soon as I heard Ash mention Emilia's journals, I got rid of them. Even though they were truly filled with nothing but boring details of the weather and her day-to-day life in Malibu Lake, I knew if I took them so he or Olivia could never read them, if I stole what the library had too and destroyed everything I could find about her, then Ash's write-for-hire job would be impossible. Olivia would go home. I needed her to give up. But even when the Emilia story fell apart, Olivia just wouldn't let go.

So what else could I do then but try to get close to her and use her? I watched her, went with her to visit Rose, listened to her theorize about Angie and Ash, and then, I used it all in my novel. She got so caught up in Angie's death, it inspired me to change the ending of *The Wife*, to publish it under a pen name, and to tell it in a confessional format, to leave just that spark of possibility that Angie herself was still alive, that she had written it all as it had happened. That's what sells books, isn't it? Intrigue.

Angie called me a coward, but I was brave on the page, with my words, in a way I could never truly be in real life. In my novel, I spun straw into gold: Angie's life and death, Ash's past, Olivia's musings, Rose's words, Emilia's made-up history, with a hint of Daphne du Maurier too. *The Wife* was an instant bestseller.

Did I steal Olivia's story? Did I steal Angie's or Ash's or Emilia's? Or even Daphne du Maurier's?

No.

I wasn't a thief. I wasn't an Asherwood. I wasn't even a liar, really.

I was just a fiction writer.

★ ★ ★ ★ ★

ACKNOWLEDGMENTS

A few years ago, I came across an article about all the different potential inspirations—and questions—surrounding one of my all-time favorite novels, Daphne du Maurier's, *Rebecca*. I was in the midst of working on a retelling (of *The Great Gatsby*) at that time, and I was already thinking a lot of what it meant to tell an original story. As Charley says in this book, there are no new stories. But are there? I truly think there are! I was fascinated by the true tidbit I read that Daphne du Maurier did defend herself (and won) in a plagiarism case in the 1940s. And also by the story of Carolina Nabuco, who wrote a novel with similarities to *Rebecca* and published it first in Brazil (but never sued du Maurier). What makes any novel unique? And who owns any story? I couldn't stop thinking about all of this, and then the first line of this novel came to me one night: *Last night I dreamt I went to Malibu again.* Suddenly, I knew I wanted to write my own modern-day gothic mystery.

In many ways this novel is extremely meta, but what is more so than a fiction writer who just wrote a retelling, writing a novel about a fiction writer…who just wrote a retelling? I had the most fun writing Olivia's story, but I should note it is absolutely nothing like my own. This is fiction, after all! I may have experienced my own share of unfortunate events, writer brain moments, and even a few surprise royalty checks over the course of my publishing career, but any similarity between Olivia and me ends there.

I owe an enormous debt of gratitude to my wonderful agent, Jessica Regel, who always encourages me to follow my heart, even when I preface my emails with, *I know this is crazy but…* The very first time I talked to Jess, in the fall of 2006, she told me she thought I was going to have a long career, and even 17 years and 12 books together later, I'm still not sure I believe her? But her enthusiasm has never wavered one bit, and I'm so grateful to have always had her with me on this roller coaster of publishing. Jess, thank you for being such a huge champion of this novel back from when I sent you only fifty pages a few years ago. And thank you for coming up with the perfect title! A huge thank you also to Jenny Meyer and the team at Jenny Meyer Literary for their continued enthusiasm and for championing this book abroad.

I feel extremely lucky to have worked with my amazing and very wise editor, Laura Brown. Laura, it has been such a joy to revise this book with you and has made me truly remember everything I love about writing fiction. I am so grateful for your support, encouragement, and brilliant ideas that really helped me make Olivia and Ash and this story shine! A huge thank you also to Erika Imranyi, Justine Sha, and the entire team at Park Row Books for supporting *The Fiction Writer* and bringing me into the fold of their wonderful imprint.

Thank you to my writing friends who read early drafts and promised me this was a book worth fighting for. Maureen Kilmer, Brenda Janowitz, and Tammy Greenwood—thank you for the early reads, the good ideas, the friendships, and the supportive and funny messages and texts. Thank you to my comadres (and comrades) on the homefront who daily help me navigate and remember the real world.

Thank you to my husband, Gregg, who puts up with my writer brain and listens as I talk about all the mysteries and stories I'm *sure* exist everywhere we go. I love you, even when you tell me to stop talking about all the imaginary murders that (probably) never happened. Thank you to B and O for being good sports when I talk about fictional people at dinner, a lot. Thank you also for letting me drag you through Malibu while I searched for Ash's house, in traffic. Thank you to my parents who encouraged my love of reading and writing as a child and my mom who bought me a copy of *Rebecca* when I was teenager.

Thank you to all the women writers who wrote gothic mysteries before me, who continue to inspire me as a writer. And last, but definitely not least, thank you to all the booksellers, librarians, and readers who continue to support my work. I am so grateful to be a fiction writer.

QUESTIONS FOR DISCUSSION

1. The prologue and the epilogue both begin with "Last night I dreamt I went to Malibu again." What is the significance of this line? How does your perspective on it change from the prologue to reading it again in the epilogue?

2. Olivia mentions the idea of "writer brain," that as a fiction writer she is always seeing stories in situations even where they don't exist. Did you think the "gothic mystery" she found herself in in Malibu was real or imagined? Did your perspective change as the story went on?

3. Compare and contrast Olivia to Angelica to Clara. Is Olivia really a thief? Is Clara? Is Angelica? Do you agree with Olivia that a story can't really belong to any writer? Why or why not?

4. Discuss the meaning of the title. Who is *the fiction writer*? Consider also the line between truth and fiction, and how that plays a role in the novel.

5. Charley tells Olivia that "there are no new stories." Do you agree or disagree with this statement? What makes a story unique or new from a story that came before it? Did you notice any similarities between *The Fiction Writer* and Daphne du Maurier's *Rebecca*? How are the novels also different?

6. What is the role of the excerpts from *The Wife* in the novel? Who did you believe was the writer of these excerpts? Did your perspective on this change throughout the book and why/how?

7. Compare and contrast Ash and Noah. Does Olivia make the right choice when she leaves Ash at LA LIT and goes to see Noah instead? Why or why not?

8. How does Olivia's family history, specifically her mother's accident, play a role in this story? How do you think Olivia's life, and her experience in Malibu, may have turned out differently if her mother hadn't died in that accident years earlier?

9. Discuss Rose Asherwood as a character. Why is she important to the story? Why do you think she tells Olivia that "magicians saw beautiful women in half or make them disappear?"

10. How does wealth and class play a role in the novel? Discuss how they affect both Olivia's and Ash's lives and the outcomes of their stories.

11. From the very first line, Malibu plays a huge role in this novel. Discuss the significance of the setting. Why do you think the novel largely takes place in Malibu? How does it contribute to the plot and overall theme?